The Man I Know

A MARRIED COUPLE ROMANCE

DAISY JANE

Copyright © 2023 by Daisy Jane

All rights reserved.

No part of this book may be reproduced in any form or by any electronic or mechanical means, including information storage and retrieval systems, without written permission from the author, except for the use of brief quotations in a book review.

The story, all names, characters, and incidents portrayed in this production are fictitious. No identification with actual persons (living or deceased), places, buildings, and products is intended or should be inferred.

Editing | Laura Davies

Cover Design | Daisy Jane

Cover Image | Majdansky

 Created with Vellum

Content Warnings:

While content warnings and advisories can be located on the Reading Guide on my website, I'd like to warn you that **this book contains sensitive material not safe for every reader**.

Please proceed with caution if you have sensitivities to any of the following **(all CONSENSUAL)**: aggressive rough sex, aggressive physical acts, rope play (light shibari), impact play, breath play, consensual nonconsent, anal, and/or roleplay of forced sex.

Please keep your heart and mind safe while reading and take these warnings seriously for the best, most optimal experience.

Tropes and other information can be found here: DaisyJane.com/ReadingGuide

Foreword

"Someone I loved once gave me a box full of darkness. It took me years to understand that this too, was a gift."
— Mary Oliver

One

LAWSON

I just stare at her, all eager energy and hard-on, enjoying all that is mine.

A dying breeze tumbles through, and my breath catches as I wait. For the life of me, I can't tear my gaze away.

"*Ooh!*" Her velvety shriek fortifies the arousal building behind my zipper, then—

"*Thank you, wind,*" I mutter, praising the universe like a hungry fool as the hem of her tennis skirt flies over her hips, exposing the underside of her ass.

Damn.

My throat ticks and my jaw clenches as I salivate at the vision before me. Impossibly flawless skin, a plumpness that makes me groan, and *no panties*. A growl rumbles through me, and I knead the length of my sternum with a closed fist to quiet the noise.

To *stifle* the *urge*.

I imagine lifting that skirt the rest of the way, her lean fingers splayed out on the window in front of her, desperately clutching for a balance she never finds. Before she's even ready, I've pushed inside of her, sawing in and out as if my next breath depends on how hard I've fucked her, how full I've left her.

How long she'll feel the burn from my savage thrusts.

Electricity jolts through my bones, and a raw fantasy appears behind my eyes. That fiery red hair all knotted up between my fingers. Her cries for help, panted appeals for respite, breathy pleas for freedom from my *cruel* grasp—sexy as hell. So fucking sexy that I'd—

Whack.

I bring my palm to my assaulted temple, massaging the pounding ache that takes hold instantly.

"*Dad!* You were supposed to catch it!"

Looking up, my two sons, Alex and Desmond, stand across from me in the yard. Both are covered in grass stains and mud smears, bits of torn out lawn poking out of Lex's hair.

Reaching down, I snag the football at my feet, stealing a quick glance at her.

My wife.

Wearing an intoxicating smirk, she tosses me a wink, her brows pinched with more than interest and curiosity. In fairness, all variations of her smiles and smirks make me a hard, lovesick fool.

Her grin says she's aware that I got hit in the head with a

football because of my lascivious staring. Well, staring *and* drooling. I am a man who can multitask after all. Just not at the same time as I can play catch, apparently.

"Sorry, boys," I say, savoring her wink before returning my focus to our sons. The focus of the football lesson today? *Never take your eyes off the ball.*

Heh. Oops.

"A few more passes, okay?" My wife says, sauntering across the lawn, running an old chamois through her hands, leaving smears of earth behind. "Then we need to get cleaned up for dinner." She sends a pointed look to our boys who, at ages ten and six, have a knack for *not hearing.*

"A few more, then showers before dinner," she reiterates, her tone adding a wordless warning.

I loop my arm around her waist, catching her before she returns to her basket of lavender. She presses a hand to my chest, her diamond ring catching the highlights of the sherbet skyline above.

"You okay over here, or do you need me to step in and catch some?" she asks, laughing a little as she teases, her plump lips enticing me.

"I got distracted by the best ass in Willowdale. Forgive me," I say, curling down to lay a kiss on her forehead. The smell of fresh lavender and soft, musky skin overwhelms me, and I pull away, shaking my head. "You smell *so good.*"

She escapes my arm prison, strolling back to where her garden tools are strewn about on the concrete near the lawn's edge. "It's the lavender."

I force my focus back to our boys, lining my thumbs along the laces of the pigskin before I chuck it back. Their auburn hair shines beneath the traces of sun as they hustle after the ball that neither will catch. My chest tightens at the sight of them and I can't help but venture a glance back at her.

Her naturally wavy hair billows over her shoulder as she cautiously crouches, collecting hand shears and a small trowel, dropping them into her basket.

"Dad!" My son howls, demanding my focus. *Jesus, I really need to focus.* How will they learn to keep their eye on the ball if I can't keep my eyes off their mother?

I raise my hands high, preparing for the optimal pass, but lower them quickly as I rush forward to catch the ball my six-year-old has flung. We go a few more rounds like this, tossing with some catching, the evening quickly stealing our light, pouring cool air over us. Less than ten minutes later, I'm rounding them up, having them gather their shoes and coats, and herding them inside.

"All the important places," I warn them as they bounce on their toes at the bottom of the stairs, anxious to rush up and argue about who uses which bathroom, no doubt.

I point to Lex, who is notorious for soapless showers. *Boys.* He lifts his arm, burying his nose in his pit. "Not even that bad, Dad."

I drop a palm to his shoulder. "Son, not that bad isn't the goal. *Clean* is the goal."

From beside his brother, Des backs up the stairs before I target him with a pointed finger. "And what do you need to remember?"

Des nibbles the inside of his cheek, peering across the house, likely looking to catch his mother's gaze. To have her supplement him with what he should already know. We've been through this too many times. "Des, buddy," I coax.

"Wash but don't use mommy's stuff."

I level my gaze at him until he finds it, latching onto the intensity, catching the importance of the message. We still do not speak of the Nair incident last summer where Des attempted to style his hair into a mohawk with *mousse*. Unrelated, it takes approximately seven months for a six year old to grow a head of hair that looks decent.

Both ruddy heads nod in unison as I say it again and a moment later, the stairs are creaking as they thunder up, racing for the hall bath. Lex makes it there first—I know because a piercing whine drifts down the stairs as Des trudges toward the master bedroom, heading into our bathroom. I call up a reminder. "None of mommy's stuff!"

A moment later, the little closet beneath the stairs rattles as the pipes come alive, both upstairs showers running. I make my way into the kitchen, stopping short in the doorframe connected to the living space. A sheen of sweat breaks out along my back beneath my hoodie, so I take my cap off and run a hand through my hair. My heartbeat echoes in my ears as my pulse thuds heavily at the base of my throat. Behind my zipper, things are happening. At my sides, my fingertips drum mindlessly against my thighs.

I reach up and grab the door jamb, leaning into the kitchen yet holding myself back. I just stare at her, all eager energy and hard-on, enjoying all that is *mine*.

We've been married for twelve years. I don't think the man I was then ever anticipated how the love I felt for my wife would evolve. I love her more now than the day I married her, but I also burn for her. She consumes me. It's a desire and need that grows over time.

Whatever expectations I'd had then, are weak in comparison to how I feel now.

She shelved her aspirations of opening her own dance studio when we got married. When we met, she'd pumped hope and happiness into the idea. But after we quickly got lost in one another and the vision of our future, she adjusted her life plan. For me. For us.

I'd already started my business and achieved success, and for us to thrive together, it would have been challenging for her to start her own business. At the time, it didn't feel possible. We discussed it and ultimately, I kept running my small business, and she never started hers. She stayed home and raised our children. Packing lunches and folding clothes, tying off goody bags and cutting construction paper hearts—she became the ultimate mother. She was always the ultimate wife, loving and caring, generous with her time and heart.

She's happy. I know she's happy. I see it in her smile, I feel it beating against me when I hold her tight, I taste it between her thighs when I make her shatter.

She's given so much, and that *should* be enough. Yet there's a part of me that doesn't just savor what she gives, there's a part that wants to... *take.*

I watch her, dipping soapy plates into a basin of equally soapy water. Steam rises from the surface, hanging in thick clouds above the sink for a moment before evaporating. I wish my needs were that way, present for a small time and then gone. Forgotten.

The window above is blanketed in darkness from outside, leaving a hint of her reflection projected in the glass. I narrow my eyes on the gauzy portrait of her, obfuscated by condensation and steam. I see more of what I love.

Her perfect lips, the arch a delicate cupid's bow. She's wearing a tender smile as she washes dishes, swaying from foot to foot, a private hum purring between her lips. A quick glance at the table adjacent to her and I spot the takeout pizza, glasses of milk at each spot, and a bowl of baby carrots in the center. She wrings her hands in the towel hanging off the counter's edge as she slides the last clean plate in the rack. Her red hair slides off her shoulder as she jolts back, spotting me in the reflection.

As she turns, I'm already busy closing the distance to get to her. I loop my arm around her waist, and tug her body flush to mine. There's no way she can't feel the hard ridge of my cock, pressing into her like a concealed weapon.

She links her hands together behind my neck, smiling up at me in the quiet kitchen. Darkness seeps in from the night closing in on us, and I find myself falling into her sway, a slow dance just for us. "You watchin' me wash dishes?" She wrinkles her nose as she teases me, and I grind my cock into her a bit more. I swallow her faint moan as I plant my mouth on hers, taking a long, wet kiss. One I've been waiting for since watching her in the garden.

"You made it hard to play catch with the boys," I tell her when I give her a break to suck in air. I love when I kiss her so rough and ragged that the tip of her nose is pink and her lips get all swollen. "You make it hard, period," I say, earning another moan. This time, it's from me as she lets a hand fall from my neck, fishing it between us to cup my aching cock over my worn work denim. "Naughty," I chastise as I smack her ass gently.

Then the urge that crawls around the depths of my consciousness, the one I push down with my boot and keep buried, *it surfaces.*

It's stirring somewhere deep in my veins. Like a dormant volcano awakening, pressure building and tearing through me. Lava scorching everything and leaving behind nothing but ash and darkness in its wake.

I've managed to tamp it down. Keep it subdued in the pit of my soul.

She rocks to her toes and finds my mouth again, this time twirling her tongue with mine as her long pink fingernails trace the ridge of my cock. Her breathy giggle wraps around me, her other hand playing with the frayed ends of my hair that curl over my collar. "You need a haircut," she whispers.

Footsteps thud above us and I pull back, meeting her gaze. Emerald mixed with molten chocolate drizzled in honey, her eyes have always been the thing that keeps me grounded here, in this perfect life, happy with everything I have.

Happy not indulging in my dark fantasies.

Exhaling with relief that her amorous gaze has suppressed the monster within me, I spin her around, pinning her to the sink. Her laughter is soft but controlled, and I love how she always tempers her passion around the boys. How she knows just when to push the gas pedal, and just when to ease off.

I bury my nose in her neck. The fading scent of her rosemary mint shampoo mingling with the lavender she's just harvested, making me frenzied with the need to bury myself inside of her.

With my hands exploring her breasts beneath her long

sleeved tee, I drop my mouth to the back of her ear, telling her just what I want.

"I crave you, Jes. I kept looking across the lawn thinking about how we've been together so long, and yet I want you more now than ever before." I brush my groin along her ass, and she whimpers at the contact. I love how she whimpers for me, so sweet and needy. It's genuine, too. "I can't believe you're *mine*. A sweet thing like you." My calloused thumbs rouse her nipples to life, stroking them until they're as hard as my cock.

"Des, you had first seat last pizza night!" Lex whines in that unhinged tone that only your kid has, *seriously*.

My hands fall to her hips, and I notice her pert nipples in the dark window, now a crystal clear reflection where the steam has dissipated. I whisper my plans to her. "I'm gonna deal with them, but I want you in the laundry room. Now." Cheeks rosy, her bottom lip tucked between her teeth, eyes wide, she nods. And then I serve the pizza at a pace that would make you think it was a competitive sport.

"Drink your milk, keep your hands to yourself. And Lex, if the seat is that big of a deal, let him have the hall shower next time, and you take the seat. Compromise, buddy." I waffle my fingers through his hair. "Okay?"

Orange grease already lining their upper lips, he nods. "Okay, Dad."

"Dude, I do not need to see what you're chewing. Don't speak with your mouth full. Now, I gotta go fix the dryer with mom." I give them both a stern look, shrugging off any perceived signs of suspicion. I think we have a few more years before that. "We will be back out here in..." I glance over my shoulder, spotting the cracked laundry room door.

The light is on, pouring down on Jes, who sits atop the dryer, still wearing that damn little skirt. Only, she's abandoned the long sleeve top and instead sits in her bra. "Fifteen minutes," I say hopefully. Though with how frequently I've been struggling to stifle my urges lately—and how goddamn beautiful she is right now—I doubt I'll need more than *three*.

They nod, their focus already on the cartoon playing from the living room. Colored animals with Australian accents talk about a tea party, and I take the opportunity to sneak away.

I prowl toward the laundry room, wishing I'd had time to shower, but knowing there's no way. The door is met with the sole of my boot as I push it closed behind me. Jes looks up, previously engrossed in untangling a stray red hair from the strap of her bra.

Our eyes meet and I realize then, my chest is heaving. Taking deep, long breaths, I exhale hard, hoping to expel the impulses clawing at me. Hoping I can battle them one more time, overpower them again.

I grab her hips, draggin her off the dryer, and spin her around. "Hands on the top of the dryer, baby," I direct, not masking my guttural tone or desperate need for her. Tugging down the tease of a skirt in one, quick motion, I tap her ankle, getting her to step out of one side. I like seeing her skirt bunched, pooled carelessly around her other foot.

Only *I* get to see that.

My pulse skyrockets as I whip my belt free, loving the metallic clank of it hitting the wood floor. She wiggles against me as I struggle with my fly, the weight of my erection making unzipping a feat. Finally, I get it down and my cock drops weightily into my palm, veiny and fat.

Gripping myself, I slide the head between her pussy lips, discovering the warmth and wetness she's been hiding. "*Fuuck*," I groan, my eyes falling closed as I give her the first inch.

She hisses, sucking in a delicate breath that only makes me want to pummel her that much harder. Collecting her hair in one fist, I give her head a tender yank. Her moan is pleasure, laced with a hint of pain, and I grow *harder* in response.

Releasing her hair, I clamp my hand over her mouth and ask, "Ready?" She nods against my palm and in one unforgiving thrust, I bury the rest of my aching dick inside her welcoming cunt. So tight, so wet, still greedy for my cock after all these years.

"Goddamnit, Jes," I grind out, moving my groin against her ass, desperate to feel her clenching around me at every angle. All the goddamn angles. "You feel so good."

My hands are everywhere, cupping her tits, grabbing at her hips, yanking and tangling in her hair. I'm fucking obsessed, and with my cock buried deep, I almost feel feral. "Come for me, baby, God, I need to feel you come," I rasp, my voice rattling with hot vulnerability. My words are dirty, but express the truth at the core of my being; I need to feel her love for me. I need to feel her come undone for me.

My climax threatens to strangle me, tamping down all nonessential thoughts. My thumb falls to her clit, sticky from her arousal, and I drive my hips toward her more urgently as I stroke her. Her thighs tremble against me, and I know she's *there*.

Ready to let go.

Ready to burst at the seams and come apart for me, let me watch her unravel beautifully like a ribbon tossed around by a heavy wind. Then wait for me to collect her loose threads and stitch her back together.

She rides out her orgasm—grinding her soft, plump ass against me—clenching around my cock with each roll of her hips. Her spine ripples with pleasure before she collapses onto her forearms, panting, gasping for breath.

I wrap my arms around her, and I find her lips. We share a breathy kiss as I still, my cock flexing in finality, giving up the fight because of the way she comes so fast for me, every time, even still.

I let a moan slip free, clutching her breasts, yanking her body to mine, my cock pounding cum deep inside of her in unrelenting pulses.

She whimpers, and I kiss along the gentle slope of her neck. She moans and stills. I drag my tongue up her skin, tipping her over the edge again.

Her pussy seizes up, clenching and flexing, torquing around me. The sight of her white knuckles gripping the top of the dryer as she leans forward again, the sound of her ragged breaths begging me to fuck her harder, the softness of her pussy all around my cock—she explodes *again*. I love how she comes again with me. I grit my teeth as she seizes around me, prolonging my orgasm and taking everything I have, whimpering in delight as she does.

I lick my upper lip, finding it salty with sweat. Reaching down, I grip myself by the base while sliding out. She releases her grip and folds her arms together over the dryer, leaning forward to rest there until I clean her up.

I *always* clean her up.

I wish I could get her dirtier, but I push that thought down as I'm dragging a beach towel up her inner thighs, kissing her as I clean. I zip up and help her get dressed. My chest expands with pride at the way her small hand uses my shoulder to steady herself as she steps back into her skirt as I hold it open for her.

I rise, and we seal the moment with a kiss, her hand cupping my softening cock over the denim. "Come on. Let's go see if there's any pizza left."

She finds my hand, then waffles our fingers together, and it never ceases to make my chest buzz a little. I trail after her to the kitchen, where we sit with the boys and dig into the cooled pizza. Her foot slides up my pant leg beneath the table, and I send a private wink to her over the grease-stained boxes.

Life is perfect. Everything I need is at this table.

I do not need more.

So why do I repeat that to myself more often than I'd like to admit?

JES

I've never been happier, and that's all that matters.

"I'm done with my banana," Des announces proudly. As I reach back, doing the driver's seat one arm crab grab, a limp peel smacks the back of my arm.

"Des, I had my hand out, buddy," I sigh, still keeping my eyes laser focused on the drop-off line. It's cut throat out here, no one using blinkers, everyone feeling more important than everyone else. You can get stuck in this line until after the bell if you aren't on your toes. Letting the peel slide off the back of my arm and plunk against the floorboard, I curve the wheel, settling my SUV to the curb.

Finally, I exhale.

"Okay, guys. Get your things," I say, lifting the gear shift to park. I turn in my seat, collecting the banana peel for the trash, and point to the water bottles about to be abandoned in the seat. "Don't forget your waters!"

Des grabs both, handing one to Lex who is already impatiently waiting on the curb. His copper hair shines in the early morning light, reminding me so much of myself at his age. Laws has a full head of dark hair, and yet our boys sport the same hue as me. I smooth my fingers through my tresses, using the elastic from my wrist to drag it into a ponytail.

Lex slams the door and they head toward campus. I linger along the curb a moment until they're behind the school gate, then head to my spin class.

Some days, driving my white SUV to spin class then going home for a latte and reading feels surreal.

I'm a housewife.

I never thought I would be. I mean, I knew I'd own a home and I'd always hoped I'd be a wife. But smashing those two together to create the title of housewife is strange. It almost feels as if, with that title, you're less important than those who work outside the home. That, because you get slices of freedom and downtime throughout the day when most people are otherwise working, you must have it easy.

The truth is, being a housewife is hard work.

Another truth? I actually really love it. Like, for real. Not convincing myself I love it because it's what I do, or projecting that it's what I want because I feel ungrateful if I don't.

I *actually* love it. I love expressing my love through care.

I read that love language book a couple of years after I had Des. I'd been in this strange headspace where I felt immense guilt for no longer having dreams outside my family. I felt like the worst woman and mom. How could I set a great example for my boys to live their best lives when my aspirations start and end in the same place I wake each day?

I realized, after reading *The 5 Love Languages*, that I'm fulfilled by acts of service for those I love. And that fulfillment is so rewarding, it's all I seek. I adore taking care of my husband and my sons. I treasure the time I spend running our home, planning meals, packing lunches, researching cleaning products, changing sheets, hanging ornaments, changing wreaths for the season—all of it, I love it.

I'm creating a life for my family that they'll always look back on fondly, and cherish their memories. To me that's far more important than chasing a dream to have my own business. Especially when that dream was made before I discovered what truly made me happy, which is... my guys.

Guilt and expectation no longer gnaw at me as I park in the spin gym parking lot. I'm comfortable in my happiness, and no longer embarrassed by how fulfilled I am in this life. This life has value and meaning, and people can naysay stay-at-home parents all they want, but I no longer worry about what anyone else thinks.

I've never been happier, and that's all that matters.

"We should've gotten breakfast," my friend Penny greets as I approach, falling into her open arms. "If Cas not being here isn't a sign that we should've gotten mimosas and eggs Benedict over spin, I don't know what is."

From her side, Ruthie reaches out her arms, and we hug. "Morning, Jes," she greets through a yawn.

"Morning ladies. And we're already here, I'm sure Cas is in there, just... on the phone or something," I say, cupping my hands to the glass, peering inside. "Ah!" From the back of the studio, Cas, the owner, traipses across the hardwood, weaving in and out of rows of black cycling bikes. "She's coming."

Penny gathers her dark hair, wrapping a satin scrunchie around the heap. She rubs sleep from her eyes, then yawns. "Fine, we're here. I'm in."

"Sorry, ladies, I was on the phone," Cas sighs, keeping the door pinned open with her hip as we filter through.

I wave an arm over my head as I drop my water bottle into the cupholder of the bike nearest me. "No worries. Though these two were trying to get me to bail and get mimosas and breakfast instead."

Cas fidgets with a black remote until music pours out of the speakers, flooding the cool, moderately empty space with life. "Well," she says, grabbing an Expo marker from the trough below the whiteboard on the wall. "I'm not gonna lie, you may wanna do that after. This workout is intense today."

Ruthie and Penny saddle up on bikes near me. "Tad being an asshole and you're taking it out on us?" Ruthie questions knowingly, running a hand through her cropped short hair.

Cas volleys her head. "It's less of a Tad thing, more of a me thing. But yeah, that was Tad and yes... we're... disagreeing," she says carefully, knowing that Ruthie remembers everything and has no problem reminding her of all the times she's been angry with her partner.

"Oh, shoot, I need my water," Cas declares, sliding off her bike, jogging back to the small private office in the corner of the studio.

Penny tugs at her ponytail, shooting Ruthie a knowing glare. "Tad," she harrumphs.

I stifle a giggle. They always tease Cas for dating a guy named Tad. The name supplies so many jokes. "Is he impotent?" "Just a Tad." "Can he give you an orgasm?" "Just a Tad." "Does he know where the g-spot is?" You get the idea.

"Tad," I retort, quietly, teasingly. But then I'm met with a pointed gaze from my two friends.

"Hey now, it's less funny when you tease because you've got Laws. The *perfect* man," Penny says, warming up her legs with a few slow revolutions.

Ruthie grips the handles and starts to warm up, too, as Cas appears, bottle to her mouth. "Cas, we're just giving Jes a hard time about being sickeningly happy with her king of a husband."

Cas drops her water in the cupholder as more women filter through the door, nodding their arrival at her as they find bikes. "Laws?" She shimmies her shoulders as if she's sunk into a warm bath and not perched atop an exercise machine from hell. "Does he have a brother?" she asks playfully.

I slide off the bike, adjusting the seat, and get back on. "He does, but he's married, too."

Cas does an over embellished snap. "Damn. Well, if you ever want a third." She wiggles her eyebrows suggestively, and the three of us laugh.

"Poor Tad," Penny adds. "He must really suck in bed if you'd rather be a side piece to a couple married for fifteen years than the main event for him."

"Twelve years married, fourteen together, and sorry, Cas, we're happy as a *monogamous* married couple," I tell Cas as I take my final sip of water before the descent to hell. "I think a third would be too wild for us."

Ruthie rolls the tension from her neck, eyeing me. "No crazy sex in the Briggs household then? Laws is a boring king, huh? All that muscle—what a waste."

My cheeks flame as Cas lifts a hand in the air, commanding the attention of the other riders in class. The girls always tease me about having the perfect marriage, because I've never been one to complain about Laws. The truth is... I just don't have much to complain about.

Sure, we bicker sometimes and we've even fought. Not much but a handful of times. But all in all, I married the right man. I love him more now than I did all those years ago. I was a twenty-two year old college graduate looking to move on from college boys, and he was a thirty-one year old self assured, rugged, sexy-as-hell *man*, who knew what he wanted and how to make a woman feel like a woman. He made me feel like the center of his universe. Safe and secure. I fell for him hard back then, and two years after we met, we were married.

But I do love him more now. "I didn't say he was boring," I say, my breath quickening as the workout begins. "But I think sexually, neither of us has any complaints. Tad's just gonna have to step it up."

A second later, Cas kicks up the workout. We're rendered incapable of doing anything but gasp for air, shake sweat off our heads like dogs coming out of a pool, and *pedal, pedal, pedal.*

Forty-five painstaking minutes later, my ass and thighs are Jell-o, but I'm headed back to my car riding the post-workout endorphin high.

I slide into the driver's seat and start my car, peeking at my phone before I pull out.

LAWS
Have a good spin class. Love you baby.

A smile curls my lips, causing my heart to thrum with a stuttered, heavy beating. I grin down at my phone, feeling like maybe the girls are right. I am blissfully happy.

I'm happy to be so happy.

Three

LAWS

Jes and my secret.

Rough and ribbed, I tug the loose end again, watching the fibers seal together as the knot tightens. Taking the opposing free end, I run it through the center of the loop before it's too taut. Another tug, and the knot's complete.

I trace the curves and edges of it with my fingertips which are permanently calloused from the trade. It doesn't matter how many times I do it, the feeling of tying a solid knot never fails to thrill me. To give me that little hit of adrenaline, that flash of accomplishment, a small raw roar of internal power.

Despite the fact I've got several guys scattered around my desk, I stare down at the Blake's Hitch knot in my hands, and I get hard. There's beauty in a knot. A simplicity that fascinates me, how they bind, restrict and tether you.

Resting my elbows on my desk, I look up at the guys waiting. "This is the knot you're going to use to climb it. Once you're at the top, you guys know what to do. Just make sure you're using this rope. The Samson ½" rigging rope takes a splice, loops through the pulleys, and can withstand what you're doing." I toss the knotted example onto the desk, and it's snatched up by one of the new guys.

Tying knots isn't complicated. Not if you take the time to learn what each is meant to do. Once you understand how the knot serves your task, achieving it is easy.

Today, the guys are heading out to a park in a neighboring county to pull out some trees, making space for a playground. Most of the time, we don't do a lot of rigging jobs that aren't in preparation for a greenhouse being built. But we never say no to readying a space meant for kids.

My foreman Greg nods, tugging his sweat stained Bass Pro Shops hat down over his sweaty dark hair. "I'll teach 'em," he gruffs out, opening his arms in an attempt to motion the other guys out of my office.

"A word before you head out," I say as Greg nears the threshold of my office door. He closes it, and stands backed up against it as I tuck myself further beneath my desk.

"Don't let the newbie wear his gloves today. He's gotta get used to it at some point," I tell Greg as I shove a hand through my hair, my work-hardened fingertips grating my scalp. That's what the newbie needs to do—toughen up his hands. "You know how it goes. He's gotta get the first set of blisters over with, then it's all callus."

Greg snorts, and I know the exact memory he's recalling.

The new guy has been wearing gloves the last few months. Rope work is rough on your flesh—palms aren't meant to handle and haul rough fibers all day. You have to harden your skin to it. There's a certain amount of pain to withstand in the process, but once you're past it, you're home free.

If gloves weren't actually more dangerous, I'd let him keep them. But last week when the guys were removing the remnants of an oak tree from the elementary school fenceline, the newbie's gloves got caught up in the line; one panicked screech later, the poor guy thought he was going to be pulled under the rope and severed in half.

The guys have been reminding the newbie of his wailing every moment they can.

"Got it. No more gloves. Anything else?" Greg asks, reaching for a can of dip from his chest pocket.

"Graham's got a project over at the college in two weeks. Once we finish the playground in Oakcreek, you guys will be back in Willowdale getting it set up. It's for the students," I tell him. Greg's my foreman—he keeps the guys scheduled and the crews on task. He also does a lot of the really hard work.

When my younger brother Graham started AgTech and I started AgDev, we shared Greg. He helped Graham revise his vision for spacious but affordable and effective greenhouses, and he helped me learn how to best build them in the least amount of time using the most effective hands.

I tip my head to Greg as he heads out to the job, and wonder if he ever is surprised that fourteen years later, we're still working together and really thriving. Bursting at the goddamn seams with growth.

"Thanks, man," I tell him as he dips out, giving me a single wave of acknowledgement before closing the door. He loves being outside, he loves the sun on his skin—he really does just fucking enjoy this work. And somehow my brother and I were the lucky fuckers who stumbled on him all those years ago.

Alone again, I look down at the remaining scrap of hollow braided rigging rope on my desk. A familiar energy courses through my fingers as I reach for it. What I feel in my chest as I knot the nodular length is something that I've only ever privately described as *primal*.

With the rope twining through my fingers, my biceps flex in reaction to the way I torque the ends, how rough it feels against my skin after all these years—goosebumps spread across the back of my neck in a torrent of chills.

My pulse quickens, and my lips even tingle a little too, the way they do when I'm about to taste Jes in one of my favorite places.

I've always loved working with ropes. It just so happens that arbor rigging goes arm-in-arm with ground preparation for greenhouse builds.

I don't know what came first. My love for discovering, tying and tightening ropes or *the other thing*.

My dark secret.

The ravenous, fierce and completely aggressive need buried deep inside my bones. The one I smother on a near daily basis, and let out rarely. And when I do let him show his face, it's only to me. In private. Alone. Never to be seen or experienced by another living soul.

Either way, my affinity for knots and my dark, primal desires, they go hand-in-hand in my fantasies. They live together in harmony a few moments a month, when I feed the monster a few crumbs to keep him at bay. Where I imagine putting my love of binding, tying and knotting to use, enacting some primal, borderline immoral act on... *her*.

"Laws?" Greg pops back in, and the fantasy gets kicked back down to lurk in my subconscious. I shouldn't have even been thinking of it here at work.

"What's up?" I ask, closing my laptop in an effort to appear as if I'd been working the last few minutes since he walked out.

Greg taps the door frame before pointing toward me. "Think you can come by the house and grab Harley for Scouts tonight?" He takes a few steps back, but remains in the hall. That's for his benefit, not mine. Greg's been going through a divorce and in the last week, they've officially made the split to live on their own. His kids have been staying with his soon to be ex-wife, and I know he's struggling.

If he steps in this office and I offer a haven of safety, where walls can come down and he can share—he'll break. If I thought breaking was something he needed, I'd let him. But that's not how Greg rolls. Known the man for many years. He needs me to be his spine, so I am.

"Sure. How about I drop him off after, swing by your new place and we have a beer?" I ask while simultaneously calculating what time that would put me home with Jes.

Something no one tells you about your forties is how much mental math you'll be doing. How long do I have to be here before I can go home? How much time do I need to put in with my friends without it coming across as the bare minimum? How long can the door stay locked before the kids get bored? Everything is a private calculation in which all I'm trying to solve is how quickly I can get home.

To her.

Greg tips up his worn hat, scratching at the bits of dark hair that topple out, over his forehead. "Don't gotta do that," he offers, but the way he keeps his eyes pinned to his toes out of necessity, tells me I do indeed gotta take him out.

Reaching into the open drawer near me, I snatch another Briggs AgTech cap and toss it to him. "That thing," I say, nodding up to his weathered hat, "needs replacing."

He makes the swap, reluctance keeping the old hat pinned between his hands as he arches the bill. "Thanks," he says, still laser focused on the item between his hands. "And thanks for grabbing Harley tonight. You know, I'm just trying to give Addie her space and movers are coming so she can't leave."

"No problem."

"I don't want Harls missing Scouts for divorce shit. Therapist says we keep the kids on their schedule as much as possible," he adds, and I think it's more to remind himself of why he isn't picking up his son tonight, but I nod along, like it's for me.

"Sounds smart. Good plan. Tell Harley the boys and I will grab him a little after five, okay?"

He nods and we share one more look, and I try my best to say all the things I shouldn't verbalize. *It's fine, I got you. It's going to be okay.* Instead, I remind him of our drink. "I'll drop him back off close to seven and come your way and grab you, okay?"

Another solemn nod. "Sounds good. Thanks, Laws."

He disappears and as I rise to call it a day, my brother

saunters in. He comes by a lot since his office building is directly next to mine. I mean, if he's manufacturing greenhouses and I'm building them, having our head offices side-by-side makes sense.

"Ten after four and you're already sneaking out." Graham shakes his head, a stupid little smirk on his lips. He flops down in the seat across from my desk. Folding my arms over my chest, I stare down at him.

"And you're here, which means you aren't working either," I deadpan. Doesn't matter if I'm forty-four and he's thirty-nine. The continual ribbing has only grown finer with age, like only a decent bottle of wine and sibling banter does.

He stacks his boots on the edge of my desk, looking at me with nearly the same face as mine. Growing up, everyone always asked us if we were twins. As adults, we don't get that as often, but I understand it. We both have the same dark hair, usually cut short. We both favor a clean shave versus stubble or a beard. And despite the fact I have a few years on him, we stand six feet four inches tall, our broad shoulders setting the stage for the rest of our physiques, which display all the signs of men who've worked hard their entire lives.

"What do you want? The boys have Scouts today, so I need to get outta here." The truth is, I have some time. In fact, I'd only planned to leave this early to snag a few minutes alone with Jes before I'm gone for the evening. I think of her little purple workout pants she had on this morning, and the fabric hair-tie thing she wears on her wrist. How I'd love to shove that thing in her mouth to quiet her cries as I tear those pants down and shove my way inside her.

I swallow, the thought feeling even more wrong while sitting across from my brother.

"Mae wants a baby."

The lust filled haze of my secret desires lifts, and my energy shifts to focus on his words. "Yeah?" I ask, tempering my excitement in case my brother isn't ready. He and his wife Mae have been married seven years. She's younger than him, only just now reaching thirty. "And does *Graham* want a baby?"

His lips twitch as he considers the question, definitely more just to put me on as he's clearly come here with news. News beyond a thirty-year-old woman who's on her way to ten years of marriage wanting a child. Because that's not news. If he's surprised that her biological clock was likely to start ticking sooner or later, then he's not as smart as I gave him credit for.

"I think I'm ready," he draws out, holding my eyes. Though his lips show a memory of a smile, I realize he's here for a go-ahead. He wants me to tell him that becoming a father will not derail his sex life—because I'm fairly certain that's the singular thing keeping him from having kids.

I say nothing but hold his gaze, my eyebrows pinned to my hairline as I wait. I know Graham. For some fucking reason, my eyes are his magic eight ball. He finds answers in me, in my responses—that's why I hold my expression and wait.

A moment passes, his fingers curl against the wooden arms of the chair then, he's on his feet. "Yeah, I'm ready."

I clap a hand on his shoulder, giving him a squeeze. "You're ready. You've been ready for a while, you were just too self-absorbed to realize it."

He snorts, as if him being the baby of the family hasn't immediately assigned him the role of needy attention whore between the two of us. Mom always babied him. And when dad pops in on us from time to time, he always pokes around Graham a little extra.

I don't mind. However, it drives Graham crazy.

"Mae's been ready, but not me." He grins. "Until now."

"What's changed?" I ask, knowing full well that Mae's been wanting to have children for quite some time. I know because the wife chain makes it impossible for me *not* to know—Mae tells Jes, and at night when we're reading our respective books or zoning out to some ridiculous news program, she recounts her day to me.

It's one of my favorite parts of the day. Listening to what happened, where she went, how she perceives and reacts to the world around her—I fucking love it.

Maybe I love the parts about Mae and Graham a little less—after all, that is how I know that Graham's greatest fear about having children is that there will be no more time for sex—but still, it keeps the gates of communication between us open.

"Listen," I say, collecting my wallet and keys from the desk. He moves for the door, and I follow him, knocking the lightswitch off. "You know Mae tells Jes everything, right?"

Graham winces, taking a hesitant step back from me. "How much is everything?"

I can't help but laugh. "Everything is everything." I clap my hand on his shoulder again, a total fucking big brother move. I hold his eyes, the ones that look like mine, only of course, less good looking. "You have to make time for sex, but you'll still have it."

He presses his fingertips to his temples. "That's not it!"

I blink, then continue walking, Graham catching up a

moment later. "Okay, maybe it is, but, well, can you blame me?" We stop just a few feet from the main entrance and Graham watches me turn off the lights and power down the computer at reception.

"I mean, didn't you worry about that when Jes got pregnant with Lex?"

Reaching for the curved door handle, I pause, blinking at my brother. "No, I didn't. I was excited and happy." It's not a lie—I wouldn't lie to my brother, but it's not *exactly* the truth.

I never worried about whether our sex life would suffer, we've always communicated well and I was going to follow her lead as she recovered after the boys were born.

However I worried about how I would control my urges. My hunger for Jes is my primary defense against my darker desires. The forbidden fruit of my fantasies was so much more tempting without her to sate me. It was a challenging time.

Graham's cup is filled with good old fashioned fucking, from what I know from the wife chain. He can jerk off in the shower for a few months and suck it up, quite frankly.

"Listen, Graham," I say, turning off the final set of lights as my brother steps past me onto the stamped concrete out front. "The beginning is hard. I'm not gonna lie. It's a lot of emotional adjustment for everyone, but mostly for her. And during that time, you're a fuckhead if you're thinking about sex instead of ways to make life better for her and the baby."

"What about me?" he asks, brows sunk between his eyes, as if I've just told him for the first time ever that Santa isn't real. Classic younger sibling reaction.

"You matter, and you're important, yes, but in the first

few months? What your dick wants is really not a smart thing to voice. Trust me."

His eyes get all beady and stressed as my phone vibrates against my thigh. We walk to our trucks as I reach for the call.

"But after that, it's solid right?" Graham asks, looping his hand through the door handle after unlocking it with his remote. I silence my phone after I see it's not Jes.

"Right," I say, because I have a great fucking life. I love my wife and kids, and everything I have I've dreamed of, worked for and achieved.

What Graham wants is to make sure Mae still cares about him after they have kids. So I nod and tell him the truth.

"Having kids makes your relationship stronger, as long as you stay honest and communicate, even through the stress." That's absolutely true. Not a single syllable is a lie. "The sex gets better. Her body changes, her wants do, too. And you rediscover her and everything she needs and wants. It's... pretty fucking amazing."

Graham hops into the driver's seat and slides the key in the ignition as I stand next to him, near my own pickup. He reaches for the door, but doesn't close it yet. "Shit. That's..." He stares through his windshield into the stream of racing vehicles filling the highway before us. "That sounds good, actually."

I shake my head. "I gotta get the boys and head to Scouts. See you tomorrow."

"Later," he says, the slam of his door coinciding with the initial roar of his engine coming to life.

I take out my phone and call Jes as I slide into my own

truck, eager to get to her. It rings just once before her silky tone cascades over the line.

"Hey babe, on your way?" She asks.

Buckling up, I start my truck and let it automatically pair my phone, Jes's next words filling the cab through the speakers. "The boys are so excited for Scouts." She lowers her tone, swapping some of her normal sugar for spice, with a hint of sarcasm. "In case you didn't know, *it's badge night.*"

I'm well aware. The boys have been running up and down the halls for the last four weeks, chanting the countdown until the badge pinning ceremony tonight. Lex is earning his Fire Starter badge, having mastered kindling and his flint on our trip a few weeks ago. Our younger son, Des, is earning his Happy Camper badge. It's really just a badge to prove a six-year-old can get through a four-day camping trip without bitching and moaning.

And he did it… mostly.

They've been practically bouncing off the walls since I told the troop at our last meeting what badge each kid would be earning.

"Oh, yeah? Is that tonight?" I ask in teasing timbre. "Actually, while I remember," I veer away from our playful moment in order to relay important information. "I won't have time to catch a shower when I get home. Greg needs me to pick up Harley tonight and take him."

"Ohh," Jes's voice fattens with tenderness and care, and it's just one of the many things I love about her. She never did get close with Greg's wife, and yet she still cares about them as if they're our best friends. "That's good. Harls could use the consistency."

"That's what the therapist told them, too," I tell her,

seeing Greg's frown in my mind all over again. "Movers are coming to get some of his stuff from the old place, so he's giving Addie some space."

"Space," Jes says sadly, like the word is the final nail in the coffin for Greg's marriage. "Well, that's very sweet of you to grab Harls. Maybe take the boys out for ice cream after?"

In the background, I hear my sons shouting, "Ice cream!" at the top of their lungs, and a smile curls my lips as I join the traffic to get home.

"I was thinking about that very thing. And then I actually told Greg I'd take him out for a beer after." I pause, not so much waiting for Jes's reaction but more so, thinking back and seeing my old friend and foreman in my mind's eye. The man is holding it together by a thread. I can see the wear and tear of his emotional stress in the bags that line his eyes, the constant yawning and the thousand yard ponderous stares.

It hurts me to see him hurting.

"That's a wonderful plan," Jes says, snapping me back to the present. "You're a good man, Laws."

I want to be there for Greg, but Jes is my wife, so I can be honest with her. "I'd rather be at home with you." The crotch of my jeans tighten as the ropes I tied earlier flash behind my eyes. It morphs into an image of Jes's naked body, full soft tits out, gorgeous legs spread, ankles and wrists bound, pink beneath the rope confining her to the bed frame.

She misses the sentiment, something in the background crashing loudly, stealing her attention from the call. "Oh shoot—Laws, babe, I gotta go. I think Des just knocked my ficus over. Drive safe. Love you. See you soon."

"Love you, too. See you soon."

I end the call, and the drive home is one of those fucking

horrific ones where you can't remember if you even obeyed traffic laws. If someone told me I'd be granted world peace if I could describe just one single car I'd seen on my fifteen minute drive, well, I'd be fucked.

Only two things fill my mind as my foot falls heavily to the pedal, knuckles drained of color from gripping the wheel so hard.

How much I want my wife… and how much I want to do unspeakable things to her.

When we married, I'd planned on talking to her about my desires, my needs. Explaining to her that some animalistic part of me has always been driven to this fantasy, though I've never been comfortable or brave enough to ask for it. I made a lot of plans to talk to her, but life perpetually got in the way.

She got pregnant. And then we were nesting. And then we had Lex.

There was never a time to indulge, and that's what it felt like after the boys were born—an indulgence. Something excessive, that was too much to ask of someone who'd given so much to me already. I hadn't earned the right and certainly didn't deserve it.

So I smothered it. And I still do when I have to. Sometimes it feels like all I do all day, every day, is fight against my own nature. Other days, it's bearable.

Today is not one of those days.

As long as you stay honest and communicate, even through the stress, you'll be okay. Look at me, the biggest fucking secret-carrying hypocrite ever, telling my brother he'll be okay as long as he communicates.

I flick my blinker on and sail around the final turn,

making my way down our street. Our shiny black garage door is visible from here, and I can't help but smile to have home in my sights. The thing is, though, Graham just has to say he wants to have more sex. That's... simple, comparatively.

By the time I'm parked and trudging up the steps to get my boys, I've completely convinced myself I'm not a hypocrite. Because what I want has to stay secret. My needs must remain concealed.

I love Jes too much to ask her for it.

It's too much to ask of her.

Four

JES

I wanna hear you beg.

The last bit of mystery mixture splatters against the counter as I shake the bottle one more time. Leaning down, I sniff the purple goo before realizing exactly what it is.

Hands on hips, I face Des. "Des, what is this?" My nose wrinkles, the scent of purple gloop is unsurprisingly violating my senses. "It smells awful."

"Miracle mix. I made it for the worm outside." He takes another spoonful of peanut butter straight from the jar before I yank it away with my free hand.

"So many questions," I say, snatching the teal lid for the jar, screwing it on one-handed. Mom's can do so many things with one hand. It's truly amazing. "First, what worm?"

He plunges the spoon onto his tongue, talking around

the viscous mouthful. "The worm in the yard I've been feeding for a week."

I blink. "Okay... and... what's wrong with him?"

"He's a she, mom," he says pointedly as he licks peanut butter from his knuckles. "And she stopped moving three days ago. So I made her the miracle mix to bring her back to life."

I swallow as I watch my sweet boy obliterate what I know is definitely more than one serving of peanut butter. "Buddy, you know once something stops moving, that means it's no longer alive. I think your worm..." I say, choosing my words carefully in case this is one of these moments he's going to recite to a therapist in fifteen years; gosh, I hope not. "I think she's a goner, buddy."

He blinks at me like I'm a complete moron. "I know, mom." He wags a peanut butter finger at the purple foam melting into the countertop. "That's why I made the miracle mix." Not spoken but I feel the burn of his silent *duh*.

"Oh, and did it work?" I ask, tearing a paper towel off the roll. The Brawny man better not choose now to tell me he's full of shit.

"No," he says, dropping his spoon onto the counter.

"Sink, please," I say, leveling my gaze at the counter to make sure the miracle mix didn't leave a *miraculous* stain. "What's in the mix, Des?"

He drops his spoon in the sink then crashes into me for the hug he knows I'll demand of him before he goes up for his shower. "Vinegar, food coloring, yogurt, syrup, perfume and some of that stuff in dad's nightstand drawer."

My eyes go wide with horror. I peel his hug off me and

blink down at him, trying to control my frantic gaze. "Why were you in our room with your mix?"

"It stunk. So I wanted to pour your perfume in there. Then I did, then I wanted to see what dad had in his drawer. So like I said, I put some of that stuff in there, too."

I sift my fingers through his hair before pinching his cheeks. "No more miracle mix, no more going through me and dad's things, okay, buddy?"

His nod is half-hearted. I think we better put a lock on Laws' drawer, and I can't wait to tell him about this. A smile finds my lips as I tell Des goodnight, shouting the sentiment up to Lex as he exits the bathroom.

"'Night, mom," he calls down to me. "Is dad gonna come up and say goodnight?"

I glance at the porch where Laws is sitting in the swing, the light holding him in a romantic haze. As soon as he got home from what seemed like a heavy beer with Greg, he'd fielded a work call.

"Fuck," he'd growled as his phone illuminated with the site owner of the next days job. He'd slammed his lips to mine, and I loved how the traces of beer and advice tasted on him. My lower half had clenched, and I loved the tremor it sent through my belly in response. "I'll be back in here as soon as I can. I missed you tonight." He'd kissed me again and gone out the door, adjusting his crotch as he did.

And now I'm wearing a smile like a complete creep as I stare at the back of his head. Wow. I turn my focus back to my son upstairs. "Yeah, when he's off the phone, he'll be right up."

The shower starts and Des begins singing the theme song to PJ Masks despite the fact we haven't watched it in two years, and I toss the bottle of miracle mix, grinning down at it atop the coffee grounds in the trash.

Lube. He attempted to bring a worm back to life with lube. And... vinegar.

After tossing it, I turn to the sink to make sure I don't have any *miracle* residue on my hands. It's when I'm sudsing up that I notice my bare finger, the subtle indentation of where my wedding ring usually rests. I took it off earlier as I cleaned Laws' office. I remind myself to nab it after.

I sleep with it on. When we first got married, I stared at it on my finger. Smiled at it, even. And then it became like a second-skin—I hardly take it off unless it's at risk of being lost.

Casting a final glance to the front door to make sure I haven't locked it from habit while Laws is outside, I head upstairs for a hot shower.

While the boys were at Scouts tonight, I decided to use the spare time to thoroughly clean their game room—which reeked of dirty socks and chicken nuggets. Now, between the purple slop and my long day, I'm dying to rinse the smell of cleaner off my skin.

In the shower, I enjoy a plethora of luxury products that I don't typically use. Some days, after cleaning up after little boys, fancy products are an absolute must. With caviar skin patches beneath my eyes, soaking up traces of my age, I lather my ends with creamy conditioner, then move to shaving my legs. Twenty steamy minutes later, and I'm pulling a ballet pink satin night slip over me, tugging at it when it sticks to the remaining moisture on my torso.

Getting ready for bed is such a calming routine for me.

Usually Laws is in bed, his nose in a book or eyes glued to a documentary on TV. When I come out, his focus is only on me, and then it becomes *our time*. Tonight, with him taking a work call, I indulge in this pre-bed ritual a little more than normal.

I take time to smooth cool lotion up my freshly shaved legs, spray perfume behind my ears and roll moisturizing balm along my lips. When I've fully pampered myself, I quietly head down to nab my ring and come back up so I can wait for Laws in bed.

The office door is closed, a subtle glow coming from beneath the door. Shit, I must've left the lights on, too. Quietly, so that the boys don't hear the squeaky handle, I open the door and step inside.

And then, my entire body tenses. I freeze, a drop of water quietly falling from the ends of my wet hair, plunking against the hardwood.

Laws is no longer on the porch.

Laws is in his office.

That's not why I'm riveted, frozen two paces inside the office, my feet immovable from the hardwood. That's not why my eyes are wide, confusion paralyzing my lungs, making it impossible to breathe. Difficult to think.

In front of me, Laws is at his desk, hunched over, a small light on his desk illuminating whatever he's got cradled in his hand. His shoulder torques, his other arm jutting forward over and over.

I know what that arm is doing. I've watched, from a different perspective, this man do that very thing, many times. Many *erotic* times.

Before I can slip out and let him have this *moment* to

himself, his raspy, broken tone slices the guilt of interrupting him.

"I will fucking destroy you. Fuck you so hard you can't walk. And I won't show you mercy, I'll make you crawl. I'll force you to try and get away. But you won't get far. I'll catch you, and tie you up—bind you—I'll get off on the way your flesh strains and rubs raw against my knots. The way you'll be marked by my ropes." He sucks in a breath, and my arms break out in goosebumps. "Goddamnit, I wanna hear you *beg*."

My mind literally goes blank. My heart rapidly fires uneven beats, panic creating chaos inside me. I step backward, desperate for my heel to find the cool hardwood of the hallway. Dying to be out of this space.

Dying to get away from him.

My husband.

But my nerves make me shaky and as I step back, my elbow connects with the corner of a book on the shelf, and it topples to its side with a quiet thud.

Quiet, but loud enough for Laws to know I'm there.

His face appears over his shoulder, eyes wide at the sight of me. Then he turns, opening his body to me, exposing the contents of both of his hands.

The moving shoulder, the busy arm—that hand fists his thick, heavy cock and even though I'm confused at what's happening, shocked by the words I heard my sweet Laws utter, my body reacts to what it sees. Everything between my thighs pulsing at the sight.

But then my eyes go to his other hand, the one clutching *something*.

Expecting it to be porn on his phone or something similar, my eyes dart up and lock to his after I realize what he's looking at.

"Jes," he says, his voice aching with unease—vulnerability and shame etched into his handsome face. "Jes," he says again, searching for strength and control, but his voice is no less brittle on the second pass. He stands, shoving his cock away, dropping the photo so he can zip and belt himself.

He can drop it all he wants. I already saw the photo he held. I saw who he was saying all of those violent, unspeakable things to.

Me.

I stumble backwards, turn, and am fleeing up the stairs with tears blurring my vision as his heavy footsteps follow behind me. "Baby, wait, please," he rasps, his smoky tone now sending a shiver up my spine.

As soon as I make it to our room, I dart into the bathroom, the place that was a beautiful safe haven just minutes ago. I slam the door closed and twist the lock before crumpling to the floor, head leaning against the wall.

Less than a second later, as tears of confusion and pain slide down my cheeks, my heart never more rattled beneath my ribs and my stomach lurching, the light under the door darkens. Two thick fingertips slide beneath, just an inch, searching for my hand.

His voice is full of gravel, low and painful, pleading. "Jes, please, baby, I need to explain."

It was a picture of me he took a year ago. The boys were at his parents house for a long weekend, and we'd decided to have drinks with his brother and his wife. It was fun—maybe too much fun. Because when we got home, I'd stripped completely naked and put on a show for Laws—one he documented for posterity.

That picture in particular was after I'd given him what he deemed *the best blowjob of my fucking life*. Only this time, I didn't swallow like I usually do. This particular time, I begged him to paint me. I whined for him to come all over my face and breasts, and then to take a photo.

With kids and swapping phone numbers with room parents, we'd never been into taking naughty photos. It's just too risky. I live in fear of sending the Scout snack schedule with a cumshot selfie.

Just not worth the risk.

But this particular day, we were both into it. Laws took them with his phone, and while we'd peeked at them a few times over the last year, I'd largely forgotten about them. I didn't know he'd selected one—the most intimate one where I was lying on my back, Laws' cum coating my belly and lips, a post-orgasmic smile on my face. My hands cupped my breasts, but the light caramel of my areolas were visible. But this photo had been his favorite obviously, since he'd printed it.

He printed that photo.

He held that photo while he jerked off.

That made everything between my legs, low in my belly, awaken with excitement and need.

But those things he'd said. The harsh desires he rasped, the cruel words he growled, the dark fantasies he promised

—the look in his eyes showed how desperately he wanted to make them real.

He held my photo while he said those things.

"Baby, we need to talk. Please, Jes, I love you. Let me explain. Please. Let me explain." He begs, his breath hitching.

The door rattles gently as a soft thud sounds and he presses a heavy palm to his side of it. A physical representation of his plea to be heard.

"Please," he asks again, and this time I wipe the tears from my cheeks, dragging myself closer to the door. I take a deep breath.

"Talk."

Five

LAWS

Without Jessalyn Briggs, I'm nothing and no one.

Fuck. Fuck!

Jesus *fucking* Christ.

"Jes," I call after her up the stairs, refusing to temper my voice for the sleeping boys. Every fiber of me painfully strains to catch her, to grab her and make her understand what she's seen. What she's *witnessed*.

The door slams and my heart leaps to my throat, lodging itself there as I turn the corner. Seeing the open bedroom door earns me a smidge of relief, knowing I haven't been locked out of *our private space*. I shut it, then spot the closed bathroom door. Her soft whimpers floor me, even through inches of wood, and I crumble. Palms bracing the floor, my forehead hits the door with a thud.

"Jes," I pant, out of breath from the chase.

I consider that a moment—I've *dreamed* of this feeling; my lungs burning from a grueling chase. Yet, the way I feel now, shaky, unstable, emotionally clinging to an edge over a void so dark and deep I can't help but be terrified—*not what I dreamed of*. Not the feelings I imagined exploring.

"Baby, we need to talk. Please, Jes, I love you. *Let me explain.*" I place a palm on the door, wanting nothing more than to see her soft smile and bright eyes. To find her lips and kiss her until *that* memory of me is erased, taste her until she realizes I'm the same man. "*Please.* Let me explain."

Everything in my torso twists with frustration, fear and anger. Why did I have to indulge tonight? Why didn't I lock myself in the bathroom, at the very fucking least? Stupid. *Stupid and fucking sloppy.* And what's more? Now my wife finds me so abhorrent she's hiding from me—from him.

The monster. *My monster.*

Despite the fact I've starved him, still, he grows. He thrives off the hunger, getting stronger, his presence taking a deep root inside me.

Tonight I couldn't ignore him.

I tried. But after having the coarse groove of ropes against my hands all day, paired with being apart from her for a few extra hours, he seized control and extinguished all rational thought.

I really felt as if I had no choice in it.

Jes's silence stretches beyond my comfort, but I wait. Because I have to. Letting the monster surface has put me in this awful, fucking uncomfortable position. I have to wait.

When she finally speaks, I'm relieved and horrified.

Relieved she's willing to hear me out after walking in on me saying vile things to a photo of her. Horrified that her voice cracks, that she's unsure of me, horrified that I let her see this disgusting side of myself.

"Talk," she says, breathing hard. Even through the door, I feel her unease.

This is why, *right here*.

This is why I kept it hidden. Because Jes is everything.

Without Jessalyn Briggs, I'm nothing and no one.

I can't breathe, eat, sleep—fuck, I can't *live* without her. I wouldn't have married her if I could. That's how tied I am to this life we've built.

And now, everything I love and have worked so hard for seems to be teetering on an invisible scale, dangerously close to tipping and upending my entire existence. I have no control. I hate it.

But she's willing to listen, so I have to be considerate with every word I choose. Try to explain what she saw, and how it doesn't take away from my love for her.

"Baby, first, I just... I need you to know. What you walked in on..." My words trail off as a vision of what she must've seen hits me. The second-hand cringe I feel causes me to jerk off the door in a wince. There's no movement on her side, not even a whisper of a breath, so I settle into my discomfort and find my place against the door. I slide the tips of my fingers beneath, dying to get closer to her.

"What you walked in on," I start again, forcing a strength I don't feel into my tone. I feel entirely boneless at the moment. "It's hard to put into words, baby... there's always been a part of me, and when I say always, I mean *always*. Like, when I was young and just discovering girls, even..."

I think back on high school. Prom, more specifically. I'd taken this girl I'd been dating for the second half of the school year. Fuck, all these years later, I can't even remember her name. Truth be told, I can't really remember too much about her.

Because it wasn't about her that night.

The silk dress she wore—I'll never forget how it felt beneath my fingers, so soft and pliable. Her hair was up in this fancy twisty thing, but she'd left a few stray pieces down. One of the stray curls kept tickling my ear as we rocked together beneath the strobe lights, and that was the first time *he* surfaced.

The monster.

The soft dress and the faint tickling of her hair, the way she giggled quietly and held me loosely—I don't know what it was but that series of events had me aching to be aggressive. She asked if I wanted to go back to her house after. *What parents go out of town on prom weekend?* High school Laws however, I was completely onboard.

Once we got there, I thought what I was feeling was natural, normal even. So I pinned her to the wall, my teenage hand gripping her throat as if I had any business doing so, my other palming between her thighs, searching for something I'd never experienced.

She pushed me off, and though I can't remember her name or what she wore, I can still see her eyes. The fear in them. She told me to leave, and I never even tried to explain. I realized years later she probably thought I was going to rape her.

She kicked me out, dumped me, and we acted like strangers the remaining two weeks of school. I remember that part glaringly, because I forever associated disgust and abandonment with *him* and *his urges*.

With *my* urges.

On the other side of the door, I hear my wife shift, and I find a way to continue.

"I've always had this piece of me. I keep it buried deep, but it's there. Always." I chew at the corner of my mouth, wondering how much Jes heard earlier. But it doesn't matter. The truth I never thought I'd need to share is laying on the proverbial table between us, exposed and raw. There's no ignoring it now. "Sometimes, its hard to ignore and I feel like I'll fucking explode if I can't indulge it."

Then, I explain to her my rationale, realizing it may sound ridiculous. But from this side of the door, honesty is my only tool. "When it starts to become unbearable, I let this part out. Feed the phantom what it wants—what it needs. And it works for a while, and I get to protect you from it. From me."

"Wh–" she starts, and my heart leaps to my throat in anxious anticipation of her words. "What is the *phantom*?" The way her voice trembles makes the backs of my eyes burn with frustration.

"The part of me that wants bad, *bad* things. I call him a phantom, because he haunts me. And honestly, it made me feel better to assign these needs to a separate identity, so I could *live*, and tell myself that it wasn't *me* who had these desires. The desires to chase, to take, to hurt. It was someone *else* wanting that shit."

"You–" she starts, stopping again, her timid words and anguished tone souring my gut, flooding my veins with concern. My entire body is covered in a sheen of nervous sweat. "You want to hurt women?"

"No, fuck no, Jes. It's *not* like that," I grind out, having to control the flare of anger in my tone. I'm not angry with her, but rather myself. But I can't have her thinking I'm angry at all.

Not after what she witnessed.

The things she heard.

"It's more like... I have this urge to be... *forceful* and..." I consider my options here. *Rapey?* A sick shiver rattles my spine that the word *rape* is something that gets my heart racing. It's not that I want to rape my wife, but I desperately want to... *play*. I want her to run, and I want to chase. I want her to resist, and I want to take. Take what's *mine*. "Aggressive." It's the best choice because it unfortunately does a blanket job describing many of the urges tethered to me.

"Aggressive," she parrots, and I envision her face tipped toward the door, red hair shiny beneath the fluorescent lights in the bathroom. My chest feels hollow at the vision, because there's a door between us and twenty minutes ago, nothing was.

All because I was too fucking weak to tame the brute.

"Like... talk to me, Laws, because the things you said—"

"Fuck," I hiss, shoving my big hand further beneath, my knuckles catching painfully on the bottom of the door. But I don't care. I'm desperate to touch her, to feel her velvety skin caress my calloused hands, to take her lips then feel her words tickle my ear as she whispers, *It's okay, we're okay, I love you.*

I don't get those things. But she does put her hand on top of my fingers, and causes my shoulders to drop with much needed relief. If she wanted to leave me, she wouldn't console me this way. Her palm strokes my fingertips a few times before settling comfortably on top, as if she knows I need her touch to find strength to admit these things.

"I'm sorry you heard those things... they're... awful. *Heinous.*" They are. I have no defense.

"But... you want them? I mean, you meant them? You..." I hate how much I have her struggling through thoughts and words. "You were picturing doing those things *to me*?"

The inside of my cheek is likely bleeding. My mouth has tasted of copper for the last two minutes, but I can't stop biting the pocket of my cheek. I'm at the point where I'm willing to be open with Jes about my desires, confess the hold they have on me.

She could run from *what I want*, from me.

And I wouldn't blame her.

"I meant them. I was saying those things and envisioning doing them, yes. Every now and then, when all these supremely fucked up urges hit me, claw at me until they're threatening to overpower me, I have to succumb. I have to indulge. But I'm ashamed, Jes. I'm so fucking disgusted that the man that imagines those things is the same man who throws a football to his sons..."— my voice begins to shake —"who touches *you.*"

"Laws." My name is a whimper, muffled by the door.

"I was indulging myself in the fantasy of what it would feel like to finally *surrender* to those dark needs... And then I planned on ignoring them again for as long as I could," I sigh. "Until I couldn't resist any longer."

There's a few moments of silence that turn into what feels like minutes, but I give them to her. I'd have given her anything before, but now, as I wait to hear my fate, I want to give her everything. If she needs to ignore me for a month, I'd barely survive it, but I'd do it.

"I never meant for you to see that part of me." My sigh is heavy, and leaves my chest feeling so empty. "I'm embarrassed and humiliated and scared." I wish I could see her eyes. "I'm scared, Jes," I admit freely, and as I do, I become more fearful, more panicked.

As if she senses it, she begins smoothing her hand along the tips of my fingers again. "I don't want you to think I'm a monster. I love you. I would never hurt you. *Ever*." I swallow hard. "I'd hurt myself before I hurt you."

Her hand is gone, and my heart returns to the lodged position in my throat. Then the lock twists, and I leap to my feet just in time. She stands there, eyes pink from tears, but laser focused on me. Immediately, her eyes pin me, prodding me for answers but I don't know the question.

I tell her what I want her to know, because it's all I can do.

"I don't need to *act on* that side of me... it's why..." I nod toward the bedroom door, alluding to the office downstairs where she found me. "It's why I get it out of my system on my own. But I promise you, I don't need it *between us*." I reach out and when she lets me place my hands on the sides of her arms, I'm so fucking happy my body nearly goes numb.

"I've gone my entire life keeping this hidden. I'm just... sorry you had to know about it at all."

She chews her lip. All I want to do is give her a bruising kiss.

"You... Do you want to talk about it? What you feel?

Those… *needs*?" Her face is so wracked with uncertainty that it physically pains me. Pulling her toward me, her softness presses into me, easing the discomfort. I smooth my hands up and down her back, nuzzling my nose into her hair. Inhaling her scent to further calm myself.

"No. I don't. I want to go back to it being a part of me that isn't for us, and us being good. Okay?" I pull back, clutching her face in my palms, staring down into her eyes. "You know I would never hurt you, right?"

The way she leaves not even a moment of silence between us before responding makes my heart throb and my dick hard.

"Of course I know that." She rocks to her toes and finds my lips, and I get lost in the sweetest kiss. When we pull apart, she's already guiding me to the bed, and she's got her hand on my belt.

Jes falls to her knees and sucks my cock, taking me deep and not relenting even when I beg her to let me shower. When I struggle with keeping my eyes on her, the shame of my desires now exposed and making me antsy—she softly murmurs, "Eyes on your wife."

She sucks me in unhurried pulls, moving her lips and tongue all over my shaft, adoring me like a fucking king. I look away a few more times, feeling so fucking guilty to be shown affection after what just happened. She rises to her feet, leaving my wet cock to bob between us as she captures my face in her palms and whispers, "Just stay focused on me."

It's the best blow job of my life, and she swallows my entire, eager load. She even licks me clean after.

She may have worshiped me like a king, but she is a

queen. *My* queen. I don't know if she's trying to prove that what she saw doesn't scare her, but I needed it.

I needed to know the monster didn't terrify her. He's back in the shadows already, chained and gagged, locked in his prison. Only this time, I'm going to try my best to keep him there.

And kill him.

Because I do not want to go through *that* ever again.

JES

He deserves it.

I slide my water bottle into the cupholder, though I've been in such a daze recently, I'm not sure I even refilled it. Whatever. At this point, I'm just glad I made it to spin.

On the drive here, I was honked at after I zoned out at a green light, and then the school called me to tell me the boys didn't have lunch today. Not to mention, I'm wearing two different shoes.

I cannot fucking focus.

And that's so unlike me.

"You seem... frazzled. That god of yours take you to pound town last night?" Penny asks, grinning at me as she leans forward to adjust the clamp around her shoe. I strap into my bike and glance around us. Empty class today. Not even Ruthie is here.

I snort. "No pound town with my god," I repeat, though it's funny because... the girls tease me about Laws and what a perfect specimen he is but... I don't disagree. When he fucks me hard, I look up at him like he is my personal god. Giving me a life so full and beautiful, taking care of me in all ways.

If that's not what a god does, I don't want to believe.

"Hey, can I ask you something?" I ask quietly, working way too hard to sound natural and not dicey. I feel dicey, and that's the part in this I hate. The sudden feeling of discomfort within my own mind, within the foundations of my marriage, to a certain extent.

She nods, tying her hair up into a heap on her head. "What's up?"

"I'm kind of wanting to experiment... explore things outside the normal... sexually," I say, knowing that my cheeks are indeed bright red. Cherries. Cherries in the fucking sunlight. I can feel the heat radiating from my cheeks. I can also feel Penny's eyes cutting into me.

"Things with Laws are getting stale?" she asks, making the assumption of the year. I can't blame her though because most would be asking this question on the cusp of a dead bedroom situation.

I honor my devotion and loyalty to my husband by keeping all of this to us. "Not at all. I wanted to... surprise him. Only, I know more about which brand of football cleats are best and what days of the week ground turkey is on sale, than the latest way to experiment with your man if you know what I mean?"

She nods, giggling. "I do know." With a sigh, she stares

forward at Cas who is warming her legs up in easy, slow cycles. Penny follows suit, turning her head to face me as she stumbles upon an answer. I can see it in the way her eyes sparkle.

She snaps, points at me, wiggling her hand. "Oh! You should take that sex quiz everyone was talking about last year."

I cock an eyebrow. "Who's everyone?" I mean, I see Penny four days a week and have for the last three years. I don't know about any sex quiz.

"Just everyone," she says, going for a quick drink of her water before continuing. "I'll send you the link after class. Basically it's this super in depth quiz where you answer tons of questions about what you like and why, and how those things make you feel. And those questions branch off into more detailed questions and at the end, you learn who you are. Sexually, at least."

Cas starts the class, and our conversation is immediately drowned out by house music. I think about the quiz. Do I need it? More so, do I know that I don't need it? Maybe I could get Laws to take it with me, maybe I could show him that I'm willing to explore anything, as long as it's with him, and as long as it means I have all of him.

That's what has me distracted and unfocused. It may even be what upset me the most. The idea that he's not wholly mine, that I haven't discovered every part of him. It feels wrong.

I think about that the *entire* spin class, and afterwards, Penny sends me the link. I save it, unsure of when or how I'll use it. But I will.

Because I just can't let it go.

* * *

After the workout, Ruthie met us at the diner for brunch, and to catch up on all the Cas-Tad tea.

"And what did you say?" Ruthie asks, the little vein in her forehead pumping. She inches her flattened palms along the table and even though the question isn't directed at me, I feel the heat.

Cas tucks a stray hair behind her ear before studying her nails, ever nonchalant. "I didn't say anything. I just left."

Boom, boom, boom. Rattle, rattle, rattle.

Ruthie's hands come down on the tabletop three times, the salt and pepper shakers rattling, silverware sliding off napkins. "Yes, Cas! Fucking yes!"

After spin class, we went out for brunch because Cas said she had news about Tad. We're all thoroughly invested in her Tad saga, as every new story seems less believable than the last. If I hadn't seen him with my own eyes, I'd have thought she made him up. He's a total theme park caricature in the flesh.

Cas told us she found Tinder and Bumble on Tad's phone last night, and when she confronted him, he asked the three words that would insult anyone's intelligence.

Are you sure?

She left him. *Finally*, she left him.

Ruthie snaps in the air to grab the waitresses attention. "Fries. We'll take a round of fries."

They're Cas's favorite. The waitress nods, and I lean back against the booth, arms folded in disbelief. "You finally did it. Good for you, Cas, good for freaking you."

She twirls a strand of blonde hair around her finger, but

drops her gaze to me more seriously. "Now I just need him to get out. Because storming out felt good, but I own that house."

Ruthie snorts. "Tad's homeless."

"Tad should have thought about that before he downloaded Tinder and Bumble," Cas adds, and I love so much that this time, she hasn't volleyed back. In the past, they'd had some... relationship snafus.

Tad thought they should split the bills 50/50, but said since Cas already owned the home, he shouldn't pay half of the mortgage. They argued about that, and Cas ultimately agreed to let him just pay his bills.

There'd been more argument worthy red flags since, of course, but every single time, Cas stayed with him. I guess the only thing that went too far was cheating. Cas is a high reach for Tad anyway, so the fact that he felt insecure enough to cheat doesn't surprise me. In truth, I'm happy for her.

She can walk away from a life she's pretending to be content with, and find what she really wants. Is there anything worse than living a life, pretending you're okay, only to be secretly dying for more?

Mid-sip of my mimosa, I choke. Like, ugly choke. Bulging veins in my neck, orange juice burning its way out of my nostrils, panic in my eyes. Ruthie rubs my back with a look of disgust on her face. "Girl, slow down."

I shake my head and speak around the tickling cough remaining in my throat. "I'm–I'm fine." I want to say I didn't drink too fast, but then they'd ask what's wrong. And just the idea that there's a real answer to that question makes my stomach hurt.

I love my life. I don't want something to be wrong at all.

Laws.

A week ago, I caught him handling himself, dark words melting off his tongue like those things are his first language, looking at a picture of me.

Initially, I'd been... caught off guard. I don't even know if scared best fits how I felt, but I admit, I was shocked. And we sat by the door and talked through it. What I learned about my husband made me... honestly?

Sad.

Sad because he's a wonderful man. A hard worker, great father, dedicated son and brother, stellar friend, beautiful partner and... a perfect lover. He deserves to be happy and fulfilled in *all ways*. Every want and whim deserves catering to. I believe that.

And to learn he's been wanting something, craving something and hiding it away all this time? To learn that he's living a life where a huge source of passion and fulfillment sits unattended?

I'm sad. I'm sad because I want him to have everything he needs.

I'm sad that he never felt like he could share.

And I'm sad that he won't talk about it with me.

But I'm not sad that he wants it. I'm not.

"You okay?" Cas asks, dusting the fresh plate of fries with a heavy layer of salt. I steal one, and slide it between my lips, the grease hot against my tongue, and nod.

Sharing things with my girlfriends is definitely still a thing at age thirty-six. And Cas, Ruthie and Penny have been through shit. They've seen things, they've dated losers, they've dealt with angry PTA moms and bad teachers. We're in this thing together.

But Laws.

What we have is, I've always believed, special. Our relationship supersedes all others in that, if I have a problem or concern, I speak directly with him. He does the same with me. We don't take our issues to a wall of friends to field advice—we go straight to each other.

It's been twelve years of marriage, without so much as one single *big* argument.

I have to say, our strategy has worked.

I take another french fry as Penny joins the conversation, no longer attempting to find Tad's dating profiles on her phone. "Know any cops? We can get one to scare him, make him think he's being forcefully evicted."

Cas snorts, dunking a fry into ketchup. "Not a bad idea. He does scare easy."

Their conversation rolls on, but I can't stop thinking about my husband. The way he's lived all this time without something he clearly wants, and obviously needs.

He's Cas and I'm Tad, living oblivious of my partner's needs. What if one day, like Cas, he leaves me? Will he get tired of stifling this part of him, grow exhausted of hiding and go find someone that can give him everything?

My heart pumps fast, causing my hairline to break out in nervous sweat. The french fries roll around souring in my gut, stress causing my energy to spike and crash. The edges of my vision darken and the breath in my lungs becomes heavy, almost unbreathable. I edge toward Ruthie in the booth, glancing at my watch as if I'd just remembered something I forgot.

A panic attack. That's what I'm having.

I don't have them often. I'm pretty sure the last time I did was when Des got a marble stuck up his nose, so I know that's what this is.

"Oh shoot, gotta grab the new shirts from the cleaners and drop them at the office. I gotta go," I lie through my teeth as I slide out of the booth, causing Ruthie to do the same.

"See you guys tomorrow morning. Cas, good for you," I say, smiling, forcing it to look as natural as possible. She dunks another fry in ketchup, beaming up at me.

"Thanks, Jes. See you tomorrow."

Ruthie and Penny lift their hands in a wave as the waitress returns with more mimosas, and I slip out of the restaurant into the cool morning. Sucking in a few lungfuls of fresh air, I tip my face to the sun and concentrate on the way its subtle warmth makes me tingle. I focus on how it can calm me, if I let it.

A few minutes later, I'm sliding into my SUV, trying to tell myself that Laws won't leave me, that he's not Cas and I'm not Tad. I look into the rearview, catching a glimpse of my eyes. "You are not Tad," I say aloud before reversing my vehicle and heading home.

Maybe a hot shower and some extra water to flush the copious amounts of caffeine will help. I've been overdoing it on coffee this week. It's been my vice. Everytime my mind wanders to my gorgeous husband, replaying him hunched over my photo, aggressively stroking his fat cock with a greedy grip, looking at me... panic surges through me.

Not at what he was doing. That may have been my initial reaction. But now, I feel panic that he wants something that I'm not giving him. That he thinks that he doesn't deserve to have it.

And then the sadness. The sadness that he feels so bad about wanting something so dark. People want all sorts of things. I mean, he was holding my photo. It would be one thing if I walked in on him holding a photo of like, a tree or something, promising to fuck it senseless.

But he wants *me*.

He wants those dark things, yes, but he wants them with *me*.

I'm hit with another wave of sadness when I realize my husband has felt like he had to hide a part of himself for so long. That he can't completely be himself. I hate that for him. I want more for him.

For us. Because there isn't a point in tying yourself to someone legally, emotionally and spiritually for the rest of your life if you can't be honest with them about what you need.

I drive home, thinking of all the ways I feel like I failed him.

I should be the person he goes to with these things, his safe place. I should be the one he wants to share it with. I should be the person he doesn't hide his demons from.

"And how many states are there?" Laws' brows fall between his eyes as he gives Lex his best poker face.

Lex nods, lips moving slightly, then answers, "Fifty!"

Laws' big hands come together in a bone-shaking clap. "Yes!" he hollars, Lex's proud grin making me smile, too.

"See? When you practice, you can remember anything. That's all memorizing is... practice."

Laws' eyes drift to mine over the table, Des's head tucked into my chest as he grows sleepy. I stroke his back while I enjoy my husband's gaze. Stubble lines his normally clean-shaven jaw, and the way he looks after a long day at work never ceases to turn me on. Messy hair from having a baseball hat on all day, fingers worn from tying ropes. The energy he gives off travels to the needy spot between my legs.

"Okay, boys," I say, ready for *my* time with Daddy. "Time to head up."

We go through our routine, saying goodnight to the boys, Laws following them up to tuck them in. We trade off on tucking in and bedtime stories, and while he's up there, I mix us each a drink and start the fire in the living room.

By the time he comes down, I'm toasty from the booze, and my legs are warming from the hearth. I pat the couch next to me and love that butterflies still spread their wings in my chest as his musky scent rains down on me. He drags my legs into his lap, running his coarse palms up my calves.

Immediately, his touch disarms any unease in me, the way it always does. My panties absorb the effects of his touch, but I gather my resolve, refusing to get lost in him when there are things we need to discuss.

I won't be made a Tad by giving in to my fears.

"Lex is getting so good with his memorization," I start, catching the hand that smooths up my leg, rubbing away the tension from Cas's brutal spin classes. I waffle our fingers together, then flip them, dragging a fingertip along the lines of his palm. Beautiful, work-worn hands. I've always loved his hands. Been obsessed with them really.

The way they're capable of hard work and tough jobs, but morph so easily into tender tools of pleasure, touching me with adoration and care. When he wraps them around me in bed, moulding to my bare breasts after a long night of lovemaking, when he cups them to my face and brings our mouths together in a kiss, when he places them along the counter on the side of me to brace himself as he fucks me—I'm obsessed.

The truth is, it's not just his hands. It's him.

But now, I'm tracing lines on his palm, wondering about all of the things these hands want to do but haven't. All the possibilities out there that we haven't grazed.

"Yeah," he says, his voice cautious. That's us. He senses more is coming, and he's not wrong. Because we've built that ability to wordlessly understand each other over time. Only, have we? He understands me, but clearly if there's a part of him I didn't know existed, how well do I know him?

My stomach turns, sending a heavy wave of unease through me.

"What's the matter, Jes?" he asks, gravel and stone, the depth and timbre of his tone causing my eyes to fill.

I blink a few times, still studying his palm, blinking away the moisture. Then I find his eyes, dark and deep pools of amber and chocolate swirling together, stealing my breath with their beauty.

"I wanted to talk about last week."

A lot of things happened last week. The boys earned new badges at Scouts. Laws counseled Greg through his emotional hardships. Graham and Mae decided they want to have kids. Cas left Tad.

We both know exactly what I want to talk about, and it's none of that.

His eyes hold mine, but I don't miss the way his chest rises with a pensive inhale, uncertainty vibrating off him in palpable waves.

"Please," I say, holding more tightly to his hand, probably feeding into my crazy subconscious thought that this thing could take him from me.

This thing that isn't necessarily off the table for me.

Not at all.

Because whatever gets him going, whatever ignites the fire in his veins and illuminates his dirty desires? I want that, too. I want that for us both.

"I just want to talk about it. I want to know more. I want to… understand," I finish, not entirely sure that I've chosen the right words. I continue to stroke his palm, silently hoping that my soft presence and careful conversation is telling him what he needs to know: that I'm here, and I love him.

He shakes his head, and I can tell he wants to yank his hand away and shuck them through his hair, pulling at the ends like he does when he's flustered. But he keeps his hand there, and maybe that's his attempt to acknowledge that I'm coming from love and care.

That I come to this couch free of judgment.

"It's… embarrassing, Jes. I don't want to talk about it. I don't like feeling ridiculous at my age. Especially not in front of you."

I blink at him, the orange flames dancing against his chocolate eyes. "Why are you embarrassed?"

Now he yanks his hand from mine, feeding it through

the side of his hair as he sighs with the weight of a thousand worlds. A weight I'd give anything to ease.

"Because it's fucking humiliating wanting these despicable fucking things. On top of that, to not be able to fully control myself—and to have that lapse be witnessed by the person I love and respect the most…" His eyes grow warm with discomfort and self-hatred, and my heart breaks in response.

He feels disgusting. He feels dirty. He feels wrong.

And I feel none of those things.

I feel worried, I feel like any secret between us is a bad thing and the idea that he wants to keep his secret buried. That's what hurts me, because it's hurting him. But as I reach for his hand again, I can sense his agitation rising with the hot exhale he forces out.

"I don't–" he jerks forward, cutting me off. 'Judge you' were the next words I was going to say but he doesn't allow it. He collects my face in those hands that I love. Those hands that I now know crave forbidden things.

"Please, Jes. Okay? Please just drop it."

I don't want to drop it, because dropping it feels like agreeing to a relationship where I don't fully know the man I love. That's not why I got married.

But his eyes are wet, and I think it's fear. Fear of what he believes it means if he truly wants what he does. And I don't even know the full extent—but there's clearly more. Because a little aggressive sex with roleplay can't have him this twisted up and scared. He looks haunted.

I want to talk about this. I want to know my husband fully the way I believed I did only a week ago.

But I don't want to break him.

"Okay," I reply softly, finding my way into his lap. Our breaths synchronize with my back to his chest, and after a few minutes of quiet in front of the fire, he lowers his chin to my shoulder, lips tickling my ear, and rasps, "Take a bath with me."

So we do. And under the bubbly surface of the tub water, his eyes boring into mine, he fucks me with his fingers. The thick, callused fingers that turn me on at just the sight of them. Water sloshes onto the floor. The rhythmic movement of his shoulder above the water as he fucks me hard, makes me heady, my temples tingling with pleasure.

When we get out of the bath, he lays me across the bed, using his hands to push my knees open, he feasts on me, slow and soft. His tongue works steady, gentle circles around my clit as his fingertips sink into my hips. My spine arches into a harsh crescent as the need to come coils tightly in my belly, his unrelenting lips on my clit driving me wild.

He kisses me, plunging two fingers in and out, bringing me to orgasm as he devours the terrain of my bare body with his hungry gaze. When I come, I crane my head from the bed, desperate for his eyes. Dying to see how he's feeling, to see if this second orgasm he's giving me is to prove that he's still him, the man that brings me to my knees endlessly.

I hold his gaze, managing to pant, "I love you, Laws," right before I spasm around his fingers and on his tongue, coming in long, almost violent waves. My thighs twitch and my shoulders roll, my entire body exploding with delight. Before I know it, my eyes are open and he's swaying over me, one hand moving between us.

Then he's there, entering me, driving his hips forward to

feed me every delicious inch of his thick, engorged cock. His eyes bore into my soul, communicating things I know he can't say. He isn't ready to talk about it and he's unsure how to get comfortable with it.

And that's okay.

I feed my fingers through his hair, eating up the groans and grunts that rain over me as he thrusts in and out. I've made love to him so many times, taken him in so many positions, and it never gets old.

Feeling him hold tight to control as he struggles not to come, as he fights to fuck me hard, to give me the experience he knows drives me wild—it makes me so wet. And he feels it.

Pulling his crown back to my entrance, he holds himself there, barely in, barely out. "You feel so good, Jes. I love how wet you get for me."

I nod, telling him the truth. "I'm close, Laws. Please, put it back in. Fuck me. I want to come." I need to come with him, that's what I left unsaid.

He sinks inside with force, and the pace he falls into is much quicker, a little more urgent than before. Laws is the biggest man I've been with and giving birth hasn't changed the fact that he stretches me every time.

Stilling, his eyes pin me, because he rarely shuts them when he orgasms. He likes looking into my eyes as he fills me with his cum, and I like it that way, too. It's brazen and intimate, something I've only ever experienced with him.

Lodged tight inside me, he begins to pulse, sending ripples of heat through my abdomen. His eyes soften as he comes, but still hold mine all the same. I seize around him, more eager to come with him this time than ever before. He groans as my pussy milks his cock, prolonging his orgasm and laying claim to every last drop of cum.

"Yes," I pant, the final burst filling me. I've never felt so warm and full and sated.

Our mouths come together in a kiss that clearly means more to both of us than either are willing to admit, and it's like a promise. A promise that no matter what happens moving forward, we're committed to getting through it. Together. With love.

He cleans me up, brings my breast to his lips, sucking gently. He carves a trail of kisses down my body, then pulls the duvet over me. Taking his spot as the big spoon, we fall asleep with his softening cock pressed to my back, his gentle snores flanking me.

I stay awake.

Because I don't want to drop it. I want to pick it up, turn it around in my hands and make sense of it. I want that for him.

He deserves it.

Seven

LAWS

I want to know your darkest desires.

She towels the ends of her hair, and I want to focus on what she's saying—pretty sure I'm on the receiving end of an update regarding Mae and Graham's road to impregnation—but I can't focus.

The way her tits sway beneath that little satin slip she wears to bed. My fists clench the balled up sheet at my hips as I nod my head, doing my very best to listen.

"I sent her the Amazon link to the ovulation tests that Penny used, so maybe that will help… focus their efforts," she says, feeding the end of the towel through the rack, hanging it to dry. Lotioning her hands, she begins smoothing cream along her collarbone, wet hair drifting around her shoulders.

Her arm bumps her breast as she lotions, and my cock goes from hard to standing.

"And I told her to be careful about using those ovulation tracker apps because they get so much of your information, you know?" A spritz of perfume on her wrists, then one behind each ear, and she's sliding into bed next to me.

Fuck she smells good. She always does but lately, I think her desire to connect with me over what I told her, it's made her even more attractive to me. Which I didn't previously think possible.

I mean, I closed up like a fuckin' *Spirit Halloween* on November 1st, but it still made me feel good that she wanted to know more. She wanted to step into the darkness and start feeling around with me, make sense of it for me.

I pull the sheet and duvet back, and my cock springs up, no longer weighed down by blankets. Beneath my flannel pajama pants, he stands, a glimpse of pinkening flesh visible from the straining fabric near the button fly. My wife's eyes go to it, then come to mine.

"You dirty old man. You got a boner from watching me put lotion on?" she asks, her lips curling playfully. A few wild strands of vermilion get stuck to her lips as she finger-combs her drying hair, eyeing me as she does. Everything this woman does is sexy, *everything*. She even looked good with her feet in stirrups, strain thick in her neck, cheeks blotchy and flushed from exertion. I'd never have told her she looked sexy giving birth because she would have likely cut my balls off. The point is, she always looks good to me.

"I think I'd get hard from watching you do just about anything," I admit, catching her hand from her hair, bringing it down to my cock.

The chest-rumbling moan she does when she wraps her hand around my cock makes me groan in reply. I pat my thigh. "Come ride."

Hitching her night dress around her waist, she reveals a bare lower half as she swings a leg over me, hopping on.

"No panties," I groan, letting the broad pad of my thumb trace the thin strip of hair she maintains, right above her pussy. A little red landing strip. "You came to our bed with a mission."

I watch her delicate hand guide my cock to her center, and tug the straps of her gown down, letting the satin pool at her waist. Revealing her luscious tits, causing me to bite down on my lower lip. "You're fucking gorgeous, Jes."

My hands cup her breasts, causing her head to fall back, a needy rasp breaking past her pink, full lips. "Your hands feel so good on me," she sighs as her hips begin to rock forward. "And yes, I came to bed hoping for this."

Her head drops forward, and my nipples harden as the ends of her hair drag against my chest. I grab her hips, watching her tits move as she rides me, barely lifting off. Her eyes hold mine, and her voice is vulnerable, soft and shaky. "I always want this with you, Laws."

With that sentence, the energy shifts. She lowers herself onto my cock again, our groins pressing together as she finds that depth she loves. All the fucking way in, as deep as she can, that's how she likes it. Sometimes, in this position, I'm even too much for her. But her hands grip my thighs as she rides, and as much as I want to get lost in her fucking me, that one sentence comes drifting back.

"I do, too," I tell her, my voice much raspier out loud than it sounded in my head. "I always want you, baby. Every second of the goddamn day." I lean forward, my mouth salivating and drool pooling beneath my tongue as I crush my mouth to her breast, sucking her nipple. She wiggles her hips, changing the angle slightly, and I palm her breasts, gently biting the stiff peak filling my mouth.

"Oh Laws," she moans, and she's a little louder than usual. When I come off her breast and look up at her, the delicate curve of her throat as her head tips back, the soft moans of accelerating delight as she writhes on my cock—goddamn she's everything.

But she's never loud, because she's always worried about the boys.

She puts her hand over mine, both of us now clutching one of her breasts. Then she strokes over my wedding band with her thumb, using her other hand to reach back and drag her nails along the pebbled flesh of my full sac.

She isn't just beautiful.

She's clever.

She wants to talk about my desires, my wants, my needs. She wants to explore. And last week I told her no. She hasn't brought it up since. But as she rides me, touching the band that tells the world we're one, teasing my balls—I know she's got me.

Whatever she's going to do now—ask me to talk, beg me to share, *whatever it fucking is*—I'll do it. I know I will.

Because the image of her fucking me, rocking back and forth in my lap like a needy little thing—it's too good. Way too fucking good. My cock is already hard to control, being strangled by her soft, wet walls.

Her mouth comes down on my jaw, and she leaves

savage kisses all over my cheek and throat, before sealing her lips to mine.

My tongue twists with hers, she keens into the kiss, causing my hips to drive up off the mattress, the need to seriously fucking impale her with my cock nearly overwhelming.

She breaks our kiss, and her swollen, used lips have me nearly coming. "I want to give you everything you need," she says, stilling over me—denying me the undulations of her tight cunt. Sweat beads along her chest, and my tongue tingles, dying to collect her flavor, to lick her fucking clean.

"You do," I croak, trying to make myself sound anything but the desperate fucking animal that I am. Attempting to save my energy and not blow before her.

"I want to know your darkest desires," she coos, her fingertips moving down the seam of my balls to the stretch of skin leading to my ass. I suck in a breath when she starts rubbing my taint, hitting erogenous zones we don't always play with.

But it feels good. So goddamn good. Now holding her hips, I squeeze her with a moment of pure force, as a warning. "Jes, I don't want to come yet."

She nods, but her eyes tell me everything I need to know. She knows I'm not going to take her off my cock because I don't want to talk.

Hell, we both know I won't do that.

Her hips resume their sensuous figure-eighting, and I bite the inside of my mouth so I don't fill her up this second.

All this shit. Exposing myself through carelessness. My gorgeous wife *wanting* me to open up about all the shit I've been ashamed of all these years. I think it's fucking with me. Making me more emotional or some shit because the soft way she's talking to me, the topics she's tiptoeing around—it's making me want to detonate, fill her with cum and hold her so tight to my body that she can hardly fucking breathe.

"I love you, Jes, you give me everything," I say, articulating everything I'm feeling the best I can, fighting the urge to come then love bomb her in my sweaty arms.

She shakes her head, lifting her hips enough to make my fat, veiny cock slip out of her, slapping against my belly with a thunk. When she grinds over me, getting me back inside her without using her hands, I know I'm going to surrender to her tonight.

"I want to know your darkest desires, Laws." She does some wicked shit with her hips, and I have to put a hand on her lower belly to slow her down. "I don't want the underside of a desk knowing my husband better than me."

I don't know what happens, but right now, in this moment, there's a shift. A give. A rupture. Whatever it is, the darkness I've buried deep... it fractures. A tiny, almost imperceptible crack but enough of an opening to allow her to see it.

Just a bit.

"Please, give me a taste. *Show me what you need.*"

"I don't need it." That's true. And I can't have her thinking that I need it, and I fucking hate that she thinks I'm hiding parts of me but the truth? I am. I have been for years.

"You do. You do need it. And I want to be the one who gives it to you," she rasps before taking more of my length. Our kiss is rich with the things we want to have but haven't found our way to just yet. I can feel it. It excites me.

It terrifies me.

But she continues on. "Please, Laws."

"You don't know what you're asking." It's true. She's got no idea that what I want goes far beyond tying her up and fucking her rough. I want her when she's not expecting it, and I want her to fight against me, to cry as if I'm not the man she loves, to run like I am the man in the shadows, the embodiment of my own darkness.

She rolls her hips, clenching around me, teasing precum from me as she rasps, "*So show me.*"

Eight

JES

I remind myself silently this *man is my husband.*

Those three words have flipped a switch.
    The very switch I've been itching to flip for the last few weeks. All I've been able to think about is this—seeing the side of him he's hidden from me. Knowing all versions of the man with whom I share a bed. Share a life with.
    One second I'm riding him, whispering, begging for his secrets. The next, I'm on my back, held down to the mattress with my knees at my ears. I blink up at him, trying to calibrate how the shift happened so quickly but then...
    I asked for this.
    I asked for this, and I have to remember that.
    Looking up at his handsome face, I take note of how

different he looks. The Laws I made love to the other night, he's gone, and in his place is *this man*.

I remind myself silently *this* man *is* my husband.

My feet frame his face as he holds me down by the undersides of my knees. His cock slides between my labia, sticky from our arousal. His eyes find mine, and they look so much darker now. The backs of my thighs already burn from the pressure he's putting on me, from the contortion. But I don't say a word.

"Open your mouth," he demands, the tension in his neck visible, thick lines of strain marking his tenuous composure.

My lips peel apart and as soon as my jaw parts, *he spits*.

Into my open mouth.

Holy fuck, why is that so hot? His eyes narrow so tightly, he almost looks like a different man completely. "Swallow it."

I do, and yet, there's no verbal reward. Instead, he removes a hand from my leg long enough to swat me right across my breast. My nipple takes most of the hit, but I don't complain. I internalize the sting radiating through my breast, and focus on his next movement.

Eyes on my pussy, he surges inside of me, thrusting on his knees at my opening. He fills me in one push, no easing in or sliding in and out and I wonder if it's because we were already having sex or if he'd do it this way anyway, rough and unforgiving.

His eyes are everywhere, roaming my tits which pinken with each swat. And he does continue swatting me. Across my nipple, atop my breast... he even slaps my pussy where he's tucked inside me.

I feel the pain of the slaps. The way the pain is my

primary focus in that moment, how my brain takes a second to realize what's to come and then, it bleeds through me, filling me with a numbing sting that hurts enough to make me whimper, but not bad enough to make me cry.

I notice around the third slap across my pussy that there are waves of pleasure that follow the bleed of pain, a moment or two where the sting dissipates, leaving a tingle of electricity throughout my skin. I'm waiting for the next slap, one that will shock my cunt and tease my clit, but this time a single sharp sting radiates across my cheek, snapping my attention back to his hard cock ravaging me.

When we make love, Laws loves watching me. Taking my gaze and holding it while he pumps and empties inside me, telling me all of the things he feels so deeply but never has an opportunity to say.

I love you more than anything, Jes.

I'm so glad you're mine.

God I love your body.

Acting on his darkest desires, Laws does not hold my eyes. He does not whisper sweet things to me.

This Laws speaks, and his words are so brutal they sting me more than his strikes. But just like those strikes, once the shock wears off, I'm left with pleasure. So much pleasure I'm swimming in it.

"I'm gonna use your cunt like the cum dumping ground it is. Do you hear that, Jessalyn? This pussy is nothing more than my wet fuck hole. I will take you hard, I don't care how much it hurts."

A full body tremble takes hold of me in response to his brutal words, and my pussy clenches the crown of his cock as he pulls back, stealing himself away. I whimper at the loss.

Another bruising hit across my cunt, this time harder. The sound of his heavy hand against my wet center has my head jerking forward, desperate to see him.

His hand wraps my throat before I can look up, but then he hovers over me, his gorgeous face growing blotchy and blurry as it becomes harder and harder to breathe.

"I don't need you to be breathing to fuck your holes, you little whore."

Oh my God. In the years we've been married, I've never heard Lawson Briggs say these words. Fuck, yes, and bitch when used in the context "son of a bitch" while watching baseball, yes. But this?

"This is *my* cunt, and you're my filthy fucking slut."

Fucking slut? My head spins, though it's pinned to the pillows by my husband's hand.

My husband is choking me while brutally fucking me.

That realization hits just as he slides his cock back inside me, no gentle care or soft strokes. He may be solely focused on chasing his own pleasure, but his engorged cock is hitting all the right places and dragging me along with him. He pummels me, crashing his hips to my ass, grunting and growling in a timbre I've never heard.

It's not just dark. It's growly and low, like smoke on gravel, emanating raw power. He sounds like he could make a room of people fall to their knees, and it's the polar opposite of the man I know.

The man I know is soft and tender. He's caring with a big heart, is private except for with me, he's smart and hard-working. Fair, honest, handsome. Gentle, sweet, loveable. Any good thing, he's it.

I see my hands clawing at his chest, the sparkle of my

ring in the moonlight reminding me who I am. Why I'm here.

He pounds into me just as my vision darkens, and right when I think I'm fading, he releases his choking grasp on my throat, and feeds his hand behind my head.

I gasp, and pant and gulp, searching for breath, desperate for air. He moves on the bed, my body pulled with him by the firm grip he has on my hair as he does.

He's not inside of me anymore. Despite the rough treatment, I recognize the hollow ache in my belly, telling me he pulled out.

Blinking, my vision begins returning in waves. The first thing I see, hazy and faded, is his glistening cock, throbbing over me. I open my mouth, needing more air, but then the salty musky taste of our sex floods my tongue, and I'm forced to push an urgent breath out of my nose.

"That's right, clean your pussy off this dick and swallow my load. That's what fuck holes are good for, right? Taking cum."

My pussy clenches at his words and aches at the loss of his cock. He hits the back of my throat, and my eyes rain tears from strain. The hand at the back of my head urges me forward, deeper, but I already have him all. My nose smashes to his groin, and breathing is difficult again.

"You think you're gagging on my dick?" His laugh raises hairs on the back of my neck, and makes my pussy pulse. "That's fucking nothing. You're gonna *choke* on my cum," he growls, and then the barbed hair of his groin crushes against my face and I realize I'm pushing against him, fighting for breath.

But he's relentless, holding me down on his cock, showering me with filthy, aggressive commands.

"That's right. Fight Me. Waste your fucking energy. But know this, slut. This mouth is mine to fuck."

Right as my thoughts start to fade and the energy in my body dwindles, he gives me an inch. One single inch, but it saves me. Through my nostrils, I take as big of a breath as I can, but before I can enjoy breathing again, he feeds his hand through my hair, the butt of his palm crushing my forehead.

"Open wide," he hisses and then his hefty cock, harder than ever, spasms on my tongue. Heat hits the back of my throat, dripping down to my belly as he slams my face to his groin, over and over. Before I know it, he's reaching for my pussy, pinching my clit with sticky forefingers and thumb.

Hips roving, dick hitting the back of my throat, causing me to gag, he fucks my face, feeding me his cum as he unravels me with just a touch.

I don't get to warn him, to tell him, I don't get to do anything but suck and swallow, be used and filled as my pussy drowns in the bliss of a forced and unexpected orgasm.

After a few moments where the only noises to be heard are rough and frantic, his groin crushing my face repeatedly, the grunts of a starved man finally able to eat, the wet center of my body where I'm gushing and spasming. A noise builds in his throat, starting in a familiar low timbre, building from a hidden depth as it reaches a pinnacle, a near feral growl, *"Fuck yesssss."*

The last wiggle of orgasm tears free, and the heady haze of roleplay and fantasy crashes to the ground like glass, immediately gone. He slides his cock from my mouth, slowly and cautiously dropping my head to the pillow. He smooths his palm around my hairline, fixing what he likely tangled with his grip.

I stare up at him, ignoring his slick and softening cock hanging over my breasts like dessert. Because I'm still kind of turned on, in truth. I didn't expect that, though I had no expectations.

Still, I wait for him to look at me. I stare up at his dark eyes, and each second that passes that he doesn't look into mine, a sadness engulfs me. When he's climbing off of me, standing at the side of the bed with my towel, then back over me, wiping between my thighs, I wonder how long it's been.

A minute? Two? Time is hard to quantify in this *after* space, where neither of us know how to behave. Or who we are.

I wonder as I watch him tug his pajama pants up. He never took them off, and I never took off my nighty. The urgency that overtook us as we began making love was so great, taking off clothes seemed to be a waste.

The aftermath of that urgency hangs in the air, only now, it's threatening to taint the experience. On instinct, I bring my knees together, trapping his hand as he cares for my used pussy. Refusing to allow him to hide from this, from me.

His wet fuck hole.

I get bumps on my arms at the thought of my Laws saying those filthy things to me. Not just saying them but clearly meaning them, being filled with pleasure at the sound of them.

Finally, I get his eyes.

I don't know what to make of them.

Unfocused, red. My heart stutters at the sight, and all the good feelings still humming between my legs disappear.

I sit up and take his face in one hand, cupping his cheek, letting my thumb part his mouth. "Hey." I don't know what else to say to him, because I don't know how to navigate any of this.

"Hey," he says, and all of the wild darkness unleashed just minutes ago is gone, dispersed, completely vanished. It's my Laws, the same Laws I made love to before all of this. He's back, but more somber than ever.

"I love you," I say, because it feels like the only smart, safe thing to say. The only sure thing to say.

"I love you, too," he says.

And though I know he means it, it still hurts when he slides into bed with his back to me and turns off his bedside light.

I don't sleep a wink.

* * *

Okay, maybe I slept two hours. Two very shitty hours where I tossed and turned and felt queasy.

We've never gone to bed angry. But did we last night? We exchanged I love yous, and that's not indicative of emotional unease.

Yet, it was there, despite the exchange of affection. He turned away from me. He didn't want to talk.

And when my alarm went off, he was already done shaving and in the shower. I pack lunches for the boys while Laws packs his lunch for work. With his hand resting on my side, thumb making small circles on my hip bone as he kissed me good morning. But he never spoke another word to me and with the boys downstairs in the midst of their chaotic morning routine, I know there will be no conversation about last night this morning.

None.

I pack up the kids and drive them to school, in a complete trance the whole way home. When I spot our house at the end of the street, my jaw hits my lap.

As a small business owner, and a man who is dedicated to his company, Laws has taken a total of six days off in thirteen years. Three days when each son was born. That's it.

But Laws' truck is in the driveway.

Nine

LAWS

I couldn't leave the house.

She fumbles with her door and keys as she slides out of the driver's seat, the garage door dropping to the pavement behind her, sealing us in.

Protecting us from onlookers, but more so, enclosing us in together.

Her gaze crawls along the wall of the garage, behind my workbench and tool chest, to the countless rows of tied ropes on display.

Part of building greenhouses is also being an arborist rigging specialist. A lot of times, we have to take out trees to clear space for the greenhouse, therefore, my entire crew is well-versed in tying knots.

They learned from me.

Sometimes, under the guise of work, I come out here when I'm grappling with my urges, and lose myself to the rough and unrelenting fibers of the rope. There's nothing like the feel of rope burning sore flesh, of a knot so strong you could suspend a human with it, of the release you feel and the sense of power that washes over you as you tighten and contort one of the worlds strongest materials.

I know she sees the displays of knotted rope differently after last night.

I didn't tie her up, but it doesn't matter. Jes has always been so fucking smart, a woman who sees the subtext and understands the plot before everyone else.

Her eyes come to mine, wide and full of questions. Full of wonder and hope, but I'd be lying if I said I didn't see a little pain in them, too. Pain that I put there.

Pain she begged me to taste.

Dressed in my work boots, jeans and flannel, an AgDev ball cap pulled down over my eyes, I had every fucking intention of going to work. Of working and thinking through what happened, promising myself by the end of day, I'd have the right words. I'd hold a solution in my hands, and take it home to her, and it'd be okay. *We'd* be okay.

I couldn't leave the house.

I couldn't even pick up my keys.

Knowing the energy was off between us last night and this morning—and knowing full well it was my fault—I couldn't go.

I texted Graham to open the doors and turn off the security system. He'd immediately called, probably assuming the worst as I never miss work. *Ever.*

I sent him straight to voicemail, sending another text before shutting off my phone.

> **LAWS**
> I'm at home with Jes. We're fine. Needed the morning off. Don't make it a big deal. See you later.

And now as she stands before me in the unlit garage, I know staying home was the right choice. I close the distance between us, my body craving our connection, our love and devotion, through kiss and touch.

Usually, we connect with words; we're not a couple that has to have sex to feel cohesive. But after last night, *I need* to make her purr. I need to feel her cum for me, I think I'll die without it at this point.

She leaps into my arms as my mouth crushes hers, our kiss needy and urgent, like I've returned to my lover after war.

Is that what my monster has done to us? Make us want to fuck like we've survived a battle? I don't want that. As good as it felt to finally give life to the urges, the extreme drop after—the drop we've *both* been crawling through for the last fifteen hours—it's too extreme.

I hate it. I'd do anything to never feel this weird, unexplainable, invisible distance between us.

She moans into our kiss, wet and noisy with tongues clashing and our exhales intermingling. Her legs loop my waist, and one of my hands slides between our bodies, going to my jeans. Before I know it, I've got her on top of the chest freezer, yoga pants dangling from her ankle, panties bunched inside, my hard cock sliding inside of her.

"Laws," she moans as I enter her, over and over, fucking her in slow, intentional strokes as my hands grasp her face, forcing her eyes to mine. Craving her loving gaze.

I should have done this last night. After I called her my *wet fuck hole*, I should have held her this way, poured my love into her and praised her for everything she gave.

I should have but *I didn't*. I chose to wallow.

I grapple with self-hatred, determined not to lose this moment between us. I dip my mouth to hers, taking another taste as I fuck her, my shoulders easing now that I have her all around me, sheathing my cock, sealing our union physically as her eyes captivate my heart.

Each thrust sends me deeper *inside us*, and as I start to lose myself, I'm assaulted by a flash from last night. Like cold water to the face, I hear myself calling her names. I hear the smack of my flesh against hers as I *hit* her. My hand aches in memory of gripping her throat and stealing her breath.

I don't try to fill her with sweet nothings. I don't make the feeble assumption that making her come now will erase what happened last night.

I just want her to know that... I'm sorry, I guess? I don't fucking know but I'm suddenly crushed by a wave of memories—*me spitting into her mouth and commanding her to swallow*. I pull out and drop to a crouch, burying my face where I left her empty.

She moans, and the sultry noise causes a sheet of gooseflesh to rise along my back. Her fingernails graze my scalp before clinging tightly to the loose ends of my hair. I've always loved going down on Jessalyn. Always. It's not just because she tastes like fucking honey and heaven, but the noises she makes. *The things she says.*

On cue, her soft murmurs settle around me as I devour her.

"I love your lips on me there."

"Yes, Laws, yes, oh taste me, yes."

"Laws... I'm so close. You're making me come."

The way her dirty talk is still so goddamn sweet has my cock dripping. Pressed against the cold front of the freezer, precum slides down the stainless steel, dripping onto the cement. The desire to ease the pressure in my cock and balls is overwhelming, and I could easily slide my hips along the cool stainless steel to do it. But I will not fucking hump and come on a goddamn freezer.

Hearing her mewls though, I'm fucking walking the line.

I slide a finger inside of her, keeping my lips sealed around her swollen clit. My tongue flicks against it as I suck, and I work another finger inside.

She comes hard and fast, and I can't deny the pride inundating in my chest; I can *still* satisfy her, even after last night. She's not turned off by me, upset with me, soured by what happened.

I cling to that notion as I seek my own release, sliding back into her after I've eaten her through her orgasm, drinking down her slick release.

The little hum that breaks past her lips as I find my momentum again, stroking deep and slow— "I love how you sound when I fuck you," I tell her, borderline panting, sweat heavy on my upper lip.

"Yes," she mewls, copper hair splayed over shoulders, eyes wide, pupils blown. Her fair skin always floods with a ruby hue as she orgasms, and I love it. I cup her face, about to come as she sucks the tip of my thumb into her mouth.

"*Come for me, Laws,*" she whimpers before giving my digit a nibble.

The small pain, the extreme pleasure and the weight of what transpired last night has me toppling over her, sealing my mouth to hers in what feels like a lifesaving kiss while I empty myself inside of her in pounding waves.

When I'm drained in more ways than one, and my legs are shaking while her lips are carving a trail down the side of my throat, I know, now comes the serious part. We have to talk. We can't fuck our way out of this uneasiness between us.

Leaning back, I find her eyes and in unison, we share a smile.

"Let's talk," she says, stealing the words from my tongue. I nod, but keep her there with my softening cock still inside of her.

Working the buttons on my flannel, I peel off my shirt and press it between her legs right as I empty her. I let my sticky cock bob against the edge of the freezer and my jeans as I take careful time to wipe my cum from her swollen, freshly fucked pussy.

Using the tip of my finger, I circle her opening, coaxing out any stray drops. She moans a little as I do, and I look up to find my bride watching with hooded eyes.

That same pride fills me again, inflating me not beyond my size but more like, returning me back to the size I felt before we did what we did. Making me normal again.

I take my time tending to her with as much care as two big hands and a flannel shirt can allow, then she sits up and redresses her lower half. I tuck myself away, take her hand, and lead her into our home.

We sit at the kitchen table after I've poured us each a cup of the untouched coffee I made this morning. I'd been too goddamn disgusted with myself to eat or drink and I'd be willing to bet last night had her abstaining from her normal routine, too. Her green juice is still on the counter.

I'm not going to be a man that unleashes his dark side to his wife, goes to bed without discussion, mauls her in the garage then lets *her* speak first. No fucking way.

"Jes," I start, taking a sip of the coffee to calm my nerves. "I'm sorry about last night."

There. That's a start. Why I couldn't have said "I'm sorry" last night and spared us both all of this emotional disharmony, I'm not sure. Maybe because *I didn't think it through.* Maybe because acting on aggressive sexual needs out of impulse without discussion is a *bad fucking idea.*

Duh.

It's my fault, though. She wanted to know. She tried to ask. She begged for me to talk.

"I'm sorry," I say again, feeling like once isn't enough.

She collects her hair in one hand and goddamn, women can do so much with one hand. I guess they get used to that when they have a newborn stuck on their tit and one arm holding them there. You're expected to do a lot with one hand. She wraps a hair band around it, and my eyes fall to the smooth slope of her exposed neck. My dick perks up like I didn't just have her less than five minutes ago.

"Sorry..." she starts, dragging it out like a piece of bubble gum stringing from her plump lips to her fingertips. Weaving her hands together around her mug, her green eyes press me, and I feel them in my gut. "About what?"

"Everything," I answer quickly, but her nose wrinkles

and a strand of fiery hair falls across her forehead as she shakes her head emphatically.

"No, Laws." She takes a sip. "What are you sorry about? That we tried to explore what you want? Or did it not go the way you wanted? Or that it's been weird between us? What *specifically* are you feeling? *Why* are you sorry?" She leans forward, dropping her hand on my wrist, massaging me softly. "*This part* is the *most* important."

Her eyes are so shiny. Sunlight pours in through the many windows of our home. The home I built, that we designed. Jes wanted windows. Tons of windows, claiming *the more natural light, the better the mood*. I don't disagree, and I love the way sunlight dances in the strands of her hair, infusing the copper with goldenrod, causing her simmering ember locks to resemble a tall, dancing flame. So goddamn gorgeous.

Everything about her draws the truth from me. The feeling of safety she projects, her soft smile, and the tender way she still strokes my inner wrist as she waits. Patiently.

"The thing is... it was *exactly* what I'd wanted. Or.. I don't know. A taste of it, at the very least. And I *did* like it. I actually hate how much I liked it. I hate that doing those things to you, treating you that way..." I take a breath before letting sour words fall from my lips. "I had one of the best orgasms of my life." Even with her, the admission is so real and so honest, it's impossible to keep embarrassment from coloring my cheeks.

I'm open with Jes. Hell, I tell her things I'd never even tell Graham, and he's my best friend—not just my brother. But talking about orgasms is just not where I'm comfortable.

But I know this is a mandatory discomfort if we want to

move forward. I know it, and I can feel it in her coaxing strokes and the way she leans into me, pining for more.

"So you enjoyed last night?" she asks, still soothing me with her touch. With her other hand she sips coffee and the ease in which she's handling all this makes my chest swell.

"Fuck yes, Jes. It was a taste of all of the things I've been holding inside and it was goddamn great."

"*But*," she states slowly, seeing and feeling the word despite the fact I didn't say it.

"But," I repeat, knowing this will be hard to say. But I think it's safe to say neither of us want to experience the *after* that followed last night's activities ever again. "As soon as it was over, I panicked." I sip my coffee too, needing a moment to find the right words. I fucked up last night, so today, it's important I don't do it again.

"Why?"

Every part of me fucking contorts as I fight the urge to drop my gaze to the surface of my coffee. To get lost in the lazy wave that ripples along the surface as I blow. But I don't, because Jes deserves better than a tail between the legs admission.

"I worried that you could feel how much I enjoyed it and that after it was over, you'd look at me differently." Suddenly my eyes are warm with fear and concern, and voicing these emotions is more challenging than I thought it would be. I refuse to blink, but I do continue. "I panicked that you'd see me differently. And that things between us..." I trail off, too damn scared to finish that sentence. It clearly hasn't happened but still, the mere idea holds so much power over me that speaking the words feels like drinking poison. They stick in my throat, choking me.

She releases my wrist to tuck the stray hair back into her bun, but returns her hands to her mug, taking a few long drinks. Finally, she says, "I do see you differently." My stomach plummets and nausea has never grabbed hold of my gut so fast, even when Jes's water broke with Lex and it made me woozy.

Reading me, she scoots her chair closer to mine and links our ankles. "I see yet another dimension of you that I love. I just need the tools to know how to fully nurture that side of you, that's all. You *are* different to me, but you're *better* than before. I know you more, and that's all I ever wanted; to know you completely. Now I do. And I've never loved you more."

Something catches in my throat. I don't know if it's my breath or my feelings, but I'm unable to speak as I stare into her eyes, processing all the things she's said. I take a moment, but my voice is still hoarse when I respond a moment later.

"You... don't think I'm a complete fucking monster?" My tone is more timid than it's ever been, more unsure than I've ever sounded when it comes to Jes.

She smiles, soft and sweet, like I've told a joke that's silly but not laughable. Maybe that's how she views my fears. Silly. After all, she's just said that she feels more for me now than before, that seeing my complexities and stepping into my shade only enriches the total package, not reduces it.

I can't believe it, but I think that's exactly how she feels.

"No, Laws, I could never think you're a monster. Never. You're the man I fell in love with, the man I'm *still* in love with, the father of our boys." Her eyes grow misty, the conviction of her words causing her voice to rise. "You're my everything. And I love you so much more now that I know *all* of you."

My throat is thick with gravel, but I manage to husk out, "Yeah?"

She nods. "Yeah."

I hold her eyes earnestly. "How'd you feel last night? How'd you feel this morning? I mean, not about me but you. How are *you*?"

I wasn't the only one struggling last night or this morning, and we need to address that. Hell, I've got some guilt in my gut that we didn't address her needs in this discussion first.

She finishes her coffee as I take another drink of mine. "I felt the same as you, both last night and this morning. I… liked it. I liked the other side of you. I liked seeing all these parts of you, so passionate and feral. Even when it hurt, I was surprised because it felt good, too. So…" Her gaze floats over the table and out one of the windows.

She's not one to look away from her issues out of cowardice, so whatever feeling has her by the heart, forcing her eyes elsewhere… It makes me nervous.

"Baby," I start, because it feels more private and intimate than saying her name. And I don't know what she's thinking or feeling, but I need her to know that I'm here.

I scoot closer and let my hand fall on her thigh, which brings her gaze back to me.

"I was afraid that you'd think less of me for enjoying it. For…. getting off to that treatment."

She came. I felt her. That much I know, though in truth, last night has already become somewhat of a blur from the gripping fear.

My hand on her thigh tightens, and I find myself scooting so close that my knee drives between her legs, twining us together. "You... you really enjoyed that?"

She nods, her cheeks flush. "I did. It felt so... I don't know. Carefree isn't the right word but, I don't know. I guess...." Her tongue darts across her bottom lip, wetting it. "*Liberating*. To be handled and taken and just *used*... I don't know, Laws, but I liked it. And don't even get me started on seeing *you* that way."

Behind my zipper, my cock awakens. "Yeah?" I think my heart is beating faster, too.

"I never knew that man was inside of you. And I get why you were nervous to show me. He's... you're... *a lot*. But it's a good *a lot*. It's a sexy, erotic, thrilling *a lot*." She leans in and I meet her, sharing a tender kiss.

"But," she says, and I nod, ready for the *we can't do it again* to come. Because... we've talked through it, we mutually enjoyed it, but... how we both felt after. I *can't* do that again.

"We can't do it again, I know." I nod, staring at my hand on her thigh, wishing I'd done more in the moment to preserve the memory of us. If I have to picture that hour forever with my hand on my cock locked away in my office, I'll cherish it. But I won't keep doing it at the hefty cost we paid after.

"Uh, *what*?" she snorts the question, kind of laughing, causing my gaze to lift to hers. "No, that's—you don't want to experience more of that? Really get into those dark fantasies you've alluded to?"

"I do, I mean, yeah, I do. But... Jes, I hated how I felt last night. And I hated how our home felt this morning. I don't want that between us. That... discomfort. The *after*. It's too hard."

"I take responsibility for that. I shouldn't have forced you into showing me that side of you that way. I knew with me already in your lap you wouldn't be able to say no. I knew it."

I don't want her feeling bad about any of this.

"No, don't say that. I could have said no. But the truth is, I guess I wanted to feel it, you know? I wanted to experience all that I've obsessed over for years." I make her gaze hold mine, imparting the sincerity of my words through intense eye contact. "It's not your fault. I knew it would be intense, and I agreed."

She nods, chewing the corner of her mouth thoughtfully. "Well, I think we both made a mistake taking part in something so big without any conversation first."

"You tried," I sigh.

She laughs, the melodic noise making my heart thump. After all of this, she's laughing and telling *me* it's okay. Goddamn, how does one man get so lucky?

"I did try. But it doesn't matter. We're here now. And I'd love to explore more of what you want, Laws, because I want to give you *everything*. I want you to have everything you need and more. Okay?"

I nod, overcome by her. Overwhelmed.

"But last night was irresponsible. What if I wanted to stop? What if you did? We have nothing set up for safety. We can explore every single inch of your darkness, Laws, we just have to take it seriously. Because what we did last night was hot as hell, but could have devastating consequences if not handled properly. Not just in terms of safety but for our relationship."

"Damn, that's the truth," I say, thinking about how I purposely woke earlier than her to slink out of bed like a fucking asshole she swiped right on, not like the man of the goddamn house. "I'm sorry."

"Stop apologizing and look at this," she says, jumping up from her chair to grab her phone off the kitchen counter. She holds it up, smiling as she unlocks the device with FaceID. A few taps and a scroll, then she's passing it to me, screen up.

My eyes lock to the words at the top.

LET'S TEST THE KINK OUT OF YOU.

I look up at her. "What's this?"

She rolls her eyes, but her lips curve into a smile. "It's a sex quiz. It's very thorough. Penny was telling me about it at spin a few days ago and, I don't know. I thought we could take it. You take it, and I take it, and we swap results."

I look at the phone again, as the first screen asks a litany of questions about who I am. My age, where I'm located, and then three selectable bubbles. The first one reads *Give me all the questions!*, the second reads *I don't want questions related to BDSM!* and the last says *Keep me vanilla [no questions relating to roles or toys allowed]*.

I look up at Jes who is leaning over the phone, reading with me. "BDSM," I say, scratching the side of my head. "That doesn't sound like—"

She jerks up, holding her hand out. "Nope. You don't get to shut anything down if you want to move forward with this, Laws." Her eyes grow serious, her brows pinching together. "I want this, so we're doing it right. We're not limiting ourselves to what we *think* we already know." She pauses, her gaze idling on me. "We didn't talk last night. Or this morning, okay? We need this quiz to help us consider new things about ourselves, understand what we're doing, and how best to move forward with it, okay?"

A lot of okay's in that speech, so I just nod, because she's right. Why am I quick to judge this damn quiz when the truth is, all my knowledge of what I like has been in my brain for years with absolutely zero exploration or guidance? "Alright," I say, confirming the head nod.

"Let's go into your office and take it on your computer. You can go first, then I'll go. We'll print and swap." She's already on her feet, waiting for me to do the same.

The office. Last time I was in there was when all of this began. Adjusting her bun, Jes's arms are over her head, fumbling with the elastic in her hair. With her arms up like that, I envision a rope binding her slender wrists together, I see her naked, strewn across our bed, limbs tethered to the posts like some sort of erotic starfish. With her fair skin, the ropes would leave her marred and raw, and my dick stirs at the thought.

"Office," I say, leading the way.

She wants to do this the right way, and I don't know how or what that will look like, but the possibility that I can get my ropes on her, that I could show her all the things I've been hiding inside me, that we could share in my darkness and turn it from something that haunts me to something of great pleasure—I stop in the hall, and Jes bumps into my back. Turning, I just shake my head. "I love you, Jessalyn."

Confusion knits her brows for a moment, but she smiles it away, saying, "I love you, too."

Then, she sits on my knee manning the mouse as we read through the quiz together.

Ten

JES

Rope bunny

Listening to Laws' rough voice read some of the questions on this quiz has caused... a tidal wave of arousal between my legs.

And sitting on his thick thigh, my center pressed against his knee—it's been like edging, honestly.

He reads the last question for the second time and I select my answer, and we sit in charged silence waiting for my results to populate.

We haven't looked at his results yet. We were going to wait and look at our own at the end, then swap. But as the answer clicker, I know how he answered his questions. And some of his answers... actually *all* of his answers surprised me.

And a secondary dose of surprise? How turned on I became at learning all the filthy dirty things my big, hard-working, sweetheart of a husband truly wants to experience.

When it's done, I click print, and both of our heads swing to the printer, watching with bated breath. I snag it once it's finished, and twist in my husband's lap, clamping my hand to the back of his neck.

"Wanna read our results then swap?" We agreed on that earlier, but now that the results are here and we're on the brink of discovery, I'm feeling admittedly a little nervous. I smile, matching his, and the way he just stares into my eyes adoringly, his groin stiff against my ass, gah. I can't believe I get to be this obsessed with *my* husband. "I'm a smidge nervous." I admit to him as butterflies flit around beneath my ribs, using my thumb and pointer finger to quantify my nerves.

His head bobs in a slow nod. "Me too."

Reaching for the edge of the desk, he grabs his printed responses before wrapping his arm around me, letting me lean back into his chest. "Come on, let's do it. Let's read."

I don't know how long it takes us to process our results, and I'm not sure if I've completely calibrated to the fact that I'm face-to-face with sexual desires I've never considered before when he nudges me.

His hooded eyes crawl over my lips as he takes his time catching my gaze. "Well, who am I married to? What do you like?" He laughs, but I can tell it's meant to ease his discomfort with the situation. "Since you already know I'm a complete fucking creep."

Our gaze idles, and I don't know what he's thinking, but I'm thinking how much it hurts me to hear him say that. He means it, too. I haven't convinced him yet that what he wants and needs is normal and okay, as long as we have communication and consent. But it's my mission to make him feel seen and safe, and I don't take this task lightly.

I walk my fingers up his chest with a teasing smile. "I don't think you're a creep, but who knows, maybe the quiz will tell us I'm one, too." I lean in for a quick kiss. "Either way, we're in it together."

His smile is small but it overwhelms me. "Okay, well, time to find out who we are. What's yours say?" he asks, the rocky edge to his voice making my core throb.

I look at my paper but I don't need to. I could never forget the top two results from the quiz. "First, I'm a rope bunny and my second result is submissive." My eyes slowly find his, and the insatiable hunger I find in them has my body going weak, the paper slipping from my fingers, sailing to the floor in a slow descent.

"Rope bunny," he utters, his tone so deep, his eyes so dark. The two words sound like *fuck me* or *goddamn*. He takes my hand that clutches the chair's arm and presses it beneath my leg, to his crotch.

What was once a hard knot is now a full-blown erection, angry and thick. I swallow hard, my mind racing. "You... you like rope bunny or submissive better?" I ask, wondering what part of my results are making him feel like railing me right about now.

"Rigger," he says hungrily, moving my hand along his length. The weight of his palm guiding me to touch him has my center dripping. Or it's him dripping from me from earlier, but either way, I'm wet. I'm drenched from seeing him like this. So aggressively turned on and unafraid to show me. "My quiz tells me I'm a rigger, a dominant rigger no less."

"Okay..." I draw out slowly as he continues rubbing my hand over his cock. My eyelids fight a flutter while my eyes betray me and roll back as I quiver at his dominance. I've seen Laws tie ropes thousands of times, bordering on hundreds of thousands, even. After all, he's an arborist rigger by trade. Tying trees, securing knots, teaching his crew how to do the same—it's like seeing a nurse loop a stethoscope around her neck, or a business man fuck about with the cufflink of his suit jacket—just part of his job.

Now though, my mind fills with questions I'd never considered. A few rush out before I can stop myself. "When you've been working with rope... for work," I start, unsure how to word my complex thoughts. "Have you ever... you know, gotten excited?"

He grunts, and I can sense his discomfort. But I love him so much for responding, for being vulnerable for the sake of us. Scrubbing a hand down his face, he responds, "A few times, yes. But never around the guys. Just here, at home."

I peel his hands from his face and he blinks at me. "That's... weird and creepy and I hate that you know that."

I pinch my gaze at him, taking a quick kiss from him to reassure him. "It's not creepy, Laws. You've had a dominant inside of you, one who loves rope play, and that's okay. You just never knew until now. But... now we know."

"Rope play," he repeats, the words potent and intense, vibrating down my spine. "Sounds fucked up—"

"You and me," I say, slowly painting a picture of something he can enjoy, without the tethers of societal shame, or whatever he's feeling. "You and me, our room, locked door, just us."

He nods, his hand no longer holding mine to his cock. Now he strokes up and down my back beneath my shirt, the scrape of his worn hands making me melt a little.

"Just us and some rope, and endless possibilities. There's nothing fucked up about a man wanting to exercise his desires with his wife, is there?" He loves when I refer to myself as his wife. No matter how civil and sweet my husband is, something primal in him awakens at the ownership of the title. I'm his wife, I'm his, and that fact has always floored him.

"I guess not," he hums, and though he's no longer holding me there, I keep my hand on his groin, for both of us. Because touching him feels as good as being touched, and that's the truth.

"Should we swap?" I ask, wanting to drive him away from the discomfort and toward the excitement. "So you can see all of mine and vice versa?"

I grab my paper off the floor and we swap. I watch his face soften as he discovers the results of my quiz. I'm not just a submissive rope bunny at heart, but I'm also a masochist-degradee. Before last night, I'd never been degraded by Laws nor had he ever inflicted pain on me, but having tasted a tiny bite of this forbidden fruit and taken this quiz, it's allowed things in me to surface... I want it. I can almost taste the copper from a hard swat to my cheek or the burn from ropes binding my limbs. My pussy vibrates fantasizing about being tied to our bed, his broad frame looming over me, desire to *take without permission* running rampant in his veins. To be his dirty little fuck toy, demanding a wet hole to fuck with no care or remorse.

God do I want to try that.

And I can tell he does too as a little groan slips past his lips as he absorbs my results. I force myself to look at his results, though I could watch him discover and dream all day —he's never looked sexier.

His results make my skin burn. I actually pinch my top, yanking away from my core for a moment as I drink in his unexpected and provocative desires.

Rigger.

Dominant.

Sadist.

Degrader.

Primal Hunter.

I blink, and reread the top five, swallowing a dry throat. I know what all of these mean, in theory, but I'm not sure how to apply them to the bedroom. The quiz has been an eye opener and I can't help but smile as I look up at him.

"We want the same things and we'd never have known if it weren't for you." That's the truth, but I see nerves vibrating beneath the surface as he drags his hand down his face, sighing.

"Are you sure about this, Jes?" He looks down at the paper, more questioning in his expression than his tone. "You really want to do all this?"

I slide off his lap, falling to my knees between his open thighs. Fanning my fingers over his legs, I look up at him, feeling his throaty growl deep in my belly.

"You want to tie me up, inflict pain, and take me as if I don't want it willingly, right?" I continue moving my hands over his legs, letting the tips of my fingers nudge his impressively hard cock, every thick inch straining against the denim. Chin to chest, he watches me with flames in his eyes.

"Right," he says. This time, there's less reluctance in his voice, and you know what? A win's a win, no matter how small.

"So let's work toward that. Let's take a week to think about our results, what we want, and what each of us thinks would be a good starting point, okay?" Watching his mind wander as he envisions immersing himself in all of his desires, even if just in thought. I swear I see some of the weight of his burdens lift from his shoulders.

That's why I'm here. To ease his stress and worries, and I can't even let myself think about what he's struggled through alone because he felt ashamed to tell me.

I rise to my feet and he sticks out his bottom lip in a pout. "Got my hopes up being down there," he grins with a wink that I feel everywhere.

"Well, I may be a rope bunny that is dying to be defiled, but peep these results," I say, waving the paper around playfully. "There's a little brat in there, too. I guess I'm just tapping into my bratty side."

"You're the most beautiful brat I've ever seen," he says, rising, twining a solid digit around a strand of loose copper that refuses to stay in the top knot. "How you feeling now?" He drops the hair, placing his palms on my shoulders, soothingly rubbing them down the length of my arms, then back up.

"Better than before," I admit, adding a crucial clarification. "Better than before I walked in on you a few weeks ago, I mean."

He blinks then just shakes his head. "I love you, Jessalyn. And I don't deserve you."

I pat his chest and lead us back to the kitchen, our empty cups of coffee still sitting on the table. I pinch them up and lower them to the empty porcelain sink as Laws comes up behind me, dropping a kiss to my cheek.

"I ought to head in now. I'm pretty sure Greg thinks you're asking to divorce me or something."

I snort, understanding why Greg would be so concerned. Laws hasn't missed a day of work outside of a few days when each of our sons were born. "It is uncharacteristic of Lawson Briggs to take a morning off."

He kisses the side of my neck as I add the mugs to the dishwasher after rinsing them thoroughly. "I'll see you this evening, Jes," he says, smiling.

I watch him leave, and I notice that he looks back on his walk to his pickup, finding my eyes through the window above the kitchen sink. He winks, and I smile. When his truck roars to life and he takes off, I immediately turn to my phone.

Opening Google, I get to work on researching how to safely fulfill his needs. And as I read about safe words and tap out procedures, excitement blooms inside me.

This may have begun for Laws, but now I'm just as invested in this voyage of discovery.

Eleven

LAWS

And you're my rigger

"C'mon Dad, he got his pick last night. I never get my pick. I never get anything I want," Lex moans, flopping down along the foot of his bed dramatically. His arm covers his eyes as he lets out the sigh of a lifetime.

He's ten.

"Hey buddy, your brother is right," I say to Des, smoothing my hand through his glossy hair. "Last night we did *Simpson's Sheep Won't Go to Sleep,* so it is your brother's night for a pick."

Des, who is sprawled across his brother's floor, a Lego truck in one hand, a headless Lego man in the other, pauses. Lifting his focus from the toys, a tremble worms through his bottom lip as he nods valiantly, pretending to be unaffected.

Lex sits up, looking at his brother. And I watch the moment unfold before me. We've been reading a fantasy series—a chapter book—and while we've let Des listen in, it has been the cause of a nightmare a time or two. Lex chews the inside of his mouth for a second, fidgeting with the end of his pillowcase. A moment passes before he turns to me and says, "Fine. We can read Simpson's sheep. But can I have an extra ten minutes with my lamp on to read alone? I wanted to finish the chapter tonight."

Getting off the floor, I sit on the edge of Lex's bed and drop a proud hand to his shoulder, imparting the emotion with a squeeze. "That's very kind of you, Lex. I know it was your turn, and I'm sure it means a lot to your brother that you gave it up."

Lex did the right thing, and at his age, it can go either way. He's on the cusp of those grouchy years of pre-teen, and he's already acting the part a little. With a roll of his eyes, he flops back onto the bed. "He owes me," he says, and I know that's a tally he's keeping track of. Unlike the amount of times he's promised to put his dishes in the sink or put his shoes in the mud room.

As I reach for the book, Jes appears in the doorway. When I'm putting the boys to bed, that's when she has her nightly routine ,but because I've been in here building Legos with the boys a little longer than usual, it appears she's finished. Because her hand is at her hip, holding her satin robe closed.

"Mom," Des says as soon as he lays eyes on her. I wouldn't call my sons mama's boys, because I think there's some bad connotations that come with that title. Like they couldn't function without her.

Well, now that I think about it, maybe we're all mama's boys because I know I couldn't do a thing without Jes. I smile as I watch her crouch to inspect the Lego man he built and is showing off. She collects a few stray pieces from the bin, adds to it, and presents him with the Lego man now wearing a hat with Viking horns. Des giggles. "I love it!"

"Now love it from your bed, because you have school in the morning," she says, holding the little Lego Viking out to him in her palm, using it like one would use a dog bone to lead a dog outside. But it works, and Des scrambles to his feet behind her.

I tell Lex goodnight, and thank him again for the compromise. I've got good sons, and I know it. "I love you, son," I tell him as I pull the door closed behind me, leaving only a hair of a crack.

"Love you too, Dad," Lex calls, before I hear him flick on his lamp to read. A few paces down, I stand in the doorway, a voyeur to the heart-warming sight inside Des's room.

He's tucked in, with Jes leaning over, smoothing his copper hair off his face. She's singing quietly, the same song she's always sung him since he was just a week old. It's really not a child's song, but she sings it so soothingly that I'm not sure Des has ever heard a single word. More so, his eyes go soft and he just blinks up at her, lost in his adoration. I lose myself in adoring her too, as I listen to the softest version of "Folsom Prison Blues" I've ever heard.

When she's done, still one hand at her hip holding her robe closed, she presses a kiss to his head. "Night, Dessie," she says, a smile in her tone.

"Night, Mom. I love you. Love you, too, Dad," he says, making Jes's head twist to find me. Our eyes lock and though we've done bedtime together for years, tonight just feels different.

Tonight we're on the verge of discovery, and my blood runs hot with anticipation and excitement. It's been a week since we took that quiz, the one that told me something I should've already known—I want to tie Jes up and fuck her. When I look down into those gorgeous eyes, I want to see fear. I want to fuck my cum into her as she cries for me to let her go, and then when I'm done with her, I want to drag my tongue over her rope burns and and revel in how I've marked her—experience how I've changed her.

Refusing to make our same mistake twice, this time, we're talking first. Jes pads out of the room, leaving Des's door open. She flicks on the light in the hall, dimming it to the perfect medium between Des needing a light and Lex feeling too old for one.

Once we're in our room, I close the door, and I swear to God her eyes linger on my hand as I twist the lock.

I installed a lock this week. One of the many things I did, in fact. Because Jes is taking my wants seriously, and it's a disservice and disrespect to her if I don't match that. First thing I thought of, before any of the details—my boys.

I don't want them walking in here with no idea of what consenting adults do together, and seeing something that will forever alter their perception of me. Fuck that.

The room already had a lock, but once we started hiding Christmas gifts under our bed, that was the time that Lex discovered all he needed was a bobby pin to pop said lock. Now we have a deadbolt.

Anyone who comes into the master suite and sees it would probably wonder why on God's green earth we'd need a deadbolt *inside* the home. Hell, if it were me, I'd have thought the same thing a few weeks back.

But now, it seems like a small gamble to take in protecting my sons from seeing me do something they're too young to understand.

"Oh," she breathes, tucking a piece of shining red hair behind her ear, exposing the slope of her creamy neck. Her skin's so fair, so pure, and all I can think about is how good it would look wrapped in rope. "The new lock is getting used." She rubs her palms together playfully, but my dick gets hard anyway. "I'm excited."

I waggle my brows. "Me too." She moves toward the bed, but I catch her wrist, and pull her to my chest. I love how slight her frame is pressed to mine, how her hands roam my chest as she looks up into my eyes. "Hey, I just want to say, thank you for... everything."

Our eyes meet, and she bites her bottom lip. "Thank you for finally opening up. I know it was hard. I can't imagine feeling shame for your desires your entire life then having to explain those desires to someone, and try to make them understand." Reaching up, she takes my face in her palm and enjoys my unshaven jaw a moment, letting her thumb discover the stubble above my lips. "That was brave."

"Foolish," I say, "foolish to keep it hidden for so long," I amend, because I'm seeing now, she would've accepted it. I just never gave her the chance. "I should have given you more credit."

I don't think her acceptance was what held me back though. I think it was how wanting those things made me view myself. But I have every faith—with only the slightest fear-driven reservations—that she's going to change that perception, one kinky act at a time.

She guides me to the bed with the way her plump ass commands that satin robe to sway, and we sit on the edge.

"I get why you didn't tell me though. I'm not mad, I'm just... glad we're here now."

She reaches behind her, uncovering a manilla folder with various colored tabs staggered along the edge. A little wince captures her face, but it's adorable. "I may have gone a little... overboard," she admits.

"Were you hiding a kinky sex folder in our comforter?" I tease as I reach into my back pocket for the singular folded sheet of paper I have my notes on.

We agreed to spend a week thinking things through. Researching things independently. Really analyzing our quiz results and trying to understand how to make the words on the paper come to life off-page.

I'll admit, I didn't know what to do. Make a list of shit I want to try? Feeling overwhelmed but completely against making Jes hand-hold me through the discovery I've put on our shoulders, I decided to pick one thing and focus on it.

Instead of the rope being my focus—though all of my heart and cock are dying to get to it—I placed all my energy on the biggest thing I've fantasized about. The darkest thing, too. I figure, start off with what I think is the most despicable, and move from there. Working forward, she'll only have less and less to process if we start here.

She shrugs, and the satin robe she'd been holding to her so tight slips past her shoulders becoming nothing but a shimmer against the comforter.

My mouth goes dry when I realize why she held it closed

so tightly. Looping her ribs, knotted thick and heavily in the front, her torso is coated in a corset of ropes.

Ropes I've never seen. Tied up around her neck, the waxy rope wraps her breasts, like a cupless underwire, followed by a series of knots descending down her tummy. Her lower half is free of rope, nothing but bare legs and pussy on display. Her eyes are full of questions and nerves as they search mine.

"I didn't go to spin today," she says, her voice quiet. "It took me twelve tries to get this, and when I finally did, well, I think I got a better workout than I would have at spin anyway." She giggles, but I feel her unease as her fingers nervously search for the robe. Is she thinking she's going to put it back on?

I grab the robe and toss it to the floor. "Don't even think about it," I warn, and there he is. The monster, the darkness, the man who wants to force his way inside a woman and hear her scream with fear. He's here in this room now, brought out to play by the sight of the woman he loves bound in ropes.

"You... you like it? It's not... too much?"

I stand from the bed, unable to take my eyes off of her. The knots are tight, all... I count quickly. Twelve. All twelve of the knots on her torso are neat and tight, the same way I'd tie them. My belt hits the wall because I whip it out of my jeans so fast. Buttons skitter across the floor as I tear open my flannel.

Jes watches me, eyes wide, full lips parted. "We...." her voice is airy, and light, and her eyes are already glazing over with desire. "We still need to talk."

"Yeah," I gruff, finally shedding the last piece of clothes.

"But right now, I need you to know just what I think of those ropes." My boxers join the other discards and I grip my fat, aching dick, pointing it toward her. I know the tip is slick with precum, I can feel it. And I groan as her eyes fall to it, her tongue swiping over her lip like the sight of my dripping cock has her ready to eat.

I shake my cock and heavy drops of precum splatter against the hardwood. "The thought of you wrapping yourself in rope makes me want to blow right this second, Jes," I admit. Her eyes widen, and her knees fall apart, her pussy lips shining with arousal.

"Yeah? You know what... I got so horny tying myself, too," she says, staring down at her handiwork. I'm so many things right now.

Proud.

In awe.

Turned-the-fuck on.

"I think I should stay here while we talk," I decide aloud, knowing if I catch the scent of her pussy right now I'll lose all control. That's what she does to me any day of the week, but wrap those perfect tits and plump ass in rope and I'm no longer a man. I'm *all* animal.

My gaze falls to the rope again, and I know it's going to be extremely hard to talk about plans and rules with her all tied in front of me. But goddamn—I step closer, my arousal now taking a backseat to my curiosity.

"Is this... 6 millimeter jute?" I ask, reaching out to pinch the rope with my fingers, smoothing over the tread a few times.

She nods. "It is. I read online that anywhere between six and eight millimeter is a great place to start. And I also read that jute—which I did not know about until six days ago—is the best starter rope for torso ties. Not suspension ties, but maybe we'll get there. Anyway, I guess I'm now a little Yoda when it comes to jute."

Too many enticing things in one sentence. I growl and yank my hand back, forcing restraint. Because we need to talk. My cock drips onto the floor and her breathy little moan tells me she's watching. And she likes it.

"Jes, I really want very much to listen to you talk about rope. Hell, I could probably masturbate to you talking about and touching rope. Honest to God. But right now, seeing you like that has me on the cusp of embarrassing myself, and I'd like that one time at the movies to be the only time that happened."

Her head falls back as she laughs, hearty and carefree, and I can't help but grin. We both remember our first postpartum date. Lex was just two months old, and my parents had come to the house to let us have a date. It was more for Jes, since she hadn't been out of the house at all since we got home. I'd been going to work, so I was seeing Graham and the other guys. But the truth was, we needed to be out *together*.

During the movie, Jes put her hand on my thigh. We hadn't made love since she was pregnant, as she had an episiotomy when she labored, she'd needed more time to heal. Rightfully.

And with doting on Jes and Lex, still working, and keeping up the parts of the house that needed it, I didn't have much free time. Read the subtext there: I hadn't even been jerking off in my morning shower to alleviate missing Jes.

I was bursting with sexual tension, which I unfortunately realized about one thigh stroke too late.

Needless to say, we left the movie, and when we got in the truck, she unzipped me and licked me clean.

"That was fun for me though," she says as her laughter subsides. I think both of us found the memory of her tonguing my cum off my groin in the dark pickup at the same time.

"Baby, that was hot but... embarrassing."

"The idea that you wanted me so bad just rubbing your thigh made you orgasm is something I masturbate to often," she says, the breathy admission taking me by the balls.

"Seriously?" I croak, my fist now stroking my length in a dangerous game of "hold it".

She nods. "Seriously." Then her hand falls between her legs, but I stop her. As painful as it is, I remember the silence the night after I pinned her to the bed and called her my wet fuck hole.

"Wait, fuck, I can't believe I'm saying this but... wait. Don't... don't touch yourself."

She snarls playful. "You either, then."

I drop my hand, and my cock bobs, veins angry and straining from root to pinkened tip. "Fine. We need to talk."

She looks down at her roped body. "This is what I spent my week doing. Researching rope play since I am a rope bunny." Her voice drops to a rasp and my skin tingles with bumps in response. "And you're my rigger."

I swallow hard. I've always been a rigger and I've always had the underlying vibration in my soul, whispering for more each time the rugged braids of rope would run across my palms and twine through my fingers. *More of this, with this.*

I'm glad I chose to focus on the thing that got us here. The primary urge, the driving force that started it all. Because with Jes on rope and me on force, I know we're going to make some insane discoveries.

"Jes, I want to tell you what I want. In no uncertain terms. And I know we've talked around it and about it a little, but now that we're here, I need you to know exactly what it is, and I'm begging you to stay honest with me. Tell me if it's something you can't do. Because I love you more than I love anything else, including these... *needs*."

She rolls her eyes, the little minx. "Go on."

The words are practiced, stacked on my tongue, ready to deliver. I take a breath, force my eyes to ignore the art of her sweet curves hugged by rope, and launch.

"I want the element of nonconsent. I want to hear you scream, I want your fear running through my veins as I fuck you, and I want to know what it's like to have you fight beneath me." I lick my lips. "I want to hear you beg." I step closer. "Pray."

"I want to give you that," she says, her confidence oozing through her tone. "But how can we make it feel nonconsensual if I consent? Just... role play?"

I reach for my cock as my eyes fall to the ropes wrapping her; the sight of her, good God. She's a perfect temple to fall at my knees before.

"No touching," she reminds me, though I notice her own hand has inched its way up her thigh a bit.

"It will always be a little bit of roleplay. But I thought of how we can make it less structured, to give it the sporadic feel I've always craved." Part of me still feels like an utter creep saying those things. Admitting those urges. But no—I have to stop calling them urges. Because the reason we're here is that I couldn't say no to this thing inside me. It's more than an urge—it's a need.

I *need* this.

I nod to the bed, where there are way too many fucking pillows stacked up against the headboard. Jes looks over her shoulder then back to me, a question arching her brow.

"That blue pillow case. The one you got when you were postpartum but still use."

She rises to her knees, showing me her naked ass as she rifles through the pillows, turning back with the precise one stretched between two hands.

"This?" she asks, lifting it slightly.

I nod.

After having Des, Jes had some wicked postpartum sweats, and after a few nights in a row of changing pillowcases in the dark hallway at two in the morning for her, I looked up a solution online. This pillow case has a light blue side meant to cool and a dark blue side meant to absorb, made for menopausal women with hot flashes.

It worked so well and she liked it so much, she kept it. Now it's in the normal rotation. And I say normal but all these years later, I still don't get why our bed needs so many tiny goddamn pillows. She peers down at it, clearly not understanding. I explain. And it's not the greatest thing I've come up with, but for now, until we're comfortable, it'll do.

"I was thinking, when you're open to the experience, flip the pillow, dark blue side up. When I come in here and see the pillow is flipped, I know I'll have... say, a couple of hours to make it happen."

She chews her lip and right as I'm beginning to grow self-conscious of the idea, she smooths her hand down the pillow and nods.

"Twenty-four hours. When the pillow is flipped, you have a day. Then I'll flip it back." She taps her chin for a second, thinking, then amends with, "if the boys are home, our bedroom or the garage only. If they're not... the world is your oyster." I know she chose our room because of the new lock, and the garage because there's a lock on both sides —thanks to Jes demanding one to wrap Christmas gifts without worry.

"You feel good about that idea?" I ask, making sure she really likes it and isn't just agreeing. Though that isn't usually her style, I still want to make sure just because I'm so insecure about all of this to start with.

Excited, sure as shit. But nervous? A lot of that too. And I don't want to fuck anything up. This isn't some shady and seedy, private room at a club. This is our home, and this is our life. I choose to honor my nerves and over ask questions in order to feel the most comfortable going forward.

She nods. "I love it."

I nod, my cock still thrumming between my legs. "Next up, safe words."

She flushes, copper hair curtaining her face in loose, sexy waves. "I'm really turned on hearing you talk about this stuff. Lawson Briggs establishing safe words." I see her visibly shudder, and another opaque bead of arousal rolls off my head.

A growl gets trapped in my throat as I take in my gorgeous wife, gift-wrapped in rope, flesh bumpy and pink from her desire for me. For this thing that we're about to begin. Goddamn I don't think I've ever wanted her as much as I do now.

But we aren't ready for that, not quite yet.

"Red is stop, yellow is slow, as in, pump the brakes unless you want this to be over." I recall the words I'd read online after a few Google searches. "Green... carry on."

Red means your submissive has reached their limit or their tolerance threshold. Yellow means they're nearing their limit and if they use this word, you should curb your behavior accordingly to make the scene or act more pleasurable for your sub.

I hope I never hear her say red, or even yellow for that matter, but in my heart, I know I might. I know once I start really owning my needs, there's a chance it could go too far for her. Or even, if she's simply had too much. What works for us one evening could go against everything she's feeling and vibing off of the next night. And whatever she's feeling, I want to know. I'd never do anything that would leave my wife feeling hurt or unsafe. Fucking never.

She nods. "Red and yellow, that's easy."

"And you need a tap out, in case you want to stop but can't speak."

Her mouth falls open but no words escape. She licks her lips, chest rising beneath the rope, her breath growing jagged the longer this conversation runs. "Wh-why wouldn't I be able to speak?" Though she stutters through the question, her expression tells me it's not from fear, but arousal. "Will you be choking me?" Her lids go heavy, and I know then that's something she'd like to try.

Goddamn am I glad she caught me jacking off to her

photo. How else would I have ever learned of all these delicious desires of hers?

"Maybe. Or maybe your mouth will be full of my cock. Maybe you'll be gagging on my full sac." I grip my balls, groaning as their heavy warmth fills my palm. "If these were in your mouth, could you beg me to quit? Huh?"

He's taking over more and more. I can feel Laws recessing, and this other man stepping forward, absorbing the spotlight, feeding off her mewls and moans, growing more powerful each vulnerable moment we spend together. "Or would you tongue them like a greedy little slut while my precum dripped from my cock and defiled your face?"

Her pupils blow wide as she considers my words, her breathy panting emphasized by the ropes constricting her torso.

Still, there are more things to discuss. As I'm about to talk about the choking she just mentioned, she reaches for her folder, passing it to me. There's only a few sheets of paper inside, but it feels like a brick.

Her voice wobbles, not with fear but with excitement. "I didn't have a ton of one color, since they're annotation tabs. But all shades of blue, purple and green are things I want to try and am good with. The lighter hued tabs, like the yellow and orange, are no's."

I don't open the folder, just look down at it, assessing the ratio of yes to no. A loud rumble tears through me, leaving my lips in a low whistle. They're almost all yes. My thumb skates over the few no's, and I lift my eyes to meet her.

"Before I know what these are, can you tell me if the reason they're a no is because they make you feel a certain way?"

The question bears depth, and as Jes tips her head to the side, considering it, I can tell she hadn't expected me to ask it.

"I wanna know why you don't like those things so I can make sure to keep those feelings or thoughts out of other things, if that makes sense."

"Yeah," she says, "I get it. Like, if the reason why I don't like—for instance—" she nods to the closed folder in my grip, alluding to one of the no's I've yet to discover. "If water sports are a no—"

I cut her off with an arched brow and flared nostrils. "I think after having two baby boys we've both been peed on enough."

She snorts "Exactly. And I don't want to be brought back to early years of parenthood while we're getting down." I join her in laughter, completely sharing the sentiment of her response. Suddenly, the folder feels much lighter. The situation feels more manageable. Less overwhelming.

Scooting closer to me on the bed, close enough that she can reach out and take my hand, her voice is low when she says, "Thanks for the levity. It reminds me that even though putting myself on display for you in some of these ways is kind of nerve wracking, it's still just you and me in this room. And I have no reason to be nervous."

I don't know if she's saying that for her or for me, but I love her for it either way.

"I feel the same." I let her hand fall to the mattress as I flip the folder open, my eyes veering to the no's. I want to know all of her yeses, but the truth of the matter is, I'm so goddamn turned on right now if I see something gnarly and know that my wife read that and envisioned us doing it then said yes? Movie date redux.

My eyes make the sad journey from her naked, roped body to the paper in my hand. On the edge I see yellows and oranges, and I search out their corresponding sin.

Fecal play.

"Oh fuck," I bring my other hand to my mouth, fist curled, swallowing down a sudden rush of acid. "People bring shit in the bedroom?"

A disgusted shiver makes her wobble. "I don't know but—"

"You don't need to explain." It occurs to me then that she should feel like she doesn't have to explain her no's to me, even if they're less abrasive than feces. "You know, you don't need to justify any of your no's. I want you to know all that matters to me is that you feel good."

Her eyes mist as she nods. I press on, going to the next item on the list.

Water sports.

Okay, we've already discussed this one. I suppose going through a list of things isn't as intimidating as I envisioned. Onto the next.

Fisting.

My eyes go to my hand holding the sheet of paper. "Fuck!" I react aloud, looking up at Jes to see her giggling.

"I see you got to the fisting." Her cheeks flush, like the idea of even discussing it makes her a little uncomfortable. But still, here we are.

I'm proud of us, but I don't say it. Not yet.

"Your hands are huge, Laws. Even if human infants came out of me, I don't really want to recreate that pain."

I shake my head. "I don't want to stick my fist in you." I don't. I don't even want to imagine it. If that makes me squeamish then so be it.

There are only two more orange tabs. Just two. The rest are all things my wife wants to try or be or experience. I look down at the opaque puddle forming on the floor. God, I haven't been this eager to fuck Jes since... shit, I think the first time since Des was born.

I keep going, so I can get this going.

Filming.

I stare at the word, imagining what it would be like to have a reel of Jes naked and covered in cum, skin stained with the sting of degradation and use. I'd watch it and come all over myself jerking off, I know I would. But then the idea that someone else could see it. Another person could see a glimpse of how intimately I know Jes, and the thought immediately sours the sex tape idea. More so, she doesn't want it.

I've gotten lucky so far. These have all been no's to things I don't want either. My breath catches in my throat as my mind races; what if this last thing is one of my primal urges? I read on, not allowing myself to borrow worry.

I exhale concern when my eyes fall to the remaining no.

Anal-to-oral.

She doesn't want to take my cock in her ass, then suck it down her throat. I get that. Fair's fair. I look up at her. "I didn't write this down but my no's are all pretty much this: if it's meant to happen in the bathroom over porcelain, it's no."

She chuckles, and I can tell the joke is appreciated. Lightening the mood is my way of getting a pulse for the situation as we navigate all of this. With time, we'll learn, and the more we learn about each other's needs, the less we'll need the levity later.

"I can go with that." Her gaze drops to her body, where she fingers some of the knots before looking at me, her eyes dark, lids heavy. "Unleash yourself and come get what you want, already."

Jesus Christ. I've never heard Jes speak so seductively. Sure, she does her fair share of dirty talk and moaning, especially when I'm eating her to orgasm.

But with the lights on. So plainly. Holding my eyes.

"Three. That's how many times you tap or pat or blink. Three," I say, remembering we hadn't established the final level of safety.

She nods, urgency making her rock to her knees, body swaying slightly as she nibbles her bottom lip.

I lick my palm and with half my strength, strike her right across her breast. The blow is unexpected and causes her to topple onto the mattress. Through a silken tangle of copper strands she peers up at me, pupils wide.

"First things first," I say, "don't speak unless you're spoken to."

Twelve

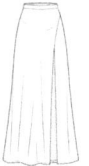

JES

The unknown is what has me nervous.

I blink up at him, my chest heavy with the breath I can't quite find. A moment passes and I finally gasp.

Laws slapped me so hard I fell back, wrapped his fist in my hair and yanked me back up to my knees, only to send me down with another harsh slap. This time my other breast took the blow.

Still just staring, I let the burn rippling through my skin connect to my brain, and the many things going on there.

Laws just slapped me across my breasts and knocked me down. He stood me up by my hair. Electric chills spark, traveling like bolts of lightning across my skin at the memory. And as pain fades, there's a pulsing left behind.

The trust he's giving me in letting himself do this—it

would make my eyes wet if I let it. But I don't, because I don't want him to think it's the slapping my tits that has me crying. But the experience brings much more emotional buzz than I anticipated.

I'm discovering that quiz was pretty damn good. One of my top matches was someone who enjoys pain, and I'm seeing now... I do. And while the slaps stung and I ached from them, the anticipation for the pleasure had me clinging to the pain, knowing it was merely the appetizer before the main course.

I never thought I'd want to pretend the man I love is actually raping me but because it's roleplay, it doesn't feel sinister. It feels like someone finally exposing the thing they guarded in silent shame for years, to finally be met with acceptance and love. It's a good thing, a life-changing thing, really.

"On your back," he growls, and I'm fairly certain this is not a new voice, but the voice of a man who's been in hiding forever. I do as he says and watch him disappear into his walk-in closet, only to come out a moment later with another rope.

One of *his*. All black. He doesn't even look at me. Instead, rocks to his toes, and reaches above his head to a spot in the ceiling. Now that I look at where he's feeling around, I take note of a thin square on the ceiling. *Is that marker?*

I realize as his fingertips press into the ceiling that it's a trap door. A tiny one. Flipping open, in the ceiling is a thick silver loop. Laws hooks his pointer finger through it, giving it a yank. It gives another few inches and all of me wants to ask him, *Did you just install that? When did you do that? Why did you do that?*

I want to ask. But I know better. Just minutes into this and I already know fucking better. And God that is *so* arousing.

Sliding the rope through the hook, he hovers over me, and while I think I know what he's going to do, I don't *actually* know for sure. He's going to use his rope on me... but how? I've tied a gorgeous corset onto myself—one that took hours, no less. My mind races with possibility as he circles the bed, his expression ominous and arousing. Electricity tears through me as he appears over me, wrapping his black rope around my wrists. Am I becoming one end of a human pulley? When he's done making adjustments and my wrists are bound, he checks his knots, tugging on the ropes everywhere. Grunting and murmuring things under his breath, his movement then ceases.

In my line of vision, he slowly wraps the loose end of rope around his fist. He's not letting go of me any time soon, I can see. Our eyes lock, and my heart beats faster at how intensely he's looking at me. Then, my head falls back with a pop as he yanks on the rope, pulling my body off the bed by my wrists. I blink up at his black rope binding my hands, and though a slow ache spreads down my forearms, my pussy seizes in delight. He's always wanted this. And it feels so good to experience it.

He yanks me higher, and my skin burns, so I scream. I can't help it. The ropes feel like thorns, paired with the urgency of his movements—I know we're role playing. I know this is, essentially, a scene. But for a moment, some part of me fails to see that portion and can only react to the man she loves suddenly being so different.

It's jarring.

But it's exciting.

Slowly, he stalks around the bed a few times, sizing me up as I hang. My knees brush the mattress but not enough to gain support, and I think that's just what he wants. Bringing his face to mine, his head blocks the light above, and his outline is illuminated. He may look heavenly but his eyes promise pain, the tight flex of his jaw paired with the sound of jute against the metal loop in the ceiling has me praying he's going to make good on what his eyes are telling me.

"I thought you'd keep your pretty little mouth shut." Another inch closer, his hot breath splays against my face, and excitement curls my spine, warmth buzzing in my lower half. "You think if you scream loud enough, I'll let you go?"

I know it's roleplay. I know it is. And I know Laws is the man I love.

Still.

There's a flicker of doubt in my belly, which I know is utterly insane. He'd never hurt me. I know that. He pulls me up higher, further off the mattress, the strain in his bulging bicep making my mouth water as he slightly lowers his arm to lift me up.

Stepping closer to me, I glance down to see his erection bobbing, way too far away. Because seeing it now, thick and glistening, flush with eager arousal... I want it. I want him to have his way with me.

But I can't move.

Suddenly, his arm lifts and I lower, and he plunges his fat cock between my greedy lips, spearing my throat before yanking back out.

I realize as precum threads between his slit and my face,

dripping down the underside of my chin to make my throat shine, that flicker in my gut isn't doubt but... nerves.

I'm nervous for this, I realize, because it's spontaneous. I showed up tonight with a manila folder, organized and tabbed. And while I'm equipped with safe words and a tap out, it's the mind full of possibilities that has me nervous.

Using the hand not keeping me suspended, he gathers my hair which flows freely behind me. My mind backfills a memory of us when we went to the fair and rode the ferris wheel. It was before we had kids, before we were married. The sky looked like spilled ink with glitter scattered over the top, stars twinkling everywhere. I remember how warm and solid his chest felt as I pressed my cheek to it, relaxing against him in the shaky old metal car. My hair dangled off the back of my seat, the harmless wind picking it up, tossing it back over my eyes and face. Laws had reached back and wrapped my hair around his hand, tugging it just slightly.

My eyes flicked up to his, and I found them in a way I'd never seen. Not just darker but possessive, and hungry, too. And the low rasp of his tone when he'd said, *Just making sure it stays out of your eyes.*

He meant it, and he held it there the rest of the ride. It made me so wet, so damn feral for rough sex with him that when we got back home, I almost cried when he'd fucked me missionary then went to sleep.

I blink at him, eyes watering as he aligns his cockhead with my mouth, and wonder if he remembers that night too. I know now that *he* was there with me that night, this other version of my husband. I wish I would've been introduced earlier.

"Open," he commands, then I'm jarred from the soft

memory as his large hand comes across my breasts again, one at a time.

"No," I retort, my denial a soft whimper. My scalp burns as his grip goes feral, jerking my head to impale me with his cock. I gag, feeling the blunt, wide head of him smash against the back of my throat. He slaps my face, and my teeth ache from the heaviness of his vast palm.

"No won't stop me'," he reminds me before jerking back, taking his cock out of my mouth. Hovering over me, his voice is unrecognizable as he glares down at me. "Keep your fucking mouth open."

I do, and I hope he doesn't notice how my jaw trembles.

A moment later, my mouth is full of his spit. Warm and thick, I can't fight the urge to swallow it, everything between my legs buzzing as it slides down my throat and fills my belly.

He releases my hair and takes a moment to rewrap the end of the rope on the other hand, lowering his arm, pulling me up again. My wrists and arms ache as his rope tightens, but a moment later, my face is near his, and I can hardly feel the way my shoulders burn and my spine stretches from how freely my body dangles.

"Did I tell you to swallow?" When he slaps my face this time, it's harder, and I gasp. I can't stop myself.

He pauses, and our eyes hold. "Give me a color."

I know he's waging war in his brain—wondering if he's gone too far? Given me too much of his monster? "Speak, give me a color. Colors override any instruction I've given you to be quiet."

"Green." I don't want to break. I don't want to be the one who calls out red or whimpers yellow.

But I'm not reaching my limit and that's not what had me considering using the words for a moment.

I'd use them only so I could hold his face in my hands and fill him with reassuring words. But we don't need to break scene that way. He's checking on me with our chosen words, and that gets me going, too.

"Head back," he orders as he releases his grip enough to allow me to recline backwards, and it's easy in this position because my head is feeling so heavy. Full of sand, at this point. It topples back easily. My ass on the bed, my arms up straight and the weight of my head forcing my back into an extreme arch.

Slowly, he moves around me until he's behind me and his proud cock nudges my cheek, warm and heavy. My pussy spasms. I've sucked Laws many times. He's got the most beautiful cock in the world, I swear he does. Thick but long, shows and grows, comes in abundant ropes, with plump balls to match.

This is the first time I've had his entire package placed on my face, like he's the dessert and I'm his plate. I stick out my tongue, eager for a taste of my treat. When I look past his cock to his dark eyes far above, I see a touch of hesitancy, like he's still lost in his head.

Trying to find the happy medium of staying true to the fantasy but also giving him the nudge he needs to reassure him, I steal a lick of his shaft. It's just a flick of my tongue—but coming from the supposed victim, it is out of character. But it's for Laws. To show him he can do this. He can keep going.

Based on how his cock drips over my face and into my mouth, I know he wants to keep going. And I'm *thisclose* to breaking character, calling out yellow, and reasoning with him that perhaps it's him who needs more time before he gets this extreme when I'm the one disoriented from blinding pain.

Is that pain or... shock?

"Fuck!" I spit out, trying to turn my head as I regroup. "You fucking hit me!" I cry out, realizing the first few times he did it, I didn't give him the reaction he needed. The reaction to keep him in this headspace, the place of captor, monster, villain.

I have to be more than here. I have to give him the verbal cues to keep him here, too. I have to be his victim, lean into this roleplay.

"You fucking asshole!" I cry out, attempting to spit at him but from the angle, it doesn't work, and the desperate mouthful of saliva lands in my own eye.

I hear him moving around the bed, and watch the rope in the ceiling move with him. Then he's on the mattress, on his knees, in behind me as I arch back.

Laws' gruff thumb smears along my lip before he curves his hand behind my head, elevating me level with his dick. "You just can't keep your mouth shut, can you?" He laughs, sardonic and deep, and I swear a tiny wave of orgasm clenches between my legs. I blink up at him, noticing the bumps scattered over his muscles and hair. His nipples could fucking cut glass, and his jaw is tighter than a virgin.

Oh my God. I don't think I've ever been this turned on.

Then he's impaling me, and my stomach muscles clench as my spine attempts to curl as I gag, gag so fucking hard that acid rushes up my throat as I fight vomit.

"Dramatic little slut. Quit gagging and suck my cock," he

hisses, and the whirr of rope against metal has my cunt spasming, dripping even. I focus on breathing, taking in air through my nose as he pummels my throat in unrelenting, harsh passes. With my wrists bound and above me, his strong hand at the back of my head, I know escaping this forced facefuck is impossible.

"You love swallowing so much, how about you swallow my cum, huh? Greedy whores like you, you must love taking a man's load." He pulls his cock out of my throat, and I gasp, desperate to collect air, to keep myself going. I get just a single lungful before his thick fingers are in my mouth. At first, I think he's holding my mouth open but then, as I feel the blunt tips of his fingers playing at the back of my tongue, I know he's not.

He's fucking my mouth with his hand, and it feels raw and foreign. The hinges of my jaw radiate heat through my face and I fight the urge to gag as he spears my throat, fucking my mouth with the same raw finesse as he did with his cock.

And I love it.

I love that careless, urgent, aggressive nature that has him in a chokehold. I don't know what that says about me, but I don't care.

We're in this together.

"What do you think? Is this slutty mouth of yours ready for everything I have to give? Hmm?" He slaps one tit, then the other, but my squeal gets trapped from his hand, still moving in and out of my mouth, keeping me in a continual state of gagging.

A moment later, his hand, coated in my thick saliva, comes up over my bare pussy. One slap, and my hips ache.

Another slap, this one harder, and my lower half vibrates with need, the pain and pleasure now so closely woven together, I can't distinguish one from the other.

"Look at how wet your pussy is for me," he growls, his words coating me in a thin sheen of sweat. My heart races as fast as my clit pulses, and the discomfort of my wrists being bound is slowly starting to fade, a delicious numbness creeping in.

"Your mouth says no, but your cunt says yes," he roars, the sound of another disarming slap to my pussy rattling off our bedroom walls. He raises his arm, and my eyes catch on his fatigued grip on the rope. Knuckles drained of color, arm bulging with strain—I realize how hard all of this is on him physically.

Sweat glistens along his broad chest, the sight of my strong, dominant husband vaporizing my willpower, making everything between my thighs pulse with urgency. I look at his cock, meatier than ever, pinker and angrier than ever. I wish I could have a photo of him this way, indulging in the things he needs most, looking sexier than ever before.

I didn't know that was possible.

His arm rises, and my body lowers, and for a moment, panic tears through me, stealing rational thought. He hasn't cum. I haven't cum. My head hits the mattress right as I yelp, "No!"

His chuckle is smoky and dark, so unlike the laugh he shares over dinner or even in the privacy of our bathroom when we're brushing before bed. This side feels so ripe for exploration, my body thrums with anticipatory excitement at all the things I love about Laws that I've yet to discover.

"Don't worry, greedy slut. I'm not done with you yet," he

says menacingly as he raises my bound arms to lie back on the mattress above my head. "Stay."

He's gone for a minute, and when he returns with a toy in his hand, I feel my cheeks blush.

It's my toy. My dildo. God, just thinking about me owning a dildo makes my cheeks flush. I bought it a few years ago when Laws and Graham traveled to the East Coast for a big job. They were gone two weeks and rubbing my clit to orgasm just wasn't cutting it.

I bought a dildo that I felt resembled Laws' cock and spent the better part of my evenings the weeks he was gone putting the suction-cupped end to the test.

I fucked myself in the shower, pretending he had me bent over. I stuck it to the wall in our bedroom and got on my knees for it, imagining it were him. I even positioned it between pillows in bed and rode it, again, always imagining him, his name on my lips as I called out who I'd seen in my mind as I came.

Him. Him. Always fucking him.

But once he'd returned home, I'd gotten so nervous about how to bring it up to him. Part of me, I remember, even worried that he'd judge me. I never got around to showing him or telling him about it and instead, I'd stashed it away in a shoebox in our closet. A few times I dragged it out, when he was gone on a weekend work trip with Graham, but I always put it away, never quite knowing just how to go about telling him.

So I kept hiding it.

My cheeks are already pink, from being hit, from arousal, from all of it. But still, I feel them burn as Laws finds my gaze and holds it.

"Take the cock away from the slut and what does she do? Wait like a good whore for her bull to return? No," he shakes his head, his throaty timbre scraping my flesh with its depth, leaving bumps of anticipation in its wake. "Instead, she buys a cock to fuck because she's nothing but a greedy, wet fuck hole, desperate to be filled."

He brings the toy to my mouth, and forces it inside. I don't know why, but I fight him, trying to keep my lips screwed shut. His grip on my head intensifies, my hairline flooding with fire and he jerks my head up. "Last chance," he hisses, eyes flicking between mine.

Reluctantly, pulse racing, residual embarrassment over the toy completely gone, I open my mouth. The end of his mouth curls into a sinister grin then—"Gag on it," he commands as he forces the rubber cock onto my tongue, the perfectly shaped head tapping the back of my throat as he impales me repeatedly.

Spit is thick in the back of my throat, earning some deep belly coughs as I struggle to suck and not swallow. The dildo is smaller than Laws, in girth and length, but close. It tastes like rubber and chemical, but I gag and suck, keeping my mouth open, desperate to obey.

When I begin moaning around the cock, he yanks it from my throat and brings his face to mine. I'm panting, lungs ablaze, pussy pulsing.

I only have a moment to breathe before his cock is in my mouth, the trimmed hair on his groin tickling my nose as he sinks all the way inside. Working the pad of his thumb down the arch of my throat, feeling his cock inside me, he lets out a wicked hiss.

"Look at that," he groans, still tracing his length in my

throat externally. "Look at how good you take cock in your throat. Like you were born to choke on dick and drink cum."

His words are jarring, filthy and dark. "My cum," he adds, his tone much quieter. And something tells me that was Laws saying that, making sure I know it's still just me and him in this room, doing this.

His cock lodges farther in my throat as he reaches forward. Attempting to moan as he slides the rubber dildo inside of my pussy only opens my throat further, and as he sinks the fake cock deep inside me, his cock reaches new depths in my throat.

"Fuck," he growls, the tight, wet heat of the back of my throat clearly new for him, too. "Goddamn, keep me this deep and you'll get a reward," he says, his words quiet as they trail over my body. He continues fucking my cunt with the toy, the noises my body is making are surprising.

I can't imagine what he's experiencing. He's holding me up again by the wrists, keeping the rope taut. Fucking me with my toy all while maintaining the unrelenting cadence of his hips as he face fucks me. It's so much. And the way I ignite at how capable he is watching him around the house or with the boys, my soul is set ablaze by him and this scene we're in.

I'm so wet, and there's no way Laws hasn't noticed that I'm far more aroused right now than usual. The man eats me with his eyes open and lights on, just to "memorize" the experience of giving me an orgasm— there's no chance he doesn't notice how my body is behaving tonight.

I'm not just wet, I'm gushing, really, and trust me— gushing isn't a word I'd normally be comfortable using. It sounds so crude and vulgar but... that's us in this fantasy.

Unlike our normal selves.

Raw, stripped to our most basic needs.

Laws' passion for this rough, aggressive connection—the desire to feel like a monster, to feel like the man in the shadows with his hand clamped over a mouth, forcing himself into her—that's what he needs. And I'm learning very quickly that in spite of some sex quiz listing my most likely desires, what I really desire is Laws.

In all forms.

His kink may be rape roleplay, ropes and dominance, and mine may very well be being a rope bunny and his submissive in the bedroom, but the truth? My real kink—the thing that has me clenching around a dildo while I'm gagging on a cock—is him.

Knowing him in all ways, feeling him take what he needs from me, use me as his vessel—being his wet fuck hole.

His words, but maybe they weren't as egregious as I once judged.

Maybe that's what's awakening me in light of his awakening—being his plaything. His free-to-use slut. The mouth to ease his erection, the pussy to keep his cum, the tight asshole to receive his punishments.

I nuzzle down on his length, sucking in his scent through my nose, which is buried in his groin. He smells like soap and just a trace of sweat, musky cedar mixing with the fresh scent of laundry.

"Fuck, that slutty little throat's gonna make me come," he says, the heat of his body radiating into my skin, causing my back to slick with sweat. The ropes around my ribs suddenly seem much tighter than a moment ago as my breath catches, a pressurized pounding twisting around my spine, my ribcage and settling between my hips.

I'm close to losing it, but really want to come with him. I always orgasm so much harder when I taste, feel or even just see his cum. Something about the noises he makes, the way desire twists and sets his features, how his generous cock pulses in his still palm, twitching, painting me, filling me, whatever it is. The warmth, the abundance. Everything about it makes me come.

Upping his speed, his hips work fast as he fucks my face, using my mouth like he would if he were filling me between spread legs. He hisses and groans, but fucks me harder with the toy, so hard that I squeeze my eyes shut, unable to focus on anything but the pulsing in my lower half.

His scent wraps my senses, the vibration of his deep register making me tingle as he growls, "Fuck, here it comes. Don't fucking swallow until I say. Don't swallow, don't—" he stills in my mouth, the hefty cock on my tongue swelling, the dildo in my cunt still pressing into me.

"Godddd," he rushes out as streams of warmth flood my mouth, rush after rush. I press my tongue to the roof of my mouth as he slides out, attempting to trap his release. To not swallow.

To obey.

I'm close. On the edge. The warmth in my mouth reminds me of what we did, what we're doing, and the reality of it is so hot, I can't help it when my thighs start to tremble, when my core aches and my orgasm grabs hold.

The head of Laws' cock is still on my tongue as he creams me with the dildo, his breathing labored. Only, when he realizes I'm nearing the edge, he jerks back. "Don't swallow," he rasps, and a moment later, he drops the rope and I drop to the mattress. Then he's over me, his still-hard cock pummeling my cunt, replacing the dildo, sending me over.

Moaning while struggling to keep my tongue pressed to the roof of my mouth, I lose myself to the overwhelming sensations. I come so hard my vision fades, leaving me blinking in darkness for a few seconds as I attempt to calibrate. My walls tighten around him as he takes, takes, takes every ounce of orgasm from my cunt that he possibly can. And when I think I"m spent, that the last of it has roared through, that's when I feel it.

Laws coming.

Again.

Holy shit, the way my pussy seizes around him, milking him, coaxing out every drop of warmth from him— I'm desperate to scream. Dying to yell. Tears slip from the corners of my eyes as I struggle against the ropes, which now make me achy and sore. I want to see his face, I want to watch him come again—he's never come twice back to back this quickly—but I can't. The jute and Laws' rope have me weak and immobilized, forcing me to motionlessly accept my pleasure, which is some sort of mental torture in itself.

Finally, when my thighs are trembling and my body can't take any more, he reappears above me, but it's not Laws. It's still *him*.

Bound, on my back in the center of our bed, his knees straddling me now at my ribs, he hovers over me. He truly looks like a phantom as the light envelops his back, his features shaded from the ominous way he lurks above.

I think I'm going to watch the phantom fade and my husband return. I think it's going to be that transformative moment where the wolf's features dissipate, and his human flesh returns, his humanity and morale restored.

Laws rests his palm along my throat and applies pressure, his gaze nailing me beneath him. Not that I could move anyway with all six feet four inches of him over five feet five inches of me. But still, his gaze keeps me beneath him with more force than his frame, or his palm. Fingertips sinking into the column on my neck as he whispers, "Swallow."

Then he watches me. I can't even call it watching. He analyzes my eyes. His pupils flare, darkness eating up the mossy earth hue of his irises. His lips part, heavy breaths bombarding my lips. His eyelids grow heavy, and his blinking slows, cheeks flushing.

I swallow, keeping my eyes on the sight above.

It's a sight, too. The way this man is enjoying the final bit of his fantasy is… emotional. And when I'd taken the quiz with Laws the other day, I had ideas of what this would be like.

Expectations, maybe. Fears, for sure. But in all of that, I never foresaw emotional fulfillment. Then again, I don't think I realized that while this is so physical to me, a lot of this is very emotional to him.

His eyes glimmer above me, making my case.

Then he crashes his mouth to mine, and while his tongue thrashes and he swallows all my breathless moans, his hands work easily first at the ropes on my wrists, then at the knotted jute running down my torso. Then the ropes are undone. A little annoying how long it took me to tie them and how easy it was for him to free me. But skill comes with practice, and he's the rigger.

We kiss, languid and leisurely. He drags the back of his

hand along my hairline, frames my jaw in his hand, takes both cheeks in his palms—he can't keep his hands off my face, he can't stop kissing me. My heart brims with happiness. Overly so, to the point where my chest literally aches. I have never experienced anything like this. At all.

It's the purest, most addictive high. There's an extreme tickle in my belly, like the stirring of leaves in the wind, or butterflies stretching their wings. The pleasant jitters and rush of hormones you feel when your boyfriend puts his hand on your inner thigh for the first time. It's the heady dose of love you feel when he tells you he loves you for the first time. It's linked fingers and soft words of wisdom in the dark. It's all of the best things you feel when you're in love, and it's exactly how I feel now, all of that rolled into one singular potent dose.

I want to cry. I kind of want to throw up. I want to scream. I want to fuck him again, give him more, find out where else we can take it.

For the rest of my life, whenever I need to feel good, I'll tap into the memory we just made. Him over me, the look of satisfaction burning in his eyes, adoration radiating off him. The happiness, the fulfillment. He let me in, and allowed his walls to come down. And this feeling wrapping my entire existence right now, it's something we experienced together.

Lost in my thoughts, Laws is gone from my mouth.

He scoops me up in his arms—not something he does too often—and the feeling I described earlier? It intensifies, it catches fire, it magnifies, it grows so fucking all-consuming and powerful that I actually let out a gasp.

I tip my head to his chest, and lose it. I don't know why I'm sobbing against him. I'm happy. I feel so good. So, so good. But I can't say the words because I'm clutching his pec and crying.

Before long, I'm resting in his lap as the tub fills slowly, the scent of lavender soothing my senses some. He knows it's my favorite. He put it in the tub. And that somehow makes me sob one last time, harder, deeper, making my core ache.

He strokes his fingers through my hair, and I can't deny the zing I feel between my legs at his romantic and tender touch. His lips rain down my hair line, placing delicate and soft kisses everywhere, all while praising me.

Praise. I've never heard my husband praise quite like this.

Sure, he's called me a good girl in the throes of passion plenty of times, maybe even smacked my ass doggy style while he said it once or twice, too. But this praise.

My ovaries actually ache as my pussy grows swollen and slick with desire again.

"You, my beautiful, perfect wife, have the most beautiful throat. You took me so well, and you held your breath so long. I was so amazed by you. And I wish you could have seen yourself, baby."

He rubs his palm down the length of my spine, the tips of his fingers teasing the top of my ass, sending sparks of arousal through my thighs.

"You looked so beautiful in those ropes. Just seeing you in them made me wanna come. In fact, I'm going to jerk off to the memory later, I can assure you."

I giggle, but don't let go of his chest, tears still streaming down my cheeks. His cock is fat and hard again beneath me.

"More than the ropes, watching you take me in your throat and fight against me, I can't tell you how that felt. And

I know that took trust. You trusted me to take what I need, but leave you with something too. And I hope I did that. Because Jes, you did so good for me, baby, you really did. I need you to know, if you never want that again, we don't have to. But know this, you made me so proud, and I love you so much. No matter what."

He rises, and he lowers us into a perfect tubful of water, the surface foamy with lavender. I settle with my back to his chest, his hard cock pressed against me.

I have to stare at our feet, mine inside of his, as I admit this. Looking at him will have me crying all over again.

I had no clue this would be so emotional.

"I want to do it again. Right now," I say, laughing hard to prevent myself from crying. "I'm kidding," I add, taking a steadying breath because I'm still trembling.

He rubs up my shoulders, and I talk myself out of grinding back against him because talking is important. Crucial, I think.

"Jes..." He sounds nervous, and that's my cue to get my shit together and make him understand... he has it all wrong.

I'm happy.

"I'm crying because I'm happy. I don't know, I think I'm having some sort of like, cathartic release or something. But I just feel so, so good, Laws. The way you looked over me, when you held my throat," I say, remembering the exact noise of my swallow. I swear it's etched into my brain. "God, I just feel so connected to you that it's almost... too intense right now."

He kisses the back of my ear. "I feel the same way."

I turn in his arms, and find a small grin twisting his lips. I splash him a little before he grips my upper arms gently, coaxing me to speak.

"How are you so calm then, if you feel the same way?" The question seems fair to me.

"I took the last week pretty seriously. And I realized, after I installed the ceiling hook—"

"I was gonna ask!" I interject, slapping his muscled chest. God, my man is hot.

"I realized I am going to behave as a dominant. Well, if all went to plan. But that would make you—"

"Your submissive." My cheeks tingle as the words leave my mouth. I like it. I like the way it feels on my tongue, and I love how it looks in his eyes.

"Yes." He swallows, and his Adam's apple dipping makes my pussy throb. "And part of being a dominant is putting your partner's needs above yours. It's part of the balance of power, if I had to guess."

I cock a brow. "Balance of power?"

He shrugs, running a hand through his hair, like BDSM relationship dynamics are a normal topic of conversation for us... while in the lavender bath together.

If I wasn't so sickeningly happy, my head would be spinning.

"You allow me to take from you, because that's part of what I need," he says, his voice not faltering. He's accepted it now and I want to cry at how wonderful that feels. I remember his eyes the night we spoke through the bathroom door. When I opened the door, I saw his shame, his guilt, and his pain and I hated it.

And now we're here.

"I need to take, I need you to be powerless, and to fight

sometimes, too. And those are big takes, those are trusting takes. So in return, there are times where I honor those takes by shelving some of my needs to give to you. I have to give to you, Jes, or it doesn't work."

My eyes water, but the steam off the water is thick, making it imperceptible to an equally emotional Laws.

He washes me while he talks to me about all the things he felt while we did what we did. Play by play, explains to me how he felt nervous, then excited - the entire gamut. Knowing how he was feeling throughout and seeing him now, it makes me feel even better.

I tell him my feelings as he dries me and dresses me.

We talk as he makes us tacos wearing nothing but low slung pajama pants. His cock is half hard and I make no secret that I'm looking at my hot older man.

He winks at me, and I finish explaining why I had such an emotional outburst, and just how intense it all felt.

Around two in the morning, we finally fall asleep.

The same bodies are in this bed tonight, but we're completely different people.

Thirteen

LAWS

She looks so beautiful this way. Helpless and at my will.

Jesus Christ, that was the absolute hardest Scouts meeting to get through. I drive to the bar, meeting up with Greg again tonight, hating myself.

He's been my foreman for ages, and we've been friends even longer. After setting up a small, tent-top residential greenhouse in town, he popped into the office to see me. He'd let the crew go, and reported that the job went well and they've even managed to salvage some spare supplies for reuse. When he lingered in the doorway of my office, I knew he needed me as a friend, not a boss.

"Think you could take Harley to Scouts again tonight? I hate to ask you," he said, and when his eyes fell on his work boots, I knew he was going through something. With a divorce on the horizon and a separation going on, even the toughest guys would crumble.

"Sure," I said, right away, not wanting him to carry any extra guilt. It's a ride to Scouts. Lex and Des love Harley, so picking him and taking him is always cool for them. "No problem. And how about I grab you after I drop Harley back off and we get a drink?"

He continued looking at his boots when he said, "You know what? I could use a drink."

Circling the desk, I slapped my hand across his shoulder blades and assured him I did, too. The truth? All I wanted to do was get home to Jes.

Sure, that's always what I want.

But in the last few weeks, my desire to be with her has increased tenfold. Sometimes I feel like I've become borderline obsessed with my wife.

I'd texted Jes that the boys and I would be picking up Harley, and that Greg and I would be getting a beer after Scouts. When I zipped by the house to drop the boys off, she'd ushered them in the house then tiptoed out to the truck with bare feet, just to tell me to have a good time with Greg.

She gave me a kiss, fed her fingers through my hair, knocking my AgDev hat off my head. She didn't straddle my lap or whisper dirty promises, but the moment felt like foreplay. Got me hard, even. Now I'm foolishly recounting the last encounter with her as I drive to Greg's.

After our first night where I hung her up and used her mouth, I thought nothing could compare. She wanted to do it again, explore more elements, keep going. I wanted it too but deep down, I made myself understand that it would *likely* be something we don't do forever. That the stress and time management required to live these fantasies would at some point outweigh the fun.

But one day last week, I texted her I'd be home late. Graham needed me to come by his place and help him install his new range hood. While I was there, I got stuck answering a trillion questions from Mae about Jes and the boys.

By the time I got home, I had just enough time to read a chapter to Lex and a story to Des. When I finally made it to our master bedroom, it was empty.

But the pillow was flipped, and as soon as I saw the shiny navy blue fabric staring back at me, without planning or thought, I stomped downstairs.

She had her EarPods in, listening to a book or podcast or something, a knitting needle and a new project splayed across her lap.

From behind, I came up and wrapped my palm around her mouth, preventing her from waking the boys. Preventing her from crying out.

My palm absorbed her pleas and begs for help. Her attempts vibrated through my hand, up my arm, and it made me hard. I told her to get up, and she did. I hooked her around the neck, my forearm pressed to the base of her throat, and led her into the garage, where I tied her arms together behind her back, and with a wax-dipped piece of jute tied around her open mouth, gagged her.

Then I *took*.

I used the end of the rope to whip her ass while I fucked her pussy, my cock getting harder and harder each shade of pink her flesh took on. Bent over my workbench, her thighs began to tremble, and I knew she was close to orgasm.

She liked me whipping her ass with rope. She liked me gagging her. Fuck, I'm hard now just reflecting on it as I pull into Greg's driveway and slide out of the truck. While waiting for him on the porch—I wave at the digital doorbell and he calls that he'll be right out—I open my phone and send Jes a text.

> I'm thinking about last week, in the garage.

She responds right away, and even though I know she's likely bartering with the boys to eat their veggies or finish their homework, I like to imagine her tucked under our covers with that dildo of hers pressed between her legs, my name on her lips.

JES

> I think about last week in the garage at least 100x a day

I grin at her message just as Greg appears, giving me a nod before turning around to lock his front door. Quickly, I send her a text back before I devote a solid hour of my focus to Greg and his troubles.

> Just grabbed Greg. I'm giving him one hour, then I'm coming home.

Then, because I feel it between my ribs, I add—

> I miss you like crazy

She begins responding, but I slide my phone into my

pocket, leaving myself something to look forward to when I drop him off later.

"That's what I didn't know," Greg says, taking me off-guard. We amble toward my truck and climb inside.

"What?" I ask, starting the engine. The bar isn't far from here and neither of us are big drinkers, even in the face of Greg's familial melt down. One nursed drink will get us through the hour. Part of me feels a little guilty about mentally being so focused elsewhere but I can't help it.

She's got a permanent place in my mind.

"How to keep *that* spark," he says plainly, earning him a glance across the cab. He stares out the windshield, shadows flickering across his profile as I drive through town with the sun setting.

"Spark? I don't know," I say, because I wasn't expecting to talk about me and Jes. I was expecting to hear Greg talk about Addie.

"You were just texting Jes, weren't you?" he asks, gripping the oh-shit handle as I take a bump going thirty-seven.

I nod. "Yeah."

He snorts. "You looked like you just had a woman stick her hand down your pants for the first time."

My first instinct is to defend my reaction to her text, but I have no fucking clue how I reacted or what I look like. And Greg has known me for a long time, so he knows my expressions. Rather than lie, I say, "Well, I guess we have kept the spark alive."

More than. We're burning our entire world and roasting marshmallows as we do.

"How?" he asks, but now I feel his eyes on me across the cab. I feel the weight of his focus, the intensity with which he needs this answer. And he needs it to be something that translates, something he can do.

He needs me to solve the puzzle of his broken marriage. I hear it in the way his tone rattles as he asks again, "How do you keep the spark after twelve years?"

The bar comes into sight, so I swivel the truck into an open parking spot. Unclipping my belt, I turn to face him, and I see it.

I see how badly he wants Addie back. How hard this all is on him. He shoves a hand through his damp, curly hair, then drags his fingers down through his beard. "I failed to keep it alive," he whispers, but he isn't trying to whisper. Grown men don't sit in the quiet cab of a truck together and whisper.

He just... lacks the energy to say it louder.

I stare at the cars stopped at the streetlight adjacent to the bar. I focus on that as I speak to him, hoping to alleviate the tension he must feel for growing emotional.

Truth is, I think he's taking it like a goddamn champ. If Jes told me she wanted a divorce, I'd probably be somewhere with padded walls, only dreaming of getting a drink with Greg. The fact that he's not missed a single day or work nor has he had the emotional breakdown I had expected, I'm impressed. But I focus on his question, because telling him I'm impressed at the way he's clearly *ignored* his emotions will do far less for him than actual advice.

"I can't tell you what happened with your marriage, or what Addie wants or needs—" I start, but Greg seizes the opportunity for sarcasm.

"Neither can I, apparently."

I chuckle, but it's short and for his benefit. "What I was

going to say is that I can't tell you any of that, but I can tell you how it is with me and Jes."

I see her in my mind, long hair shiny beneath the fading sunlight, laughter in her eyes, the boys in the yard around her. Jesus. I think for a split second my eyes warm when I picture it.

I love Greg, but I'm not crying in a truck with another person. It's just *not* happening.

I clear my throat. "Well, she's my friend before she's anything else. And I think that's why it works so well with us."

"I thought Addie and I were friends," Greg says, his voice still quiet.

"I mean, when I say we're friends what I mean is, we are friends before we're anything else. Before I'm Lex and Des's dad, before I'm Jes's husband, before I'm the Laws that owns AgDev..." I blink at him, imparting how true this is.

I don't know if this is the secret, but it sure as hell seems like it's kept us so damn in love.

"When I say before everything else, I mean it. Above all, I'm Jes's friend. When I see something funny, she's the person I want to tell. If there's a new book she's reading, I'm the person she texts about it. And you know what? She doesn't always wanna hear about the shit I think is funny, I'm sure. Same way I don't particularly give a shit what book Reese Witherspoon recommends women read. But you know what she does? She cares. And I do the same. We give each other our focus and care, the same way we're doing right now."

I wave two fingers between us. "We're friends, so we're there for each other, right?"

He nods.

"I think sometimes it's easy to think that because your wife is your wife, your relationship has to be reserved for talking about finances, planning trips, buying appliances, deciding where Christmas will be." I shake my head. "That's a bonus you get with marriage, getting to do all that hard shit with your partner. But we made sure to not stop being friends. When you date, you're friends. Really, that's what dating is. Friends who have really good sex."

It's the first time I've spoken about sex with another man. And even though we're not really speaking about it as much as I am using it as a tool to drive home a point, I still flinch a little.

I would almost rather talk about politics. Shit.

"I don't think Addie would want to be my friend though. That's the thing." He scratches the back of his head as it bobs, like he physically can't hold still as he sorts through this scenario.

"It's not just texting and hanging out. You have to be there, you know? Don't have your phones out. Be engaged. Be present. Really give a fuck, because if you don't—"

He faces me again, wearing a smile that I know does not reflect happiness. "Then you end up like this."

I don't know what else to say, but as I imagine Jes's legs draped over my lap, hair draped over the couch with the fire flickering behind her, I keep talking.

"I don't know if you're trying to get right with Addie, or not. We haven't talked much about it. But all I know, man, is that Jes is my best friend. I don't speak against her to anyone, not even Graham. And I listen when she talks. I recognize her moods, what she needs. I'm in tune to her because I've built my life around her. She's mine, and our entire life depends on our happiness. If we're solid, that success trickles down."

He nods, smiling at me with his brown eyes looking solid green. "Well shit."

I laugh, and he does, too. The heaviness in the cab seems to dissipate.

"Do you want to win her back?" I think he's going to say no, because in the last few months, he hasn't mentioned a reconciliation. Not even once. "Not for Harley. But for you. Do you want to be married to Addie?"

His neck seems to snap as he drops forward, face parallel with his lap as he clutches his head. "Yes," he says, not emotional but more so... exhausted. "Yes, I want to be married to Addie. I can't even believe I'm here right now, Laws. I can't."

Truth is, I didn't imagine Greg and Addie being here either. They were two years into marriage when I met Greg. I was envious of their life. Throughout my twenties, all I wanted was to settle down. When thirty came and I hadn't gotten there yet, I was nervous I wouldn't. But a year after that, I met Jes. And at just twenty-two years old, she boasted an old soul and the desire to settle down. I remember thinking when I met her, we could be like Greg and Addie.

Fuck. My head whirrs at the cataclysmic change. "Let's head inside," I say, hopping out of the truck. I wait for him at the tailgate, and we walk up.

I let Greg talk while we drink beer.

He vents, he complains, he stares blankly at the peeling label on his beer bottle. And I'm there for all of it, wishing I could take his hurt away but knowing full well there's no quick fix.

Relationships aren't like that. Ruts aren't easy things to pull yourselves out of, it takes time and effort. Instead of telling him what he already knows, I encourage him to invite Addie to have a conversation. No arguing, no past, just conversation.

Around the one hour mark, we pay the tab and head out, and less than twenty minutes after that, I'm pulling into the driveway at home.

The house looks dark as I sit in my truck, wondering if I did Greg right with what I said tonight. Now I know why women give you advice then say "but that's just what I would do" when they're done—they're covering their ass in case it doesn't work out. I scratch the side of my jaw. Well, I guess I don't have to worry about that in Greg's case since they're already separated.

That's when I see the bathroom light flicker on.

I kill the engine, and even though I know nothing for certain, the hairs on my neck rise with suspicion. I grow thick and heavy between my legs as I close the distance from the truck to the door.

Quickly, I check my text message from earlier.

Can't wait to see you tonight.

I smile, and it's the last sweet thing I do.

Moving inside, I lock the door and head straight for the stairs. The boys are fast asleep, a sound machine filling the hallway with a quiet dozing coming from Des's room. I push open our bedroom door, the room dark, my heart thundering a mile a minute. The shower is on, the bathroom door barely cracked, but the small sliver projects a streak of light across our bed.

The pillow.

It's turned over.

My hands are on my belt buckle in no time flat, my work boots a crooked heap in the corner after I kick them off. I know I should be more careful but as I rip open my flannel, buttons go skittering.

But that pillow is flipped, and when it's turned over, I'm not worried about ruining my fucking workshirt. I can buy more.

I'm not careful, or intentional.

I'm not even me. And as I glance back at the pillow, shucking my jeans and boxer briefs down, I know that *he's* in control. The more I let him out to play, the more I like him.

After making a quick pitstop in our closet, I kick open the bathroom door, my cock hardening at her breathy shriek when the door bashes the wall.

Yanking the curtain back, I step inside, finding her in a ball at the bottom of the shower, knees drawn to her chest, arms hugging her legs.

"Please don't," she whimpers against the chaos of the shower stream. My dick bobs in front of me, the veins in my shaft plump, the head a deep shade of red. Jesus, I want to fuck her so bad right now. I look down to my hand, where I'm gripping her dildo. Slamming the suction end to the wall, I step under the spray, then reach down and collect her.

Fist in her hair, I yank her up, my dick thrumming at the sight of her fiery hair made darker by the water, wrapped around my knuckles. Her hands fly up, gripping her scalp, clawing at my hold.

"Ow, ow, *oww*," she whines, her voice wobbly and raspy. My dick loves wobbly and raspy.

"You're gonna be a screamer, aren't ya?" I ask, my own tone somewhat foreign. I sound... menacing, like an actual intruder. I look down at my hand, my wife's head in my clutch. I don't just *sound* menacing.

I drag her face to the shower wall, lining up her mouth with the cock. "Open your eyes," I tell her, standing at her side to make sure she obeys. When she blinks them open slowly, then sees the cock, she clamps her mouth shut tightly.

I want to smirk and whisper good girl in her ear, because the more she makes me fight her for it, the better it fucking feels.

But I don't break.

Instead, I position myself behind her, loving the way my arm looks stretched across her wet naked back. I tug hard, and she yelps, and while she does, I shove my groin to her ass, sending her forward on the cock.

She attempts to yell or scream, but with the dildo spreading her mouth and filling her throat, it's just garbled pleas. My dick likes garbled pleas.

"I saw the light go on up here when I was in my truck outside," I recount, truthfully. I don't know if she will realize this part is true, but I plan to tell her afterward. I want to let her know just what I was thinking when I pulled up.

She whines around the cock, so I press my groin against her again, my fat cock slipping in the split of her ass.

Angling my shoulders to the side, I let the hot shower rain over her backside. I jerk her head back again, then forward. She gurgles as she takes the cock to the hilt, and at that moment, with my other hand, I slap her cheek, *hard*.

"I knew there'd be a tight little cunt up here, naked just waiting to be taken. I fucking knew it. And looky what I found," I say, pulling back just enough to let my cock slip further. As the head aligns with her cunt, I drive inside, taking her in one single push.

She impales herself, gagging in spine curling waves as her pussy pulses around me, adjusting to the all encompassing presence of my dick.

Attempting to pull back a little, I shove her farther forward again once before yanking her off the dildo completely. She's so fucking hot and wet all around my cock, when I push her back down on the dildo, she tightens on me, and I swear I wanna fucking blow.

I slap her ass, and fuck her pussy in short, fast strokes, pounding into her with such force that she bobs on the dildo the same way.

I blink, staring at my knuckles in her hair, replaying her whimpering *"please, no"*. And though it seems too soon, goddamn, I can't help it. I tear her off the dildo, jerk her to face me, and shove her down onto her knees. I shove her hard, my other hand gripping the base of my cock so tight it hurts. She splays her hands, attempting to steady herself against the slick porcelain where she kneels.

Still fisting her head by the hair, I force her to steady and face me, but she won't open her eyes.

"Open your eyes."

She fights my fist, trying to get to her feet, but I push her down again, loving the way my arm looks flexed above her. Adoring her, wet and helpless at my feet.

When she opens her eyes, she looks straight into mine. Holding her gaze, I pop the dildo off the wet tile, and crouch, bringing us nearly eye to eye. I'm still bigger, hovering over her, but our faces are close. I put the cock between her legs, aligning her spread pussy with the head.

Using her to help me rise, I press a palm to her shoulder and shove her down, rising to my feet with force. She attempts a whine as she impales herself on the cock, but my cock keeps her mouth too full to be heard.

I feel it though. Her wild cries and hot gurgles. A shudder wracks my groin, and watching her pussy lips seal around the fake dick as she chokes on me, sucking me tight and deep— I crumble.

She looks so beautiful this way. Helpless and at my will. Yet, not at all, not really.

I yank my cock out of her mouth and order her to hold it, to wrap her hands around it.

I come violently.

She strokes me fast, my head pulsing, ropes streaking her tits in tantalizing, breathtaking waves. The veins in my forearm bulge and I can only imagine how her scalp feels. It must burn.

Sinking down, she stays there, not bobbing up to take the stray drops of cum that leave me as my orgasm subsides.

Then I realize.

She's coming.

I release my grip on her hair, and her relieved sigh is beautiful. It tells me she was in pain. She suffered while she found that orgasm.

And I know for that, it must feel a thousand times better.

It's how I feel when I come after I've fucked her when she's tied up.

Two nights ago I did that. The pillow was flipped. I found her in the closet, tied her entire torso up, wound her up so fucking tight, strung up by the hook in the roof, then came across her belly as I shoved my balls in her mouth.

She nearly passed out.

Said she wanted to try that again.

As I came, I had this sense of purpose. Like, that particular orgasm was a beacon of light shining through the clouds. A meaningful song chanted into my ear after having smoked the enlightening shit. That soulful second where it all makes sense.

All that time I thought wanting what I did was bad. Immoral. Dark. Depraved.

Not something a good man wants.

But the way she gave herself to me, my love for her deepened, intensified—whatever it did, I'm more in love with her than ever. And how can more love be a bad thing?

She blinks up at me, bare tits glazed in my cum, her hardened little raspberries coated in icing. My mouth waters for her. Her pink lips are swollen, partially parted, but curled into a shy smile. I reach back and shut off the water, knowing full well she still needs to shower. No more water wasting until she's ready to clean up.

And just like that, the phantom is gone. And now, I just want to care for her.

Reaching out, I hook my hands under her arms and lift her slowly, bending to watch her body slowly release its grip on the fake cock as she rises. My dick stirs between my legs, not yet flaccid, and twitching at seeing her glistening release coating the dildo. But this isn't go time, it's recovery time.

I slide her past me, turn the water back on, and let her soak up the spray as I wash her.

I wash her hair, and condition it, knowing by now, after all these years, just to do the ends.

It's strange, this shower. Jes and I have showered together so many times. I've washed her hair. I've shaved her legs. I've put her foot up on the edge of the tub and eaten her pussy. I fucked her in the ass for the first time in this very shower. Then I washed her hair.

But this particular time, the way I'm slow as I sink my fingers into the place that I know must be sore on her scalp, is a first.

She relaxes back into me, and we begin a slow, easy conversation around what we just did. Last time, it was the same way. First, "Did you have a nice time?" or something like that. This time, I ask, "How was it for you?" and her answer is quick. Immediate, even.

"*Amazing.*" Her voice is all dreamy when she says it. My chest burns at her inflection.

From there, we ping-pong thoughts, and ask more questions. And when we're both under the covers and the lights are out, she yawns and says, "Hey, babe?"

Grinning against her back in the dark, I ask, "Yeah?" After the best night of sex and fantasy, I *think* I'm on the brink of being told how loved I am.

"Next time, pull me out of the shower by my hair and drag me across the floor." She yawns, settling against me with her soft, bare ass. "Goodnight."

"*Goodnight.*"

Fourteen

JES

We've been... spicing things up.

"Why are you glaring at me?" I slide the ponytail tie off my wrist and over my hair. With my feet already locked in, I start warming up my legs.

Ruthie squints her eyes, and it makes me feel naked in front of the class. I shy away from her as I reach for the handles on my bike, ponytail firmly in place.

"Your face is scaring me."

She narrows her eyes even further, and I wonder if she can even see me now? That's her commitment to being dramatic, alright.

"*Your* face is scaring me," she deadpans. "Why are you like, glowy and chipper and shit?"

I bounce on my bike as I get adjusted, stretching out

the last pre-ride jitters. Grinning back at her, my ponytail still swinging behind me, I ask, "I don't know what you mean?"

She looks at my ponytail like it murdered her entire family.

"Why are you so *ponytaily* and—" she presses her pointer fingers to her cheeks and lifts, making a strange clown smile. A clown if it were also a murdering mime. "That," she says, grabbing her handles after she's through mimicking me. *Allegedly* mimicking me.

"I'm not," I defend, but my lips curl anyway.

From behind her, Penny nods. "You do seem very... *Christian YA novel after the big side hug.*"

I'm certain it's not a compliment, but I'm on the fence as to whether it's a burn.

They don't have to twist my arm too hard. I look around conspiratorially before leaning away from my bike to catch the space between them. "You wanna see?"

I reach into my side pocket, and retrieve my phone. I always keep it on me, even when cycling, in case anyone from the boys' school calls. I tap the photo from last night.

Laws spent an hour tying me after he kicked open the back door and fucked me against the kitchen floor, his forearm at my throat.

I begged. I spit in his face, even.

And he fucked me so deep that my ass burned from sheer proximity. My belly ached with fullness. And my core burned as he fucked his release into me with passionate anger.

After we came, he tied me up, grunting and growling obscenities the entire time.

Laws' filthy mouth makes me so desperate and wet, I'd likely let him do anything to me.

But I fight him every step of the way, and that makes me wetter yet.

Last night, with my wrists and ankles tied, held together with a carabiner pinched through the looped rope, I swung from the ceiling as he berated me.

Spoke few but electrifying words. Spat on me. Came in my face, smeared it into my flesh with the rough tips of his blunt fingers.

He unhooked me, and I begged him—literally begged—to take a photo of my bound body. From behind, no face. Nothing showing it was either of us. Just my body bound and at his mercy, completely used.

He did.

And I'm fucking obsessed with it.

I blink down at the image that I still can't believe is myself, turn the phone, and show them.

Ruthie's eyes don't blink for a disturbing amount of time. Penny's head bounces up to me then down to the phone several times, and then, I put the phone back into my pocket.

"We've been... spicing things up."

"That's you?" Penny questions, staring blankly at the space where I'd held my phone, as if the image of me holding the phone out, the picture of me on the screen—she's committed it to memory. Forever.

My legs start moving, and even though we're best friends, a part of me wonders if their current shock is the only thing keeping a barrier from their disgust.

What if they find being bound and used as degrading?

My mind spins faster than anyone in the class is on their

pedals as I consider what to say. I've already shown them the photo. Lying about it now isn't an option.

But before I can qualify what they'd seen, Ruthie starts a slow clap. She nods toward a woman on a bike adjacent to us, one that we always say hello to but don't actually speak with often.

"Suz," she says to the woman. "Clap with me, just... trust me. This one." She nods at me on my bike turning cherry red. "She deserves it."

Penny joins in and Cas does, too, neither of them really having a clue as to what they're applauding. I smile shyly, and press my hand down in the air, hoping they catch the universal sign to stop fucking embarrassing me.

"Finally. Using that man of yours for something hot," Ruthie says once Suz and Cas have given their focus back to the workout.

"Hey," I giggle, full of relief knowing that she accepts it. Though in truth, I love what we're doing. I love what I'm discovering about the man I've shared a bed with for years. If Ruthie and Penny didn't understand, or if they judged—would it matter?

It's strange. I think before I knew this about Laws, I would've judged people engaging in role play like we do. Doing the things we've been doing. Ropes? To the point where my skin is left looking like raspberries wilting under a harsh sun? To the point that my flesh physically feels marred and torn for days after? I'd have judged that shit harder than Judy.

But now, being in it, I look at judgment so differently. Had Ruthie come at me with a, *what the fuck*, instead of her actual response, it would have hurt. And I would have internalized it for a hot second. Then I would have led myself to the truth: people that judge the sex you have in the privacy of your own home, speaks more to their own happiness and contentedness (or, ahem, lack thereof) than actual disapproval of your behavior.

I'm glad that they aren't judging though.

I glance at Penny, realizing that only Ruthie has spoken. Penny's focused forward now, cycling like she's trying to win the Tour de France, despite the fact Cas is calling for a slowdown, saving energy for a big hill.

"Did I weird you out?" I ask her as my breathing grows a bit more erratic from the uptick in cycling speed. She looks over at me and shakes her head, wearing a sad smile that makes me feel bad for her, not me.

"What's wrong?" I ask, realizing that my moment is now her moment. But I'm okay with that.

"It's just... Laws *wants* to do all that? I mean, he actually wants to use ropes and stuff?"

Then I realize what's wrong.

Penny isn't satisfied. *At all.* Without prompting, I envision Penny in the arms of Garth, her partner. They've been the couple so hot on PDA that they've actually made me feel weird before when we've done group dates. He's always whispering things into her ear and touching her, and she's never without a blush on her cheeks and a grin pasted on her lips. Yet I see it. I see that they don't have that behind closed doors.

"Yeah," I say, speaking honestly while respecting and protecting the truth. Because the fact that Laws has battled the desire to live in a rape fantasy complete with ropes and binding? That he's into impact play while in the midst of his fantasy? That's for us, and only us, like the first words shared quietly after your child is born. They're private. Some moments are only ours, some information meant only for our souls, and this is one of those things. "We actually took that quiz we talked about a few weeks back."

"And that got the ball rolling?" she asks hopefully, her legs slow as her interest increases. Cas doesn't pick on Penny the way she normally calls out cyclists for losing focus.

I nod. "Yeah. I mean, we talked before, we took the quiz, and we talked a lot about the results. Then we each took a week to kind of... I don't know, internalize the things we'd learned not just about ourselves but each other, too. Then we came back and just... started doing what we enjoy."

She looks like a million words have collected behind her lips, her eyes almost frantically searching mine. "And that's... him tying you up?"

Rigging, I think to myself but don't dare say it aloud. Cas leads the class toward an on-screen hill, and all the women rise to their feet in unison as they adapt to the ride. "Yeah, among other things. We kinda have a handful of interests that align, so we have fun with it."

The class sinks to their seats, lurching forward off their bikes, taking the hill together under Cas's commands. I can't speak anymore—I'm too winded, but for the rest of the ride, I keep thinking about Penny and Garth.

Once we're off, high-fiving for surviving another ride from hell, Penny pinches my elbow and pulls me aside. Ruthie joins us, clearly not forgetting what she saw on my phone. She grabs my hands, inspecting the insides of my wrists like she'll find some evidence of filthy, naughty sex. The truth is, there isn't much to be seen.

Because while I've been tied up, spit on, covered in cum, whipped, spanked, slapped, pulled apart, filled and forced to fuck, I've also been tenderly cared for afterward, rubbed with lotions, filled with electrolytes, wrapped in soft blankets, and physically tended to the next few days. When I see Laws with the tube of lotion he uses to ease the redness and achiness in my skin after he's tied me up, I swear I get turned on all over again.

"So tell me how you got Laws to take the quiz," Penny says, still catching her breath, but completely focused on me. Ruthie is still checking me out like she's going to stumble across something.

"I told him about it and then just said, let's take it together. So I sat in his lap and we took it. Then we talked through it all."

Penny nods, eyes wide, as if I'm telling her the world's biggest secret. She stays transfixed as I explain how talking through our results and taking time to process them both helped us have yet another conversation, where we figured out what we wanted together. That the key really isn't any quiz, but moreso, honest conversation.

"You have to be honest with yourself about what you want and equally, what you don't want. And then, be honest with him," I say, no longer pretending I'm explaining me and Laws, I'm just flat out giving advice now.

It hits me then that communication about sex is likely difficult for some couples. Had I not walked in on Laws in the office that night, and I'd approached him about the quiz randomly, I'd love to say we'd still be right here. But it's likely we wouldn't.

The thought makes me shiver. I hate thinking of Laws

going his whole life without his needs being fulfilled. And I really loathe the idea of not knowing this separate, sexy, hugely complex side to my husband, either, or myself. That's something I'm only now realizing. There was a whole side of myself I was never aware of, and Laws' phantom led me to it.

"I know it can be hard. But if you guys can work past the uncomfy aspect of... facing things... you can have everything you want." I mean that. I *believe* that.

"Maybe for you and Laws," she sighs, all hope in her eyes replaced with disappointment.

Ruthie snorts. "You didn't think it was magic, did you, Pen? You gotta talk to him about what you want. You thought she got that big, fine man of hers to tie her up with a pill or something?"

"No," Penny draws out defensively, shoving her water bottle in her gym bag.

"You did. You clearly did because you're over there pouting," Ruthie says, still wearing that playful grin. It's how she's allowed to so blatantly call people out—she does it with a smile, and in truth? She doesn't mean harm by it.

"It's just talking. And I know that can be... hard," I admit, remembering locking Laws out of the bathroom that night. Scared to have a name put to the thing he was doing. Scared to hear what he wanted. "It's scary at first because it means change. It means your partner has secrets, to an extent, right?"

She nods, and I wonder what it is she wants from Garth that he's not giving. Because she's wearing the same baited, starved, lonesome expression I found in Laws' eyes when I opened the bathroom door that night.

"But if you indulge in those hidden wants, your bond

really intensifies. Because Laws was my best friend and a wonderful spouse before, but now, we're like..." I shake my head, and know the flush in my cheeks isn't from the exercise. "I'm just annoyingly smitten."

Ruthie, ever the sarcastic one in the group, grins and hits me with an unexpectedly kind and completely sarcasm-free comment. "Jessalyn Briggs, you keep me on my toes, you know that?"

Unsure of her meaning, I draw my palm to my chest. "I do?"

She nods, peeling damp strands of hair off her neck, finger combing them into her ponytail. "I always pegged you as the missionary type. And Laws is such a traditional good guy, troop leader, looks at you with heart eyes, all that stuff. I just assumed you two were having some *'let's make love'* kind of sex on repeat."

I can't help but snort at the way she's sized us up because... she's not wrong.

Laughing I say, "Well, we do make love. But even before we took the quiz, we had fun. It wasn't all just *making love*."

Penny nods, but glances at her watch then out the window, and I know she's itching to leave this conversation. She slings her bag over her shoulder, and smiles. "Well, this has been... *enlightening*. I will talk to Garth but... I don't know, I'm not setting my expectations too high."

I want to correct her, or at least, reroute her expectations. But she's hugging Ruthie and saying goodbye to Cas before I can. As Ruthie and I wipe our bikes down, I think about how long we've been friends with Penny and Garth, and how I've always found them to be, outside looking in, so happy.

You just never know what happens behind closed doors. I know this now more than ever.

"What do you think she wants to do that she's afraid Garth won't be into?" I ask Ruthie.

She smirks as we push through the double doors into the sunlight. "Easy. She wants to fuck him in the ass."

I slide my shades on and stride toward my SUV, Ruthie at my hip. "Well, she won't get his ass if she doesn't use her mouth first."

Ruthie tips her shades down, peering at me over the top of them. "Jes, that's quite possibly the best thing you've ever said."

I slide my aviators up my nose and jump up into the driver's seat. "What can I say? Tie me up a few times and I'm a slutty little Yoda."

She laughs. "Slutty Yoda. Is that what Laws calls you when he's got you tied up?"

We're both in our vehicles now, windows down so we can finish this conversation. "When I'm tied up, the man can barely speak."

Ruthie fans herself, we roll our windows up, and I drive away with a heady pulsing between my legs. When I get home, I ease the ache while looking at the pictures Laws took of me.

He didn't want to take it, but I'm so glad he did.

LAWS

I don't know what I did to deserve this life, but fuck me, I'm never letting go.

"This seat taken?" I look up from my tranquil haze to see Greg staring down at me, a half grin perched on his lips.

I take the pile of coats off the plastic folding chair and slide them between my legs. "Nope, just the boys' coats." I look up at the stage which is still dark and empty, and back to Greg. "Harley in the show? He didn't mention it at Scouts this week."

I face Greg, and watch him scratch the side of his hairy jawline. He's got a beard these days and I don't know if it's a style change as much as it is *his* life change, but I don't ask. His fingers, worn from a day of rigging trees, are cracking around the tips, knuckles dry. Bags line his eyes and his shirt looks like it came off of a bedroom floor.

He looks like shit.

I didn't take him out for a beer after Scouts last week but I did take Harley with me. Apparently, he and Addie were going to have a talk.

I've seen him here and there since, mostly in the office over a few minutes of work. But here, tonight, is the first time I've really had a chance to look at him since he had that night with Addie.

I'm no Dr. Phil, but something tells me it wasn't a great talk.

He looks... *worse*.

"He didn't wanna do it," Greg says with a heavy sigh. So full of the weight of his pain, that I feel his sign deep in my bones. "He doesn't want to do anything right now but... hurt."

I swallow hard but force myself to engage. He's uncomfortable, I can feel it, but I also know that I'm likely the only one he has to talk to. "Addie wanting to go through with the divorce?"

He smooths his hand down his chin, plucking at the end of his beard a moment before he nods. "Yup." He doesn't look at me, and from his profile, I see his eyes shining with the pain of reality.

I face forward, taking the heat off of him, but grip him at the back of the neck. "You'll get through it," I say quietly, squeezing him once before I switch to a reassuring pat. With my hands back in my lap, still facing the darkened stage, I add, "You will get through it."

His voice is uncharacteristically rocky when he asks, "Is

this gonna ruin Harley? Will he ever recover from this? Because right now, it's feeling a lot like he won't. And instead of being the dad he looks up to, I'll forever be the man that couldn't save his family."

Now I'm leaning forward, pressing my knees to my elbows, assaulting him with my gaze until he barely peers over at me.

"Kids don't think like that, and you shouldn't either. It's just not true, Greg. Sometimes, shit doesn't work out the way you think. And it doesn't make you a failure," I say, staying focused on him despite the fact that the stage lights have come on, and the murmurs of the audience have started to wane.

"And you're experienced with failure?" he asks, though I see it's more of a fuck-you rhetorical than an actual question.

"I know what it's like to believe that your happiness is tempered, and that you'll always be where you're at. Now I'm not saying I've been in your shoes or been unhappy, because I haven't. I don't know what you're feeling, Greg. But I do know what it's like to think you can't have more. To think you gotta just smile, even though there are still things you want and need."

He blinks, like he's trying to sort out what in my life could possibly be lacking. I shake my head. "Just trust me, okay? You're gonna be alright. If you don't work it out with Addie—"

"She wants a divorce," he sighs over the top of me.

"Nothing's final until it's final. But if she does go through with it, you'll be okay. And so will Harley. Just keep communication open, and if you just can't bring yourself to talk to him about it, go with him to his therapist. But he will be okay. And so will you."

I believe what I'm saying, but I can't say it with certainty. From this point on, it's up to Greg. And I hate what he's going through, but as I sit there and watch my sons sing, their mother off to the side of the stage, pinching her cheeks to remind them to smile, I can't help but think that I could've been Greg.

My secret isn't a secret anymore, and that other part of me I kept hidden so long is now something we enjoy together. But had she not forced the topic even though I'd shut her down a few times, we wouldn't be here.

Would I have ended up like Greg without this? I want to say no. My bones rattle with a resounding *of course not*. But the truth is, I just don't know.

I lean toward him, imparting one final bit of advice before we watch the concert. "Just keep trying to talk to her. Never stop trying to talk."

"I'm so glad we practiced that part again right before he went on stage," Jes says, smoothing lotion around her elbows, standing next to the bed. With her hair draped back, she smooths her palm beneath the strap of her nightgown as she applies cream to her shoulder.

I'm hard just watching her get ready for bed.

"Don't you think he did so good?" she asks, beaming at me.

"Oh yeah," I say, knowing she wants to bask in how good the boys did at their school choir concert. She sets the lotion bottle down on the nightstand, letting her arms fall heavily to her sides.

"Laws, are you even listening?" she asks, head tipping forward in a disciplinary way, like I'm being scolded by the teacher.

I swallow, despite the fact that my mouth has gone dry. "Yes and no. The boys did good. That's where my brain stops." Lying on my side, arm bent to keep my head propped in my palm, I use my other hand to pat the bed. "Get in here. Watching you lotion up has been one-sided foreplay."

She slides under the covers, immediately tangling her legs with mine, but whimpers softly up at me, hands splayed across my bare chest. "As much as I'd love to meet you there," she says, reaching down to cup my erection. "It's... *that* time of the month for me."

With my palm on her face, I bring her lips to mine and kiss her slowly, torturing myself as I discover the warmth of her mouth. Her gentle moans have me pulling back, because we can't take this any further tonight. She grips my cock, and I groan at the way her fingers don't meet.

"Then," I say, trying not to focus on the way she lazily drags her fist up and down my sheathed cock. "Tell me about your day."

She looks into my eyes, holding my gaze, still stroking over my boxers as she recounts her day to me. "It was kind of a weird day, in some ways. I mean, normal in that I made the boys breakfast, packed their lunches, and took them to school. Went to spin, got groceries, made the choir concert flyers then cut them all. We had the concert and now we're here."

I stroke my thumb along the length of her bottom lip, and

I know the next time her fist slides up my cock and over my head, she'll find my boxers damp. "What about that was weird? Sounds normal to me."

She leans in and takes a chaste kiss from my lips, cricketing her feet with mine. "Well, at spin, I told the girls that we took the sex quiz."

I feed my fingers through her hair, loving how silky it feels against my rough palms. Sliding my hand all the way through, I tug an end before kissing her lightly. She smirks when she discovers the mess I'm making, stroking over my head. "And?"

She stills, almost like she was expecting a different reaction. "You don't mind that I shared we took it, do you?"

I shrug, my eyes falling to her plump lips, and I envision them sealed around my cock. I clear my throat. "I trust you." Three words thrown together so easily, but ones that hold such power. I do trust her. If she wants to talk about sex with her friends, I want her to have that.

Laws a few months back maybe would've gotten angry. Then again, despite the fact we were never lacking in the bedroom, maybe a few months back she had nothing to tell them about. Maybe she needed more, too?

"Were you happy?" I blurt out, surprising us both honestly. "Before we started with the consensual nonconsent fantasies, the rigging and impact stuff, were you happy?"

Her hands still splayed on my chest, she digs her nails in, narrowing her eyes up at me. I have the strongest urge to roll her onto her back, so I do. Over her, I hold my body above, on my elbows. She moans at the weight of my cock resting at her center.

"Very happy," she says, sounding so sure and honest. "But I'm even happier now."

"Yeah?" I ask, my heart suddenly flying.

She nods, then brings her hands to my hips, sliding her fingers beneath my waistband. I hiss in reaction, not prepared for her smooth hands to touch my bare cock. She fills one palm with my balls and the other with my shaft, stroking me root to my swollen head.

Neither of us acknowledge what she's doing. Instead, I reroute back to what she said earlier. "Why was the day weird?"

"Well," she says, bringing her hand to her mouth. Slowly, the wide pad of her tongue brushes over the tip of her thumb, licking my arousal away. I groan, and make no show of hiding it. "Penny as much as said she wants to try things with Garth but she's concerned he won't want to explore."

I find myself nudging her legs apart with mine. Why am I getting comfortable between these beautiful legs when I know I can't have her? Still, I keep on, this time, dropping my mouth to the spot on her neck between her shoulder and throat. So soft, so sweet. I lick as I kiss, and her whimpers do nothing for the leaky pipe between my thighs.

"I just," she starts, sounding a bit out of breath as I nuzzle her neck, then the curve of her jaw, then lips again. "I just thought they were so happy. They're all about PDA. But today, I don't know, I got the idea that maybe they have some problems."

Staring down at her, I admit to her that my day was a little weird. Though the weirdest part of my day is talking about Greg while my dick is hard.

"Greg said Addie wants to move forward with the divorce."

She licks her lips and takes her hand from my balls, bringing it to my chest. her thumb strokes my nipple, and that's another thing I didn't know I liked until my wife. She started pinching and rubbing my nipples before I'd orgasm and now, it gets me there.

"Oh no. I'm sorry to hear that," she says softly, as if she isn't jerking me off and flicking my nipple, driving me to the point where I want to blow all over her little satin nighty.

"I told him not to give up. Well, I didn't say it like that. What I said was, keep talking to her. Never stop communicating." My balls ache, missing her soft tugging, as she pulls down my boxers. Pressed to my belly by the elastic, I look down to see the wide head of my cock peering back at me, opaque liquid smeared around my slit.

"Good advice," she says, using the back of her knuckles to stroke my cock.

"What did you tell Penny?" I ask, wondering if she was in the position to give relationship advice today, too.

"I don't even remember. I know, that makes me sound like a bad friend. I was just so taken aback that I'm the kinky one in the group—"

"How do they know how kinky you are, Jessalyn?" I ask, my tone dark, my hips grinding down on hers, cockhead smearing precum all along her little dress. She moans and bites her lip as she looks down at my angry head sliding against her.

"I showed them the photo you took of me tied up."

I freeze, and around me her legs open wider, knees drawing closer to the mattress as she opens her body for me.

"Don't be angry, okay? It made me feel good to share, and they won't tell."

"Okay," I say, placing my trust in her. I've never gone wrong there before. I didn't want to take the photo, especially because it was one of the rules we agreed on at the start. But I'm trying to be amenable to things, and let her enjoy what we're doing in her ways. If showing them a photo of her tied up means anything, it means she likes what we do so much she can't keep it secret. I don't know how I got so lucky.

"I'm just so in love with you, Lawson," she murmurs, and suddenly, the grinding and casual conversation falls away, replaced by a more serious, powerful undertone. I feel her energy shift, her body softening beneath me, legs giving way completely. "Make love to me," she whispers, staring up at me with heady eyes and hard nipples under that satin. I lean down and suck one into my mouth, tasting our fabric softener.

She moans, fingers falling to my hair, tugging gently. I lift up and look at her. "You never want to have sex while you're on your period," I say, because it's true. In all our years together, the only time Jes ever is not in the mood is when she's bleeding.

Nodding, she says, "I know. But feel me, Laws," she raps, taking one of my hands. Leaning my bodyweight onto one arm, I allow her to drag my hand down to her hip, finding her lower half lightly trembled. "I'm shaking from how much I want you inside me."

I don't know what having sex with her while she's on her period is like. We've never done it. But I'm hard—dripping—and she wants me. She wants me as much as I want her and even though it's new territory, now feels like the right time to try.

"Get a towel," she whispers, cheeks pink with anticipation and arousal. Maybe even nerves, too, but at that idea, I press a kiss to her forehead.

"You're sure?" I keep my eyes locked to hers, searching for anything hiding in them. But nothing but lust shimmers back at me.

"Fuck yes."

We both get out of bed, me heading to grab a towel and her slipping out of her nightgown. She uses the restroom as I spread the towel across the mattress, folding it to create more barrier. When she returns, she climbs into bed and I climb in over her. We leave the comforter and sheets balled at the foot of the bed.

I don't know what part of me is coming out right now. I've always thought it was just me and the phantom. But as my cock falls naturally to her opening as I shift above her, I look down, desperate to watch this. Maybe that's the voyeur in me, or maybe it's the part of me that Jes has created. The part of me that now thrives from exploration. I don't know, but I find her eyes again as I ask, "You're sure?"

"I don't know if I'll like it. I don't know if you will either. But... I want you. I want to feel you inside of me. I want your lips against mine as you empty yourself in me. I'm dying for that intimate connection."

Reaching between us, I position my cock at her center, and ease in slowly. She winces, but the way her body accepts me with wet warmth has me clenching my teeth.

She whimpers when I'm fully in, my groin brushing her swollen clit as I begin deep, slow strokes inside of her. "Yes," she pants, her hands coming down against my biceps in urgent slaps. Rolling my hips, I fall into the motion of making love to Jes. It happens that way, I sink inside of the safest, sweetest place, and my body takes over, my mind wandering free.

I think of all the dirty ways she loves me, and all the sweet ways she pleases me, too. I stare down into her shining eyes as she whimpers and moans, calling my name in the sultriest tone I've ever heard.

I'm moving slowly inside of her, reaching between us to rub her clit, when I glance down. Sliding back, shaft partially buried, I notice the faint traces of crimson smeared up my cock. Still watching, I sink back in as she begs for me to take her to the edge, cries against my ear to make her come. I can't come yet, though, because as I slide in and out, I become obsessed with the way her body has marked mine.

The way that she's giving herself to me at such a private time—in twelve years of marriage, I've never so much as discussed her period with her. She's told me she's on it, and she's told me when she's missed it, but outside of that, Jes is private about it. And I get it. Some things our bodies do, like the cycle for life and make waste, are biological traits not meant to be shared and spread open for everyone to see.

But she's letting me take her while she bleeds. She's allowing me to see her at a time she's expressed that she doesn't feel beautiful. And I know it's not the same as me exposing my phantom to her—but it's still unveiling a confidence that wasn't mine to hold before.

I stroke into her faster and her nails sink into my back. "You feel so good, baby," I tell her, wanting her to know that for me, making love to her now feels better than ever based solely on the emotional connection. "Goddamn, Jes, you're so beautiful like this."

Straining up from the pillow, she looks down just as I slide out of her, leaving just the throbbing head of my cock inside. Blood streaks my shaft, and she moans at the sight. Her head thunks against the pillow, heady, heavy-lidded eyes finding mine.

"It's so sensitive, everything is so... I feel so good," she moans, drawing her knees up, giving me more room. Changing my angle, I lean off her torso a bit, taking in the sight of her raspberry-tipped breasts bouncing as I slide in and out of her, over and over.

She whimpers, she slaps at my biceps, claws my chest and lurches forward as she tightens around me, all of her wet warmth strangling my cock as she orgasms.

"Laws," she pants, as if I don't know. As if I can't feel that heavenly vise around my cock, bringing me to the breaking point.

"Fuck, Jes, I'm gonna come, too," I pant, almost embarassed that it's been less than five minutes. But the feel of her coming hard around me is too much, and I pump in a few more times before my hips rock to a stop.

Pulsing, thrumming, throbbing, I pump my release into my wife, watching her eyes grow dizzy as I fill her. She presses a palm to her lower belly as I empty myself, moaning filthy words as I do.

"Every drop," she pants, "give me every drop, Laws."

I do. I twitch and pulse in her, coming hard for what feels like an eternity. When I'm spent, the liquids between our bodies have me slipping out onto the towel. Quickly, I bring the loose end of the folded towel to her pink, swollen pussy, and press it there.

"When you're... on your period," I start, trying not to sound like this is the first time in forty-four years of life that I've discussed this, But it is. "Do you like to shower or take a bath?"

I scoop her off the bed, keeping the towel pressed between her and my arm. "Shower," she says, letting her head fall against my chest.

It's when I sit her down on the toilet and drop the towel in the hamper that I realize, all sex deserves aftercare. Not just the wild sex we've been having lately. I start her shower, and stand naked against the wall as she uses the toilet.

"I think I should've been taking care of you after sex a lot better," I admit aloud. I never admitted that kind of stuff aloud before. But all this openness is seeming to breed more openness, and I'll admit, women might be right. Talking about shit does make sense.

"You've always been a really good lover," she says, wiping then flushing. Crimson spins in the porcelain before it gurgles down the tubes, and I've never been more in awe of my wife than now. Even after she gave birth to our boys and fed them with her body, right now, something about our connection is just so intense.

"Can I get in there?" I ask, not even because I'm slick and sticky from sex, but because I want to be near her.

She giggles, and yanks the curtain open the remainder. "Better with you in here. Then the floor won't be soaking."

I slip in behind her and take the washcloth from her hands, taking over the job she had yet to start. Washing her, I keep my voice low when I ask, "Did you ever want to try that before now or was tonight the first time?"

She turns as I smooth the warm terry cloth down her spine. Bubbles cascade down her soft skin, and even though she's clean, I continue touching, rubbing, wiping... worshiping.

"Actually, I wanted to make love to you plenty of times when I was on my period. I just..." she trails off, pumping shampoo into my hands which rest atop her shoulder. With the spray raining down on her, I sink my fingers into her hair and start massaging. She doesn't need her hair washed—she just showered before we had sex. But neither of us want to leave, and if staying in this steamy stall helps say the hard to say things, the way the bathroom door afforded us before, then we'll stay in here and get squeaky fucking clean.

"Tell me, Jes," I whisper softly, hoping my words don't get lost in all the noises of the shower. She twists beneath my hands, and I drop them to my sides, sudsy as hell, and listen as she stares up at me.

"Honestly, I was embarrassed. I obviously know I have nothing to be embarrassed about—it's my period. It's biology, I can't help that. I think if I'm being honest, what I was embarrassed about was that I couldn't even make it five days without needing sex. That you'd think to yourself, Jesus, what a slut she is that she needs to be fucked so bad that she's willing to do it while she's bleeding." She finds a cluster of freckles on my chest and analyzes them, as if willing herself to say this next part. But what she's already said has me nearly spinning.

"I thought you'd think it was gross, but do it for me

anyway, and then start to associate having sex with me with an obligation. So I never asked."

Her words are soft and shy, but they impact me as hard as a slap across the face. I take her face in my hands. "I would never think that. I would never have said no, I would never have thought having sex with you is gross and more than that? I can't believe you had those feelings all these years." I try as hard as I can to not sound shocked, but I am. And I'm disappointed, too. Not in her, but in myself, for creating some world for her where she felt she couldn't tell me what she really wanted.

"Wild, right?" she asks, then slowly she arches her brow, and *there it is*. The parallel has been drawn and holy shit.

"Baby," I start, gripping her more tightly, pulling her even closer. She giggles, diffusing the urgency rampant inside me out of nowhere.

"I know, I know, it was in my head. The fear, the worry, all in my head." She rocks to her toes and kisses me. "But I guess you know all about building something up for years only to find out you're actually wrong."

"I've never been so glad to be wrong," I tell her. She turns to face the water, and I continue washing her hair.

"Me too," she murmurs.

When we get out a few minutes later, Jes cuddles in my arms, against my chest, and we fall asleep happier than ever.

I don't know what I did to deserve this life, but fuck me, I'm never letting go.

Ever.

Sixteen

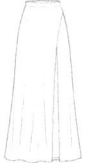

JES

If it were possible to fuck a smell, I would. Instead, I'll just fuck the source.

It's not that I don't love my sister-in-law because I do. I totally do. Except, I didn't necessarily want her to tag along with me today on my *errands*.

I ran into Mae while grabbing my morning coffee after dropping the boys at school. I'd *planned* to head to the mall as soon as it opened. I have a list of things to buy for tonight.

Our *surprise* night away.

Well, not a surprise for me but for Laws. I have his parents watching the boys until Saturday morning, a hotel room booked in the town over, and lots of wicked plans.

A few days ago, we had an extra heavy rigging and impact session. Laws spent over an hour tying me up. While seeing his handiwork in the mirror after he's done does steal my breath, there's something so erotic about *watching him work.*

Sometimes I think watching Laws rigging me is as hot as being his wet fuck hole, rope bunny.

I'm obsessed with watching him rig, dark eyes full of focus, sweat peppering his forehead. His thick fingers brushing my skin, each scrape of his work-worn flesh against my softness enticing a valley of goosebumps over my body.

It's erotic but beautiful, it's arousing but somewhat emotional, too. All these years I could've watched him this way, had this side of him... but he was afraid to tell me.

I planned this weekend as a filthy getaway, yes, but also as a step forward in our discovery journey. We both enjoy the rigging and the impact, but the quiz both identified us as explorers. When we researched how that term was defined, we learned we may want to experiment with our consensual nonconsent roleplay fantasy in public a little. Really make it a scene—have him follow me, have a hotel room, two key cards, shadows and suspense. Ropes and gags.

Privacy.

And all I wanted to do was buy copious amounts of tiny lingerie to pack, but now that Mae has sidled up to me while grabbing my pre-shopping coffee, I'm nervous I won't be able to shake her.

"Grande almond milk sugar cookie latte for Jes," the barista calls out. Stepping to the counter, I thank the girl and take my drink, meeting Mae at the table where she's sitting. Staring at her phone screen, she looks up as I approach.

"What're you up to today?" she asks brightly.

Though I want more than anything to shop for naughty

things alone, I realize that if I lie to her, she'll know. Mae has always been one of those sleuths that pinches her gaze on you and simply knows. Her bullshit meter is unbelievable. And anyway, there's nothing wrong with buying filthy dirty things for my husband to enjoy.

Knowing it would probably turn him a thousand shades of crimson to know his sister-in-law knows about our sex life, though, makes me smirk. Laws is a god in the sheets, and a shy hero in the streets. And I don't hate it.

I find a happy middle ground, respecting his comfort but being real with my sister-in-law.

"We're going away this weekend. The Briggs are keeping the boys and I was just about to go to the mall and buy obscene amounts of lingerie that cost more than is logical considering it will cover very little." I take a sip of my latte. She blinks.

Rising, she puts her purse over her shoulder and says, "I'm in."

"Give me thirty minutes to finish getting myself ready, okay? Then I'll come check your bags," I say to my sons who stand in the hallway outside my bedroom, excited eyes pinned to me.

Lex nods. "Okay, Mom." He goes into his room.

I wag a finger at Des. "Thirty minutes." He nods, too, and I know that I have more like twenty minutes rather than thirty. But that's okay. The truth is, my bag is already packed. My outfit is picked. The reason I need time? I'm itching to get started on my second surprise for Laws. A secret tie beneath my clothes to edge him with, all night.

On our night away, I thought a long maxi skirt with a thigh-high slit and a simple blouse would do the trick. It's one of those outfits that Laws has told me in the past is torturous. He can catch glimpses of skin, but is largely *left to drool* as he so adorably puts it.

The skirt with the high slit gave me the idea for the hidden tie.

Grabbing two loops of thirty foot jute and one fifteen foot from the shoebox in my closet, I pull up a YouTube video from a creator whose focus is simplifying basic ties for beginners. I'd already binged a few of her videos, and even kept her on while shaving my legs the other day.

One I remember well is her booty bondage.

This is primarily a decorative tie, so it will be a perfect surprise under my skirt for Laws tonight. I also remember her saying this tie was best for standing, as sitting on the booty bindings could be uncomfortable. Another sign that this is the perfect surprise for my man.

Passing the rope around the back of one thigh, I begin the deceptively time consuming process of feeding and running the rope around my thighs, mimicking the pattern on the screen.

Ten minutes later, the nape of my neck is damp from the amount of effort, but as I take in my reflection, my heart races. He's going to love this.

I continue the wrap on my other leg, completing this one a bit quicker. When it's all done, I pull my skirt up over it, adjusting the satin fabric to best cover the jute. The truth is, with the slit and the flowy style, the rope really isn't visible at all.

Hiking the slit up to expose the jute, I peer at my reflection again.

"Damn," I whisper, chills sliding down my spine at the erotic image. The pattern forms a ladder of jute Laws will have no issue climbing later, probably with his tongue. He's going to lose his mind when he glimpses this. Now I need to get our boys ready.

* * *

"But you told them it was okay, right?" Des asks, shoving way too many stuffed animals into his overnight bag.

I nod. "Yes, Grandpa knows you're allowed to use your Kindle at bedtime. Don't worry," I say, smoothing my fingers through his auburn hair. He nods and my heart swells as he stuffs his eReader into his bag.

He's six, so he can read. But not well enough to need his Kindle unless someone is reading with him. It's cute because he knows Lex will read at bedtime, and he wants to be just like his big brother. And who is his big brother mimicking? I glance over to the hearth, where a photo of Laws rests framed. It's my favorite photo of him, and one of the only ones I have of just him. He's got a paperback spread open with one hand, eyes focused, fire roaring behind him. Once Lex was old enough to read, he wanted to be just like Daddy. Now, they're both readers, and I couldn't be happier that they're into bedtime reading. I know it likely won't last forever—once video games and cell phones are a thing, once being like Dad isn't as cool as it is at age ten—but for right now, I relish it.

"Des, did you pack your trunks?" Lex calls to his brother from his room next door.

Russell and Ann, Laws' parents, recently invested in a heated pool and jacuzzi. Though they're in their early seventies, I know they did it for the boys. To entice their grandsons to come stay, and to entice future grandkids, too.

And it worked.

Ever since they got the pool and jacuzzi over the summer, the boys are obsessed with going over there. When I told them after school today that they'd be spending the weekend with Grandpa and Grandma, they nearly screamed. Honestly.

Laws is the only one who still doesn't know.

I glance at my watch, seeing he'll be home in less than five minutes. I'd planned to take the boys right as he was getting home, so that he could say goodbye. I'd like to stick to the plan.

I grab Des's overly full bag and sling it over my shoulder. "Lex, you good?" I ask, letting him pack on his own because, "I'm not a baby" is all I hear anytime I try to help him do anything.

He appears in the hall, his bag thrown over his shoulder. "Yup." He peers around me, looking hopeful. "Is Dad home?"

"He should be pulling up soon," I reply, smiling. When I was his age, my dad was home so infrequently, I never gave a crud where he was. But Laws is so present and engaging with his boys, it's beautiful.

And I can't wait to let him fuck me senseless all weekend to show him how thankful I am for him.

We stomp down the stairs and head into the garage. I tap the button and as the door rises, Laws truck appears in the gravel drive, headlights shining despite the fact the sun is still high above us. Through the windshield he squints as he watches me load two bags into the back of my SUV.

"Daddy's home," I call to the boys who are filing out of the house as slow as molasses. Instantly, they're bolting through the garage to his truck, Des bouncing like a puppy at the driver's side.

"Daddy! We're staying with Grandpa and Grandma this weekend!"

Lex puts his hand on Des's shoulder, slowing but not stopping the bouncing. "We're going now. You wanna ride with us?"

I close the hatch with the button on the edge, and stride over to the truck, a flutter moving through my body at just the sight of my husband after a long day at work.

I can only see his lap, but his blue jeans are covered in dirt and clay, a day's worth of stubble coating his sharp jawline, AgDev hat tipped back. His flannel sleeves are rolled up and what is it about a hardworking man with his sleeves rolled up? Between my legs, a small part of me pulses with desire. His scent wafts toward me from the cab, and I discreetly suck up the smell of deodorant, soil, aftershave and musk.

If it were possible to fuck a smell, I would.

Instead, I'll just fuck the source.

"Hey, baby," he says, his eyes making a quick and inconspicuous pass over my body. He can't eye-fuck me the way he wants in front of the boys, and we both know it. I smirk at him.

"Surprise," I say softly, stroking my hand through Des's hair as he bounces endlessly. The excitement of a child on the cusp of a sleepover is incomparable. Lex grabs Des around the arm and yanks him back from the truck playfully.

"Race you to the mailbox," he offers, wiggling his eyebrows.

Des nods, and they take off toward the top of the drive, giving us exactly one hundred feet of sprinting child's worth of time to talk.

He shifts the truck into park, the muscles of his forearm torquing. My pussy flutters.

"My parents are taking the boys tonight? Is that surprise for them or us?" he asks, voice husky as he takes me in again, this time more slowly. "You look gorgeous." His eyes catch on the slit running up my thigh.

I definitely thought of that when I put this on.

"Last time you wore that to the Scouts meeting I couldn't fucking focus," he chuckles, the huskiness of desire heavy in his tone.

"The surprise is for both of us," I reply to his earlier question, then add, "And thank you. I know you like this skirt."

"I like you in anything," he says, peering out the window in time to see the boys circling the mailbox and heading back. "In *nothing* especially."

I lean in, attempting a quick kiss, but he seizes me by the back of my neck and yanks me in the window a tiny bit. "Trying to get away?" he rasps against my lips, using the voice he uses when he's my captor and villain. My skin heats, and my spine goes a little wobbly under the dismantling glare of Laws'.

"You know it," I say, kissing him hard and fast before sliding out of the window, right as the boys approach. "I thought you could catch a shower while I drop them off at your parents, then we'll head into Willowdale. I got us a hotel. I planned a little night."

"Two nights or one?" he asks.

"Just one." I lean in. "We'll make it the best night away ever."

He groans. "Now I gotta hug the boys." Scrubbing a hand down his face, he looks at his lap then back at me. "Load them up. Give me a minute. I'll come say goodbye in the SUV."

"Alright, boys," I call to them as they whiz past, apparently now racing to the garage back to the truck. "Get in. We're going to go. Daddy's going to come say bye once you're buckled in."

"Buckle up!" Laws calls to our sons from his rolled down window right before he reverses the truck, drives forward into his parking spot, and gets out.

A smirk tugs at my lips as I watch him through the truck windows, standing next to the driver's side, pulling at the crotch of his jeans, cursing. My arousal intensifies, and I don't know if it's just the baseline of how I feel for Laws since we've been exploring so much or if it's the fact we have a night completely alone in a city to play however we please. Either way, I keep my thighs together beneath the wheel as I buckle up.

A moment later, he opens the back doors and reminds the boys of the rules, goes through a list of things he knows they need to sleep (a sound machine and Minecraft stuffed plush toy for Des, and a plug-in night light for Lex, under the guise that it's actually for Des), kisses them, and closes the door.

He stands in the garage, all work worn and hunky, waving us off. My heart races the entire drive to his parents' house and on the drive back home, I'm nearly shaking.

This is going to be the best weekend ever.

Seventeen

LAWS

She's my painting. I can't look away from her.

I'm coming down the drain before the water is even warm.

A night away with Jes definitely requires pregaming in the form of masturbating at least once. Because the way she had me hard in that fucking long sexy skirt, alluding to the weekend –*fuck*.

I hop out of the shower after a thorough washing, knowing in just a few hours I'll likely be dunking my balls into her mouth while she's tied and choking. With a towel tucked in at my hip, the terry cloth tents as I get bricked up at just the thought of her walking the city sidewalk, me a few short paces behind, fingers drumming against my thighs with delicious foreboding, pursuing her, prowling.

The more we'd enabled the phantom and the more she

gave me this rape roleplay fantasy I'd been so starved for, the more we enjoyed it together. I thought for sure when she said months back she wanted to try this, it would be something she did for *me*. Not for *us*.

But I'm learning so many things about her because of all this. I realize my secret was holding us back. Now, we're fucking thriving.

The front door downstairs swings open on the noisy hinges that I've WD40ed plenty of times, and I hop into a fresh pair of jeans. With a black hoodie and a plain black baseball hat, I put my black work boots on, grab the bag of stuff I threw together before the shower, and head down.

She's waiting at the bottom of the stairs. Escaping the high slit in her skirt is her exposed thigh, foot perched seductively on the bottom step. Though it's only the edges, my roving gaze comes to a grinding halt at the sight.

Rope.

She's got her thighs tied up beneath that sexy skirt, and my cock thickens painfully at the sight. I want to see it all, I want to tear her skirt off and trace the jute with my fucking teeth, but I know it's part of whatever she has planned. It's a device meant to torture me, to enrich the scene we're bound to engage in later, and I honor that by showing restraint. My fists clench at my sides, and I have to force myself to look away from the gift waiting for me on her thighs.

A flick of her wrist has her long hair cascading down her back, picking up the setting sun pouring in from the windows. She glows standing there wearing a smile, waiting for me.

"Goddamn it Jes, you look so beautiful." I drop my bag

and just stare at my wife in awe. I remember the first time I laid eyes on her.

We were in the parking lot of a restaurant, she'd just finished a meal with her friends and I'd just taken my parents out to dinner. She dropped her lipstick and didn't realize, and I handed it to her.

Our fingers didn't touch but when our eyes locked, I fell.

I knew right then she was someone special. That she'd change my life, one way or another. She was only twenty-two when we met, and as a thirty-one-year-old man I thought for sure she'd use me to play out some *age-gap* fantasy or work out some *daddy* issues and break my heart.

But somehow, I got her to fall for me.

And now we're here, and I'm falling for her all over again, the way I did in that parking lot all those years back.

"You already said that before I took the boys," she muses, her cheeks wearing the compliment.

"I can't say it enough. Plus, now I can openly eye-fuck you while I do." I take the steps two by two after grabbing my bag again. I bring her mouth to mine, and the way she tastes like everything I've ever wanted makes me hard. Again. Peeling myself from her, I ask, "How'd dropping off the boys go?"

She tucks hair behind her ear, and I collect her bag from the bottom of the stairs, following her out to the SUV in the garage.

"Good, they were so excited to be there that they hardly said goodbye to me." She pops the hatch and it lifts slowly.

"Were Mom and Dad happy to see them? Did they ask you what we're up to?" I toss the bags in and catch her smirking.

"Yeah, I told them we're going into the city for a night so you can follow me around like a stalker then tie me up and fuck me while I scream no." The way her voice remains so light when she says it is what has me growling, pinning her to the now closed hatch of the SUV.

"Now I know you didn't say that but hearing that's what you've got planned?" I hum out a pained growl, letting my lips brush against hers as I sink down over her, sealing my body to hers. "I can't wait to hear you scream. I can't wait to watch you *writhe* beneath me."

She melts into me, spine going soft, legs unsteady. Heaviness rests in her eyelids as her lips fall open but she doesn't speak, only smiles.

"How scared do you want to be tonight?" I ask, my mind a literal playground of possibilities. After all, I'd wanted this forever. I've jerked off to every single imaginable fantasy of Jes. And I know she's loving this. Thriving, evolving, exploring her desires, all of it. We'd discussed pairing our consensual nonconsent and rigging with some more public scenarios. Though we knew we couldn't really do anything publicly because we live in a small town, we have children, we don't want to be arrested—the list goes on. We did, however, decide that going out of town and only enacting the safe parts in public would be okay.

I suppose I thought, despite her agreeing to it, that we wouldn't do it for ages. That we'd continue our play at home, but that largely, we'd never level-up.

She ducks beneath my arms, and slides around the SUV, jumping into the passenger seat. I open the driver's side door, and find her grinning across the cab.

"Scared, and I'm gonna keep you on your toes. I'm gonna

make you really work for it tonight." The tip of her tongue traverses her bottom lip, leaving it shiny. My mind goes to dark places, like my cum glistening across her rope-marred chest, tears of pain and pleasure shiny on her cheeks.

"Good," I say, unable to control the flare of my nostrils. The phantom is awakening, he's surfacing, and we need to get the fuck out of here before we can't. "I'm gonna double check the lights are off and the doors are locked, then we're going."

She reaches into her oversized purse and produces a banana. Peeling it slowly, she brings it to her mouth before stopping to look at me. "Good," she smiles. "I can hardly wait." Then she slides the muted yellow fruit past her lips and my cock howls in agony.

I zip through the house, checking light switches, the stove burners—all the usual things I like to check before we leave. When I close the door and see her sitting in the SUV waiting for me, I can't help but think of Greg.

He wants this type of relationship with Addie, the honesty and the openness, I can tell. When I get behind the wheel, I tell Jes, "If we're going to make it to Willowdale without me painting the window in cum, we need to talk about other things."

I bring up Greg.

"He says he wants to work it out with Addie, but she just doesn't want to talk about it," I say, watching Jes key in the address of the hotel. The navigation begins, and I pull out of our driveway, a short thirty-minute drive, the last thing between us and deliciously chaotic freedom.

"I'm sorry, Greg's a good guy. Oh, Laws," my wife says, utilizing her most gentle tone, the one she uses when she accepts, listens to or delivers bad news. "I don't know that you'll want to hear this but... I saw Mae today. She actually went shopping with me for an hour or so while I picked out some new lingerie."

My eyes widen, flicking off the road ahead to peer at her. "Mae went shopping with you?" Panic rises, haloing the collar of my hoodie in heat. Jes knows me well. I'm a private person, and Graham and I, while close, don't talk about sex and stuff. It's just... not how it was in our house growing up.

She folds her arms over her chest and though I'm focused on the road, I feel her eyes on me, poking me like knives. "Lawson Briggs, you do realize we have been married for twelve years and have two children, right?"

I wince a little, knowing that it's me, I'm the problem. "I know, I just... I don't know. It's not like that with me and Graham. Him knowing you're buying lingerie to wear on our weekend away... he's gonna know we're having sex and—"

Her hand comes down on my arm, and it's a soft touch, nothing abrupt or forceful. I glance back over and find her attitude has dissolved, and all that's left is understanding.

"Babe, Graham knows we fuck. Graham fucks Mae. In fact, they're having a baby. I'm not asking you to swap blow job stories with your brother, but I am telling you that you're wasting your energy being uncomfortable." She tightens her grip, and my heart flexes. "Us exploring your secret and finding a way for us to enjoy it, isn't the end of our new found communication. It doesn't stop there."

"No?"

She shakes her head as I flick on my blinker, finally getting onto the main road. I've never been so eager to go thirty-minutes out of town. "I think it's been a long time coming but... we have to talk more openly about sex in general."

I think about what she's said, then— "Wait, Mae's pregnant?"

She smirks. "Yep. But act surprised when he tells you, okay? She swore me to secrecy."

I nod, smiling, trying to imagine Graham as a dad. He'll make a good one. When I look over to Jes, to see her excitement, I'm thrown a little. She's watching me, wearing a wince, chewing on her thumbnail.

"What? What's wrong?" I start to imagine the baby, and all the potential complications.

"No, I'm sorry, I don't want you to worry. Mae and Graham are fine. The baby is fine. She's telling him this weekend, actually."

"Okay, so why the face?" I ask, reaching across the center to rest my hand on her inner thigh. Immediately she flips up the console, loose change and old pens tumbling around inside. She slides into the middle seat, giving me access to both legs. I drape my hand on her outer thigh, resting it there.

"It's Greg." She leans against my shoulder, wrapping her hands around my bicep. "Addie's not looking to mend fences because she's...moved onto *greener pastures*."

"She's with someone else?" I ask, voice hoarse as I picture my buddy and all the pain he's been wearing. "Fuck." I think for a moment. "Does he know?"

She shakes her head against me. "I doubt he knows. But either way, Mae told me Addie told her, so we can't tell anyone."

"Damn." I hate that for Greg. I do. I look over at Jes,

whose face is still twisted up with sour words left unsaid. "Fuck, what else? When I said I wanted to talk about something else on this drive, I didn't know it would be—"

"Depressing?" She sighs, settling against the seat. "Well, that's being in your thirties and forties. Some are starting their families, others are ending theirs. Outside of that, it's mostly just retirement and vacation talk." She sighs again. "Shit, now I'm kinda depressed."

I snatch her hand, and move it to my lap. With one hand perched on top of the steering wheel, lazily guiding us down a long, empty country road—the main road leading into the heart of Willowdale—I enjoy the feeling of my wife snuggled up next to me.

"Well, how are Penny and Ruthie doing?" I ask, hoping for some positive news.

She shifts away from me, grabbing her phone from her bag. "Actually, thanks for reminding me. I didn't go to spin today, you know—lingerie shopping—" she wiggles her brows. "But I wanted to talk to Penny. She's been having issues with Garth."

"Wow," I deadpan, having never been the biggest fan of Garth. "A grown man who made his partner pay the hospital bill for the epidural when giving birth to their child is causing issues for his partner, eh?"

Jes's head tips to the side, and when she pushes her hair over her shoulder, I get a whiff of her shampoo, her perfume, her. Beneath my denim, things happen. Talk of Garth easily extinguishes that, though.

"I know. I agree with you, Laws. Garth is... *different*."

"Different?" I snort. "Different is someone who pours the milk from the cereal back into a container and labels it cereal milk. Different is not 'you couldn't do it without the meds like we talked about so now you need to pay the $8k hospital bill on your own', okay? Why do we let this guy off the hook so much?"

"Well," Jes says, her fingers skittering across her screen. "Penny lets him off the hook because marriage is give and take. She can't fight everything. Not every fight is worth fighting."

"But—" I start but stop myself. "Well... what's the problem now?"

She finishes her text, hits send, and tucks her phone back into her purse. She stays on her side of the truck, and I pat my thigh, trying to coax her back.

Sliding back over, I wrap my arm around her shoulders, keeping one hand atop the wheel. Lights from the quiet town come into focus, and I flick on my headlights as the sun sinks into the mountains ahead.

"There are sexual things she wants and before you ask, I don't know what they are. But she wants to try new things, and Garth isn't open to conversation."

Fuck, suddenly, I can't judge because, and it sickens me to say this, I have been Penny. Tied up in my own insecurities and fears so tight that I couldn't fathom coming clean.

"Did you tell her to ask him to take the quiz? It's a pretty good ice breaker," I admit, peering down to catch Jes smirking up at me.

"It was, wasn't it?" she sighs, draping her hand on my inner thigh. Both of us stare forward, watching town swim past the window as I navigate through slowly, the GPS telling us we're just a few minutes away from our hotel. "Hey, enough about that. I want to talk about tonight."

Then she's sliding back, putting distance between us, but this time, the space makes me hard. It's necessary space. Planning space. Space wherein we decide how cruel and devious this night will go.

"You brought rope?" she asks, then answers before I can. "Nevermind. Stupid question. Okay, I'm a little nervous."

"Why?" I ask, chancing a look at her as I approach a blinking four-way stop.

"New environment. It's... exciting. And I'm just a little nervous."

"Me too," I admit, not realizing that I was nervous until now. I've never trapped her cries and slapped her skin outside our comfort zone. We've never done this roleplay beyond our four walls, and now that the hotel is coming into view, my palms slick with perspiration, and my stomach clenches. "But maybe we set some parameters now, so we can focus on the excitement, and not worry, huh?" I reach across the cab and stroke my hand through her hair.

"The museum. I'm going to go to the museum. I want you to go too but not with me. Sometime after me, and I want you to follow me. Like... you're stalking me," she says, and the way she delivers these details so precisely and slowly, like she's crafted them carefully, makes my cock pulse behind my zipper. It's not even the scene she's laid out, it's the passion she has for doing something new and exciting with me. *That's* what has me aching.

"I like that," I say, pulling into a parking spot and throwing the truck into park. With my shoulders and back leaned up against the window, I unclip my belt and get comfortable. "You got a stalker fantasy, baby?" I wink, and my cock turns to granite at the pretty shade of pink spreading through her cheeks.

She shrugs. "I mean, the idea of you following me before you—" she pauses, and though we both know the fantasy we're partaking in, neither of us say the exact word. I know why I don't say it and it's likely the same reasoning for her. "Before we *play*," she offers instead, and the tension around the word dissipates, "seems like it would make our play that much more exciting."

I stroke my hand down my face, and she watches, seemingly entranced. The darkness inside me rears up, and as the day turns to evening around us, the phantom works on clawing his way out. "Are you picturing this hand on your throat?" I ask, my voice husky.

She nods, biting her lip, sliding further from me in the cab until her back presses against the window. "I want lots of rope, lots of impact play, and lots and lots of raw Laws."

"Raws," I say, putting a name to the phantom. She's named him the raw version of me, and I like that much more than calling myself a monster. "That fits."

"Same as always. Red for stop, yellow if I'm nearing my red, and three taps or three solid blinks if I'm incapacitated but need to stop."

The way she says incapacitated has me envisioning tears streaming down her temples, face beet red, my cock lodged in her throat as I straddle her face and slap the fuck out of her cheek. I love feeling my cock in her mouth when I slap her.

Hatred and self loathing attempt to creep into my brain when I envision the fantasy. She reaches out and pats my thigh. "I want this, just a reminder." I trap her hand against my leg and squeeze. Continually hearing her consent is something we both know I absolutely need. Continual reassurance, that's the only way we keep this option open.

"Thank you," I tell her, because she sensed the perfect time to deliver her consent. She always knows what I need, and when. God, I can't wait to make this night everything she wants and more.

She peers up at the hotel. "I'll go get the keys and check in. I'll bring one out to you but I'll take your bag up with mine. But after I hand over the key— that's it. We're... strangers."

My mouth goes dry, my cock thickens and my heart races. "Okay. So... museum, dinner, hotel?" I look at the time and see it's nearing seven already. She digs in her bag, produces a sandwich wrapped in cellophane.

"No dinner. Eat this while I'm getting the room keys. Museum then hotel. I want to maximize the fun and I didn't think a restaurant would lend itself to the fantasy."

I nod, knowing I'd agree to anything she planned for us, knowing how it's all going to come to a head. "Sounds good. I love you, Jes."

She slips out of the cab and shuts the door, so I lower the window. Collecting her hair in one hand, she frees it from beneath her purse strap as she smiles. "I love you too."

By the time I've eaten the sandwich—which I'm sure was delicious but because my mind is racing, I couldn't even taste it— Jes is back at the window. I roll mine down, she presses the black room key into my palm, but doesn't let go.

Our eyes lock.

Her breath hitches, lips part. The wind lifts her ruby locks, tossing them across her face. She bats them away, and holds my gaze. "Ruin me, baby. Make me everything you've ever wanted in your dreams." She releases her hold on the card, turns, and disappears into the sea of people moving through the crowded downtown streets.

And just like that, Raws takes control.

* * *

I swear I can already *feel* the rope against my palms as I watch her peer up at the lit canvas on the wall. I can feel the loose, coarse fibers breaking free from the wax-slicked rope, scratching up the insides of my fingers as I work knots into the length. I can feel her hot breath flanking my face as she cries for me to stop. *Begs me to quit.*

Taking two steps back, her heels connect with the bottom of a curved wooden bench. She falls into it, gaze cast up at the art as if she can't be bothered to look away long enough to sit safely. She's so... engrossed.

She's my painting. I can't look away from her.

Crossing her legs at the ankle, her skirt falls open along the slit, exposing her thigh and teasing me with a glimpse of her hidden ropes. Heat ambles through my core and I find my fists clenching at my sides. Quickly, I take in my surroundings, making sure no one is watching me.

If someone is, I may end this night in a cop car, because the way I'm watching my wife feels illegal. Like a starved man presented with a feast, I'm swallowing mouthfuls drool, salivating, choking it down, struggling to trap my grunts of feral desire but coming up short. Tonight I am playing a part, assuming a role that every fiber of my being is desperate to act out. I look the part of *a man unhinged...a predator.*

I feel like a man who's about to grasp the arm of a beautiful woman, press my lips to her ear and hiss private, dangerous commands for her to obey. I feel like a man who's about to force his way into his wet fuck hole, fill her against her will, and leave her a used heap.

I have a love/hate relationship with the phantom and the cruel things he enjoys. But as I watch Jes lean back on the artistic looking bench, hands splayed along the knotted wood behind her, I remind myself that *she* wants this.

Traversing the space between the impressionist exhibit and the sculptures of hands, I end up in a poorly lit corner of the museum. Fitting for my mood. Pretending to care about the canvas with muted tones splashed across it, I peer through the sparse crowd to locate Jes.

She's no longer on the bench, now she stands before a column in the middle of the room, a large glass orb on top. A man wearing a navy-blue suit, fitted and tailored to every gym-chiseled ridge, is standing at her side, wearing a slick smile that fills me with rage.

It's a smile every man wears and every man knows. It's his *I want to fuck you* smile. Every single molecule of me wants to be good, wants to stay in character, to make this night feel every bit of the fantasy we've built it to be.

But that's my wife.

And he's *not* me.

And the way he's tossing his head back to laugh, how he's eyeing the slit in her skirt, and how he checks out her tits when she gazes at the glowing orb—I can't fucking take it. I storm across the museum, but as I approach, Jes's eyes come to mine.

Don't, she says without saying the words. Her eyes flare,

as do her nostrils, and with one menacing look, I freeze. Blue suit follows her gaze, and the douche and I lock eyes.

I have a choice here.

Live out this fantasy and do the right thing. Watch this man drool over what's mine, then snatch her off the street and show her who owns her cunt.

Or ruin the plan—the one we have sitters for and everything—and storm over there like a jealous prick and engage in an alpha tango of *mine, not yours.*

Her eyes return to him and I watch as her hand falls to her thigh, slightly hiking the soft fabric of her skirt, exposing the edges of raw jute twisted around her skin. She's fucking *baiting* me. Baiting *and* teasing me, and goddamn. *I fucking love it.* My slutty little brat will pay for that later.

I turn abruptly, and find the men's restroom. Standing over the sink, I ignore my reflection and instead focus on the constant flow of water. It's okay that he's talking to her. Hell, men likely talk to Jes when I'm not around all the time. At the store, when she gets the car serviced, everywhere. Because she's gorgeous. And sweet, and fuck, isn't that the ultimate compliment to my decision making? Other men wanting what's mine?

After a few palmfuls of water, I pat dry my face and head back out, resolute. Tonight is about exploring more of what we love, not about proving something we both already know: we are solid.

I take a few steadying breaths and enter the fluorescent space again, eyes working to find her. I see *blue suit* first, but this time, he's talking to someone else. Another woman.

From the corner of my eye, there's a flash of crimson and an intoxicating laugh that makes me ache bone deep and I know it's her. I turn, positioning myself behind a pack of older folks who appear to be reading a pamphlet in a huddle. Through them, I see her.

Talking to another man, this time wearing black cigarette pants and a white button up. His hair is slicked back, and peeking through his collar is a gold necklace. His wrist glitters with the same jewelry, and when I study his face, I don't see fine lines or salt with his pepper. He's young, and he wants my wife. I can see he wants her with the way he holds her eyes as she speaks, how he reaches his arm out to touch her, but instead smooths his hand through his hair.

My dick grows heavy between my legs, fattening with the idea that *I* get to have what they want. They're laughing with her but in a short amount of time, I'll be licking her tears as she pleads for mercy, pleads for her freedom.

I have to admit, coming out like this intensifies the role play, and I know without a doubt, this world building is going to lead us to the best fucking orgasms of our lives. *I feel it.*

We spend the next hour playing the most dizzying game of cat and mouse; I watch her weave through crowds, turning heads, garnering smiles. Sweat slides down the hollow of my spine as she makes her way to the large entry doors.

Finally.

We're going back to the hotel.

I trail behind her a hundred yards, knowing if I can hear her heels clicking along the pavement, I'm too close. I stay far enough behind that she can't hear my labored, ravenous breaths and I can't hear her delicate, unsuspecting steps.

I stand outside the hotel, watching through foggy glass as she presses her room key to the elevator, and the doors slide open. She steps inside the car, and as she does, I surge forward, suddenly overwhelmed with a near unquenchable thirst to touch her. To start the next part of this incredible fucking fantasy we're living.

With one foot in the lobby, our eyes lock just as the elevator doors seal her in and carry her up, away from me. My stomach goes sour and my fingers curl inside the kangaroo pocket of my hoodie. We've technically been apart all night but now the idea of not tying her up this fucking second is driving me mad.

The phantom takes over completely, as I race up the stairwell, taking them two-by-two. I can't beat the elevator, but it doesn't stop me from charging through the halls like a racehorse.

When I see the painted red 3 on the plaque nearing the door, I push it open, stumbling out into a dimly-lit, quiet hallway. Chest heaving, I peer around, trying to orient myself. I pull the black card from my back pocket and blink down at it until I spot the number. 323.

Squinting, I read the number off the door nearest me. 317. As I'm about to turn the corner—I'm at a fork of two hallways—I hear the heavy closing of a metal door, and spot her.

Feet now bare, long hair pulled up into a loose ponytail, Jes sways down the hall, a bucket of ice at her hip, a soft hum on her lips.

So innocent.

So unsuspecting.

I'm quiet as I close the distance between us, and with the ice shifting in the bucket, I really don't think she hears me as I get within a pace of her. Without a second to think, I knock the bucket with a closed fist, startling her, sending ice skittering across the maroon and gold matted carpet.

Her breathy little gasp instantly makes me hard. Looping an arm under hers, around her chest, I cup my palm over her mouth, the vibration of her first panicked cry absorbed completely by my hand. My other arm loops her waist, yanking her against my chest hard.

She jerks in my grasp, throwing an elbow into my abdomen before I capture her by the wrist, keeping both of her limbs immobile as I bear hug her.

"Help" is muffled by my hand, but she does cry for help, and goosebumps rise on my neck in response sending pulses of electricity down my spine. My hands don't shake and my voice is steady as my lips press to her ear.

"No one can hear you, so stop wasting your breath."

My mouth is filled with her hair as she struggles to turn, to face me, and for a moment I wonder if she needs to see me, to know that it *is* me, that this is what we planned and that it isn't some terribly timed coincidence and she's truly being abducted.

I nudge my knee into her lower back, causing her body to crumple forward. Lifting her before she can fully fall, I keep my voice private as I force her to walk. "To the room. Don't try to run or I'll fucking hurt you."

She goes limp, her last tactic to escape my grip, but it doesn't work. I'm so fucking hard from the struggle—one I didn't expect, either. That's part of what's got me so keyed up—how far she's going to make this real.

I fucking love it.

I love her.

"Stand up, don't fucking play with me," I hiss, jerking

her to her feet once again. This time, she walks, but still, she thrashes.

Her torso twists in my grip, ruby hair flying and the little moans and grunts that slip through my fingers over her mouth have my heart fucking soaring.

"That's right, tire yourself out so you can't fight," I press my mouth to her ear, "when it counts."

She lifts her leg and stomps with force, her heel coming down right on the toe of my black boot.

My *steel-toed* black work boots, to be specific. I let a maniacal laugh dust her ear as we approach the door label 323. "Steel-toed boots, but nice try." She whimpers, and beneath my forearm, her pulse rockets and her chest heaves. "Now get the card out and open the door." I don't say or else, but it's there, hanging between us as a cruel warning.

She shakes her head vehemently, and since we're at the door of the room, I take a chance and remove my hand, realizing she can't tap or blink if I can't see her.

And what if she needs to use a safeword? What if the footstomp was a real cry to stop?

But when my hand falls away and she gasps for air, she doesn't try to speak or turn to face me. Instead, her shaky hands go to her purse, which dangles lifelessly at her side. Digging around a moment, she produces a black card and presses it to the reader affixed to the door.

The red light turns green, and I reach out, pushing the door open for both of us.

Inside, the room is undisturbed. Two bags lie at the foot of the king sized bed, and the curtains are closed. If I were a real intruder, truly an abductor and rapist, I'd likely leave the lights off.

But I need light for what I have in store.

I walk her to the bed and push her down, face first, keeping my knee to her back as I snatch the bag. Digging through, I find the pre-knotted ropes I'd readied just for this moment. I pull out the double-loops, slide her hands through, and tighten at the wrist. Makeshift cuffs that are quieter and honestly, way fucking sexier than metal handcuffs. With her arms unusable, I flip her to her back and it's the first time we've laid eyes on one another since the museum.

Emerald tones shimmer beneath a glaze of tears. She blinks, thick lashes driving moisture from her eyes. Tears coast down her temples. My chest heaves with anxious, excited breaths. Hers does, too, though I don't know what she's feeling. Beneath her blouse, her nipples are hard.

Her lips tremble and right as I'm about to break and ask her if she's sure she wants to continue, quietly she says, "You followed me. I saw you at the museum."

I turn my focus to the unzipped duffel bag, and begin unloading the three loops of jute I brought with me. I know my wife. As much as she likes being helpless to my whims, she loves watching me tie. Fuck, had I known that, I'd have let her be the front desk girl down at AgDev all those years ago when she asked. Maybe we'd have gotten to this place sooner.

Heavy rope stringing between my hands, I stare down at my canvas. Her clothes concealing what I know to be smooth, satin soft skin. Beneath her silk top, the peaks of her breasts are pebbled, either by desire or fear, both of which make me hard. Like she knows what I'm thinking, her eyes fall to my crotch for a moment, then she pulls her knee to her chest and I realize what she's doing just in time to catch her heel in my hands, rope falling to the bed.

"Fuck," I mutter, immediately looping the rope around her ankles. She's still getting the full body diamond tie up I had planned, but it'll have to wait. "Every time you kick, fight me, or struggle, you dig yourself deeper. Quit being a little brat and lie there."

Yanking, my muscles burn from how tightly I pull the ends of the rope. She shouts, actually shouts. The walls vibrate a little, I swear to fuck they do.

But she doesn't scream yellow or cry out red.

She just whimpers and trembles as I take a gag from my bag and stuff her mouth, muting her indefinitely. Tears are streaming freely now, but I hold her gaze, giving her the opportunity to blink. A subtle shake of her head, small and almost imperceptible, but I know what it is. She's not tapping out.

With her wrists and ankles bound, I retrieve my shearing scissors and hold them up, the dim overhead light twinkling off the unused, sharp blade. She moans against the gag, words, likely *please* or *don't*, I'm not sure. I press the blade to her thigh and her entire body stills. Our eyes connect, and through the fear and eroticism, I manage to find the trust. It's a glittering moment followed by a blink, but it's enough.

I shear off her blouse and cut off the slitted skirt that had so many men interested. Then the teasing outfit is nothing more than scraps of fabric in a heap on a hotel floor. I finally reveal the intricate ropes lacing her thighs. A lattice of mouth watering bindings that ignite the phantoms' burning desire to devour her.

With her revealed to me, I can get to work.

A smile rolls through my lips, curling the edges. "Hishi Korada," I tell her, calmly, wiping the glaze of sweat from my upper lip with the back of my wrist. She writhes on the cheap comforter, but she's fucking beautiful. Gorgeous. My cock is hard, full of release that I want nothing more than to pump into her right this second.

But tying rope and rigging is an art, and it often takes time. I've been reading.

"That's the name for how I'm going to string you up." I hold her eyes as I slip the jute beneath her, gentle to tug it out on the other side. I'm going to score her skin, I won't lie, but I want that to be in the thick of it. Not the preparation.

"It's a diamond pattern with ropes. Some have knots," I say, tugging the jute through a loop I've formed, starting the pattern. "Some don't." I continue, looping and knotting, my triceps beginning to ache around the eighth time.

Only twenty-two more.

"When I'm fucking you, I want you helpless to me in all ways." I lean down, nostrils flaring, her green eyes glistening up at me. "You won't be able to fight me when I fuck your tight little ass. You won't be able to escape me when I ram my cock down your throat and force you to taste yourself," I rasp, leveling up out of nowhere because the more knots I complete, the more feral I become. It's as if the sight of her fair skin trapped beneath the chafing jute flips a switch in my brain. The last of logical Laws bleeds out, and rising up from his ashes is *this man.*

The man who wants to be pushed against, punched and cursed at while he steals access to whatever he pleases.

I lick my lips and continue working with the rope. I don't miss how her eyes stay on my hands, and how her thighs tremble ever so slightly. "I know all about rigging," I say to her, my voice a quiet roar, holding power but not volume. "I love ropes." I cinch this knot extra tight, and she spits out the gag in a reflexive exhale.

She looks over at the rubber ball strung up with leather. I hadn't gotten a chance to buckle it yet. Before she can look at me again, I pluck her nipple between my thumb and finger and twist.

"Fuck!" she screeches. Her nipples have been so sensitive ever since she breastfed years ago. But I know she likes it. Glancing down, I see a dark spot in my jeans, and groan up at her, hands working from memory as I continue the pattern.

I've been practicing with the ropes and specific ties. Reading a lot. But that's a conversation meant for Jes and Laws, not... whoever *we* are right now.

I'm nearing the end of the pattern, and can't wait for the last piece. From the bag, I retrieve another piece of rope. Her eyes widen as I lick my lips. "I'm gonna tie your neck to your feet and fuck your cunt and tight ass. It's gonna hurt, I'll make sure of that." I seal the words with a slap across her cheek, hard enough to turn her head, but soft enough to not leave a mark.

As soon as I'm done putting her in a shrimp tie—back on the bed, legs pulled to her torso by the ropes, exposing her cunt. I shed the remaining barrier between us, shucking off everything wildly. My hoodie tips the cheap bedside lamp, and it clatters to the floor. I kick out of my boots and shove my jeans down, sending them into the armoire as I shake them free from my leg.

Naked, my cock bobbing between us, pink like lipstick

with how hard and restrained it's been. I look at her pussy, and my mouth actually fucking *salivates* at the matted thin strip of ruby hair lining the split of her lips, coated in her arousal, ending at her pubic bone.

"I watched you tonight. I watched you and told myself, I'm gonna take her." I stroke my cock, bending to bring my mouth to hers. I spit, and watch her gasp in shock. Her pupils swell, and she blinks a few times before spitting right back at me.

I wipe my face, then slap her pussy. "Watch me take what I want. Then watch me turn your sweet little pussy into a swollen cunt, dripping with my cum." I slap her ass, hard, five times, my cock weeping at the sight of her harnessed tits bouncing.

I make use of her mouth, plunging my fingers inside. She gags but I force her to wet them, and when saliva strings between her and me, a groan tears through me.

"Fuck, you want it, don't you?" I give each breast a hard slap, her nipples bright red. "What kind of slut wants to be fucked by her abductor?" I lean down and spit into her mouth, but this time, she swallows it. "A dirty little fuck hole, that's all you are."

Gripping the base of my cock, I spear into her puckered hole, fast, rough, knocking free a deep cry.

"Noo!" she whines, breath jagged, bottom lip trembling. "Please, not there, *please*," she cries, shaking her head violently. I look down at where my cock is one inch away from being completely tucked into her ass.

Fucking tight. Smothering. A warm vise swallowing my dick, dragging me to the edge of orgasm almost immediately. I steal my hips away, my cock bobbing, and spit on her hole.

My mind flies to our intimate moment last week, when she wanted me to have sex with her while she was on her period. She'd said she'd been ashamed to ask for it. Afraid I'd think it was gross. A flash of my dick, streaked how it is now, only then with pinks and reds, and I'm groaning.

My chest tightens and suddenly I'm desperate to find her eyes. Still twisting and turning, it takes a moment before she catches me watching her, and she stills.

A singular moment, no blinking, just contact, and I'm encouraged to resume. I just needed to see my wife.

The phantom apparently has a weak side, too.

"Please," she sputters again, resuming her arching. With her neck fastened to her feet with just a few feet of rope between the two, she's forced to watch the movie taking place between her legs.

"Please what?" I push the final inch inside of her, my eyes rolling closed from the intensity of her tight heat.

"You—you're too big, please, let me go."

I arch a brow as I feed my hand beneath the jute, gripping the knotted rope at her neck. "Let you go?"

Her head trembles. "Please," she whimpers.

With one hand tight on the knotting, gripping her hip with the other, I give her one final warning. A singular ounce of mercy before I hammer her into oblivion and make her nothing but a swollen fuck hole oozing with cum.

"You can scream all you want, but I'll just stuff your mouth. So if you want to breathe, keep fucking quiet and let me fill this ass like I came here to do." Saying these things to her—things I know for sure I've uttered to her photo in the privacy of my home office more times than I'd like to admit—feels so goddamn surreal.

She cries, she attempts to rock away, though even if she got off the bed she's so tied up, she'd still be helpless.

On that note, I thrust into her, my hips finding a motion of their own. Relentlessly I pound into her, but after a few seconds, her cries take on power, her voice rattling the walls with her pleas for help. I tuck my fingers in her open mouth, no longer holding the rope. Without holding it, her body writhes against the jute, and I watch her skin grow pink as I slam into her repeatedly.

I love the way the creamy fairness of her skin is all but gone, an aggressive blush left behind. The shrimp tie is somehow loosening, and though it's the first time I've tied it on her, I've practiced the concept a few times before. I note to myself that the shrimp tie needs work, but continue railing her.

She gags on my fingers and I stare down at her body, thrumming behind the ties, feeling my cock twitch inside her ass, and I've never felt more connected to my wife than I do now.

The vulnerability and trust she's shown me in letting me have her this way. I'm taking, and even though I know she's enjoying it and that means I'm also giving, I know what I'm taking is huge. And I fucking worship her for giving it so freely.

Emotions clog my throat, my eyes burn with satisfaction and I still my grinding hips, leaving my glistening cock resting against her lips as I take my fingers from her mouth, loving her breathy gasps for air.

I don't want it to end yet, but stalking her, abducting her, taking her this way—I'm fucking teetering here. On the edge. And it's crumbling, falling away beneath my feet like soft earth.

I'm close, I'm so fucking close.

And I know this is about to be the best orgasm of my life.

Eighteen

JES

What a fucking mess.

Oh my God. Oh my ever loving God.

Laws using my own sex toy on me? Hot. Being passionate enough about rigging and exploring the desire to make me his rope bunny by researching shibari? Hot. Installing the hook in the ceiling at home? Hot. Wanting to continually make sure I'm okay? So fucking hot, because care is pussy-melting. S*woon.*

But tonight?

Having him follow me through the museum, then down the city streets, into the private halls of a hotel room—hotter than the actual sun, I'm fairly certain.

Ten minutes into the museum visit, I was drenched.

Like, so wet that my thighs were sticky and I thought at one point, I'd actually chafe.

Now, being in two ties more complicated than anything he's tried with me in the past, I'm on the brink of explosion. Watching him tie me up in a diamond-patterned rope bodice? Lord help me. I think if his broad thumb had even stroked my clit once during the tying I would've gushed all over the comforter. Seriously.

I've always been hot for Laws. Always. The only reason we don't have ten children instead of two is because of how hard childbirth was on me. Not because we aren't fucking like bunnies to this day. And like the king he is, he had a vasectomy so I didn't have to bear the responsibility of birth control and he gets to fuck his cum into me as often as he likes. It's a win-win.

But seeing him in his element has transformed my highest opinion of him. He's no longer just hot. He's something else entirely. Godlike, with how he carefully handles the trust I've placed in his hands, with how he lets his dark side run free when it's just me. That trust he gives back to me is so... beautiful.

I know it's roleplaying rape. And I know if there was a fire in this hotel room right now, we'd be in a pickle. But the logistics and titles aside, we're living our deepest sexual fantasies with emotional ease, and despite the erotic nature, I'm feeling the feels from all of it.

I manage to blink away the heat in my eyes, and focus my energy on the present. I can get lost in the beauty of us and what we're doing in the aftercare. Now, I need to be here, in this scene that he's crafted, living in this night I've shaped.

"I'll never forget your face," I rasp, my belly tightening with need as he fucks me in deep, determined strokes. "I'll report you. I'm going to report you after this," I cry, letting my emotional tears slide down my temples, playing them off as part of the scene. He growls, literally, a roar erupts from deep in his chest, making the walls tremble with his strength.

"Time to forget," he rasps. Grabbing me with both hands by the knots on my body, not the tie between my neck and feet, he quickly flips me, as fast as a waiter would tug free a table linen, leaving the silverware and plates intact.

My nose fills with the scent of cheap detergent as my face is buried in the comforter. He slides his cock inside me, this time my pussy, and a moan of pleasure flies past my lips, getting lost in the bed.

But he hears it. He hears it and I'm met with a resounding thwack as he spanks my bare ass, all while fucking my pussy from behind. My toes lose feeling as he pummels me with his cock, my groin burning with fullness each time he enters.

"You're torn up from these ropes," he hisses at my back, sliding a thick finger beneath the jute to touch my marred skin. I can feel where the ropes burn me. It hurts, but right now, it hurts *good*. The heat of his finger over my tender skin makes me shriek in pain, and then he's gripping the rope at the back of my neck, yanking me to my knees.

"I'm gonna come all over your torn up skin then leave you here. The hotel maid will come in here and find you, nothing more than a used, bound *cum dumpster*."

Cum dumpster. Definitely not a term he wrote in his vows, but hearing my good man, my Scout leader, upstanding member of our small community say those wanton, nasty words? I begin to slip off the edge.

He yanks back on the rope, and my neck lurches back, but without him holding the tie between my neck and feet, the pressure is off-center, off-balance, causing my neck to stay straight now, and my shoulder to jerk back. The motion is jarring, and as he plunges inside me again, that's when I feel it.

A sharp burning. A tear. A pop even, maybe? I don't know what it is, but suddenly, my world goes red with pain. So much fucking pain, it's nearly blinding. It hurts. It hurts so fucking bad.

For a moment, the pain is so great I'm rendered speechless.

His long, thick cock slaps down against my ass, a hot ribbon of cum streaking my skin. And then, my vision returns, the pain centralizes and the moment of shock wears off, leaving me in nothing but splintering, all consuming pain.

"*Red!*" I scream into the mattress, though my neck is hurting so bad I can hardly turn my face to get the words out. "*Red! Red! Red! Laws!*" I scream. God do I fucking scream.

Heat splashes against my back, but he's not grunting, he's not spitting dirty words over me as he does. Rather, he grabs me by the harness and flips me back onto my backside, sending another dose of searing pain through my shoulder. I scream, and it's not a role I'm playing.

I'm hurt, and I open my eyes to find Laws staring down at me, eyes wide, his cock still bobbing as his orgasm leaves him, no longer with his permission. He's coming, but his brain is already through with it, realizing I'm saying... *the word*.

"Red?" he's breathless. "You said red?"

I try to nod, but find myself screaming again. *"Red! Untie me! Laws! Laws!"*

I have never seen him so panicked. His slick cock resting against my leg, he begins untying me, elbows jutting out over and over as he works as fast as humanly possible.

But it took time to tie me up. And it will take the same amount of time to untie me.

"Fuck!" he hisses, sweat peppering his upper lip. "Fuck, fuck, *fuck!* Where are the fucking shears? Fuck! What have I done?" he growls, stumbling through the knots in a panic.

The pain in my shoulder radiates to the front, and even though I'm feeling more agony by the moment, I know I need to center us. Because he's going to lose his mind, and that's not going to help.

"My shoulder," I breathe, trying hard to steady my tone. "I think my shoulder is..." I swallow, my stomach growing sick at what I'm about to say, "dislocated."

He stops his untying, and his eyes come to mine. "Oh my God, baby, I'm so sorry." Then, at lightning speed, he begins working the ropes again. This time, I don't get lost in the way the jute twines his thick digits, the sound of the coarse fibers wearing against his tough skin.

All I see now is a man desperate to help his wife, and I focus on my breathing to get a better idea of what we need to do. *Calm.* We have to calm down.

But Laws is more flustered and panicked than I've ever seen him.

"I knew this was a bad idea! We fucking jinxed

ourselves. How could we think we could do this? We said no photos, I took a photo! *I broke the fucking rules,*" he says, throwing his fingers into his chest, absorbing all the guilt, everything a panicked, stream-of-consciousness brain dump wherein I see, for the first time ever, my husband is scared.

Then, startling us both, there's a heavy knocking at the door. The distinct rap of a curled fist hammering. Our gazes lock, then Laws' eyes crawl over my body. Cum sprayed everywhere, ropes knotted in places and untied in others, my hair strewn across the pillows, clothes littered about.

The door rattles from booming knocks again.

Using the edge of the comforter, Laws throws it over me, covering my body, then grabs his jeans off the floor and trips twice as he hurries to step in them. "Just—fuck," he says, swiping a hand through the top of his hair. My lips tremble as the pain radiates, God does it fucking radiate. "I'm fucking sorry, baby, just, hang on for me, okay?"

Nerves rattle him from the inside out, doubt and fear in his expression. He pads toward the door, and while the pain is all-consuming, my breath catches, waiting to see who is there. And what they want.

The mechanical twisting of the deadbolt releasing has me straining off the bed, or trying to, but I'm still half bound and my shoulder—fuck, my shoulder. I bite into my bottom lip, a futile attempt to stop my cries of searing pain.

Hinges squeak quietly and then— "Hello… *Officer.*"

Officer? Fuck. Oh God. *Oh my God.*

"Everything okay in here? A call was made to the front desk about the noise." The voice is deep, low, and the worst part? Questioning. Like he's staring into the eyes of a bad guy, not into the eyes of my husband.

If I weren't writhing in silent pain, I'd be bugged eyed, going, *what the fuck?* But the pain is getting worse, and now, unlike mere minutes ago, the ropes burn. They tear at my flesh, sending judders of agony everywhere they touch.

"I know this is going to sound...." Laws' voice trails off for a moment before he clears his throat, "cliché, but, my wife and I were... having some fun and... that's likely what someone heard."

There's silence, and I'm dying to know why.

The officer speaks, his voice unwavering. "I'm going to need you to step back sir. Put your hands on the wall there for me, let me check you for weapons. You're not under arrest, you're not detained. Just making sure we're all safe here."

I hear him spread his hands against the wall, and bile rises in my throat.

A moment later I hear, "Alright, hands down. Now. Front desk showed me some concerning footage. I'm not accusing you of anything, but I'd like to speak with your wife."

He isn't asking, he's telling. And my stomach lurches— "I'm naked!" I croak. "Please, I'll talk to you but please, just... Laws!" I rasp, my eyes stinging with a sudden onslaught of tears.

"Ma'am," the officer calls, "I'm gonna step inside and take a peek, alright? Then you can get dressed. Are you... presentable?"

I have to snort. Laws orgasm drying on my skin, ropes everywhere, sweat making me slick and uncomfortable. "Um, no?" I offer through a wince as pain pinches my arm.

"She's um... tied up," Laws supplies, his tone thick with

shame. My heart splinters. This was our first big roleplay outside our bedroom at home. And it's gone spectacularly to shit.

"Tied up?" he asks, the door closes with a loud thud. Nerves strangle me, knowing a stranger is feet away and I'm lying here naked and exposed.

But their voices stay where they are. "Oh my God," Laws breathes. "I'm... we're... we're into..." his exhale rocky and turbulent.

"Relax, okay?" the officer adds, not really soothingly but more so, a command. Something about this guy's voice makes me think he's got a great poker face.

"Okay."

"What's going on? Why did I see you knock an ice bucket from a woman's hand then grab her and force your way into her room with her?"

"Oh my God," Laws breathes, likely full of panic. I'd be panicking too... if my arm weren't hurting so bad that I'm nearing the point of vomiting. "I'm into rape roleplay," he says, his voice quiet. "And rigging. I like to tie her up. We got a hotel and decided to have a... roleplay night."

There's a pause. Then, surprising likely the both of us, the police officer asks, "Is that right?"

"Tonight we went to the museum. I can show you both of our stubs. This isn't real, I'm not really a fucking rapist abductor. I fucking swear, man."

"Why'd you go to the museum?" the cop asks, confusing me for a moment.

Laws sighs, the last of his soul leaving his body. My husband barely got comfortable talking about this shit with me, and now he's emptying the contents of his diary to a stranger. A cop, no less.

What a fucking mess.

"She wanted me to... *stalk* her before I grabbed her. So I watched her, followed her around– God you must think I'm full of shit. You must think I'm an absolute monster but I swear, man, I swear, I'm not lying. Separate us. Do the cop shit you gotta do but I swear to you, I'm telling the truth." He sucks in a breath, then adds, "We need to go to the hospital. She's hurt. The ropes– it slipped– I grabbed–" he stops, and I hear a shaky exhale.

"Get her dressed," the cop says, "and let's talk."

Laws appears a moment later, eyes wide, shiny, hovering over me. "Are you okay? How's your shoulder? What are you feeling?" Sweat shines on his forehead, dark eyes no longer filled with passion, only fear. "We're going to get these ropes off, get you in some clothes and get you to the hospital, okay? It's going to be okay, I promise Jes. I love you."

"Laws," I whisper, not even willing to address the accident right now. "Before the ropes," I lower my voice again, "wipe me off."

The cop clears his throat and I think Laws and I both die a thousand deaths. "Okay," he whispers, before disappearing a moment. There's movement and bustling but I keep my eyes closed, trying to wrap my mind around the pain. When cool cloth brushes my skin, I scream. Literally scream.

The rope has left me achy and torn, and the cool water paired with the cheap terry cloth of the hotel towel has me howling.

"Oh my God! Fuck!" I scream, my spine curling as my upper half shoots off the mattress. Jarring my injured shoulder, the sudden movement makes me scream again. I fling my arm across my chest, covering my breasts, gripping my bad arm just as the officer steps into the bedroom area.

There's the rough clearing of a throat, and because my gaze is fixed on Laws, I know it's the cop.

My husband blinks down at me, and the cop clears his throat again. Laws' head twists, his gaze going to the cop.

Laws reaches back, exposing the arm of the officer, silver shears shining in his curled grip.

"I can't give these to you, man," he says, and my entire body tenses when his boots shuffle, indicating he's stepping closer.

"Laws!" I shriek. He turns back to me, gathering the sheet with his hands. His eyes pin mine as he carefully and slowly covers my exposed areas.

"We gotta cut you out, baby," he says quietly, but not in an effort to conceal his words but more so, out of shame. Guilt and pain pinch his features as he tucks ends of sheet beneath my body with care. "It'll be faster. But the officer has to do it, okay?" He nods until I do, too.

The subtext of the moment hurts worse than my shoulder. The officer won't give Laws the shears because he thinks Laws has intentionally hurt me. Abused me.

What's worse, I think *Laws* believes him.

He turns away from me again. "I'm holding the sheet," he says, and though only one of the men in this room has a gun, my husband wants the officer to know who's in control.

A beat passes, and there's a snapping noise, but my head is turned, eyes studying the shitty hotel art on the wall. I can't look, I won't watch. I can't believe this is happening.

"Hold still, ma'am," the man says. Gloved hands slide

beneath the ropes and then the cold press of steel against my sternum before a moment of pressure then release. The same pattern continues, the gnawing of a blade against jute not as loud as all the worries stomping through my head.

The sheet shifts, and Laws is there, adjusting it to protect my body from the officer's sight.

"My eyes are on the blade of these shears, and only there, Briggs," he offers to Laws. When I risk a glance at my husband, his jaw is set with anger, eyes pinched on the blade moving up my chest.

Then his gaze flicks to mine, and his anger and guilt morphe to tender sadness. "I should be cutting you out," he says but before I can say anything, the officer is done.

"I'm gonna hang onto these shears," he says, and then his boots move through the room, hopefully giving us privacy.

"Her shoulder is dislocated," he says facing me. He stands me up, and then turns, standing protectively in front of me. "I'm going to put her clothes on, can you please give us a moment?"

The cop, who has a thick dark beard and black rimmed glasses, a dark baseball hat on his head, nods. He turns away, both hands on either side of his utility belt, a warning for Laws, no doubt.

Digging around in my bag—since he cut my clothes off —Laws gets out a pair of yoga pants and a tank, and carefully eases me into each, all while assuring me that everything will be okay.

"We'll take you in right now, they'll help you, okay? And whatever happens with this, it'll be okay, alright?" His hand comes to my cheek, his thumb resting on my bottom lip. His eyes implore mine, begging me to be okay, pleading with me to show him that it's okay.

"Okay," I nod. "Hey, it's going to be okay, alright?"

"Is it?" he whispers. "A cop is here, I'm on camera assaulting you, and now you need medical attention." He shakes his head, but the shame and guilt still cling to him when his eyes return to me. "I'm so sorry. But it's going to be okay, alright? We just... we need to get you to the hospital." He slips the shirt on so carefully, and does the same with my pants.

"She's dressed," he says, still holding my eyes. Through the surge of pain rolling through my left side, I tilt my chin up and steal a kiss from his lips.

"I love you," I whisper, and I don't care if the grumpy cop hears or sees. "It's going to be okay, alright?"

He nods. "I should be telling you that."

"Ma'am, what's your name?" the cop asks, stepping toward the edge of the bed. His eyes stay on mine, and I'm grateful he doesn't analyze the mess around the room. Laws picks the lamp up off the floor and feeds his arms through his hoodie, toeing back into his boots.

"Jessalyn Briggs," I tell him, narrowing my eyes on the nameplate resting below the embroidered letters that say WILLOWDALE PD. "Officer Drake, this isn't what it looks like. This is my husband, Laws, and we were doing some stalker, aggressive style roleplay and we had an accident." I swallow hard, and the room is so still that I know they hear. "How can I prove it to you? I'm not a victim. He's not a stalker or rapist. This is just... a misunderst–" I don't get the last word out as searing pain shoots through my shoulder, making me hiss in agony.

"How about I take you both down to the hospital? We'll talk on the drive over," he says, eyes moving from me to Laws, then back to me again. "Let's do that. Okay?"

He asked, but I know it's not a question. "Okay," I say quickly, and then Laws is at my side, easing me carefully off the mattress and onto my feet. He bends, sliding my feet into a pair of slippers I'd shoved into my bag.

Officer Drake holds my elbow as Laws scurries around the room, shoving everything into his duffel bag. A moment later, he's got me by the waist as we walk toward the hall, the police officer holding the door open for us. Once in the hall, Officer Drake lets the door close then turns to face Laws.

Nervous, Laws says, "I'm not really a stalker. It was… just part of the whole… thing."

Officer Drake's eyes narrow on us, and I swear for a split second, he smirks. But it's gone as quickly as it appeared, and then he's hoisting our bags over his shoulder and nudging us on. "Come on, let's get to the hospital."

For my whole life, I will never forget the look on the concierge desk clerk's face as we ambled out, Officer Drake a pace behind, my arm held tight to my body, a worried, disheveled husband at my side.

Quite the look for a stay-at-home mom of two.

Out front, the cop car sits in the half-circle drive, and Officer Drake opens the front passenger door first. "Jessalyn, I'd like you to sit up here," he announces, only looking at me for a moment before his eyes raise to Laws. "I'll need you to ride in the back."

The back.

My pulse skyrockets. "He can drive our car separately, can't he?" Do I sound like a lying victim to him? Does he believe us? God, my arm hurts.

"No, he can't. Mr Briggs, go ahead and get on in for me, sir," he says, not with condescension, as he pulls open the rear door. There's no reassurance in his voice though, either.

The car shifts as Officer Drake helps me into the seat, and a moment later, he's slamming both doors closed. We're alone in the car for a moment as the officer walks around the back of the vehicle, speaking to a hotel worker who stands at the entrance, hands cupped to mouth.

"It's going to be okay," Laws says, reassuring me. "If I go to jail, call Graham to come bail me out, okay?"

My eyes fill with tears. "You're not going to jail! This was consensual!"

He leans forward, his fingertips stroking down my arm. "Baby, listen, we know it was all consensual, but... they don't. Okay? So I might go to jail tonight and–"

Officer Drake opens the door and positions himself behind the wheel. The radio on his breast chirps with coded directions that my brain can't compute, and I don't know if it's the pain or if it's not meant for civilians, but I let my head fall back.

"We're going to go to Willowdale Hospital," he offers, tapping away on the keyboard mounted to the dash. He twists the wheel, and we're headed there, and I almost can't believe that our big night has turned into this. From the cupholder, the officer grabs a cellphone that illuminates silently, and answers.

I guess cops can talk on the phone while they drive. I wonder what else this guy gets away with?

"What?" he answers, and somehow he sounds less friendly to whoever is calling him than he did to Laws or I. I want to turn around and find my husband's eyes, speak wordlessly to each other, but my arm is killing me and moving isn't an option. The side mirror reflects a shining window, and I can't find Laws through the glare. "And that's my problem, *how?*"

A muffled voice comes through the line and while I can't hear what they're saying, I know it's another man. Lights dance over my lap as he drives us through the town, the hospital just a few minutes away. "Fine, but why did you call me now? You know I'm on shift." Another pause while the voice on the other end runs on. "Dude– I said fine. I gotta go, I'm rolling up to the hospital," he says as it indeed comes into view.

I don't know if he drove fast or if my nerves have time passing quickly, but either way, it feels like we flew here. I want my arm to get fixed, but I don't want to go inside the hospital yet. I'm not ready.

I'm... scared.

Officer Drake pulls up right in front of the double doors and throws the car into park, still on the call. I'm grateful for that call, because it's buying us a few precious seconds. Laws fingertips graze the back of my arm, a sneaky comforting touch. But I needed it. My eyes water, but I blink away the emotion.

"I'll tell her. I gotta go, Mally. Bye." He hangs up, rears back against the seat, and shoves his phone in his pants pocket. Facing me, he says, "Listen, Jessalyn, there's a nurse here I'm going to take you to see."

"Like a rape nurse? Oh my God, he didn't— we're just– it's not what you think! I swear!" I cry, tears streaming abundantly and freely down my cheeks. Behind his glasses, the cop glares at me. Twisting his gaze, he looks at my husband. "I'm going to take her in, and I'll be back."

Then he's out, moving around the car, and I'm panicking. I don't want to be separated from Laws, I don't want to be interrogated without him. I don't want any of this. And all the calming vibes I tried to muster back at the hotel explode, and my tears and fears erupt violently from me.

"Calm down, Jes, please, baby," Laws coos from the backseat, but his voice is rocky, too. "Let them fix you and just... breathe. Okay?"

Before I can respond and give him any assurances, put his mind at ease, Officer Drake is there, gently aiding my exit from the car. He doesn't hold me how Laws did as we made our way from the hotel room, rather, he hovers a palm at my lower back.

"Don't worry, okay? I just want to talk to your husband. And while I'm talking to him, there's a sort of specialist nurse you should talk to. And no," he says, "it's not a rape nurse."

Can cops lie? They can't lie, can they? If he says its not a rape nurse and this isn't some big trick to arrest Laws, then I should believe him, shouldn't I? I stop, and Officer Drake stops too, allowing me a moment to turn back.

Laws is pressed to the window, dark hair messy, hand pressed to the glass. One last look at the love of my life, and Officer Drake is ushering me inside.

"Where's Sam?" he asks an aged nurse sitting at the

nurse's station, eyes pinned to the computer in front of her. Without looking up, the woman waves an arm to the left. "Curtain 3."

He takes me back to curtain 4, and helps me sit on a table wrapped in medical tissue. "Sam will be right in, okay? I'm gonna go talk to your husband."

And he leaves, and I'm left with a dislocated shoulder, a stomach of nerves and a mind spinning out of control with what-if's.

Not the best night of our lives, after all.

Nineteen

LAWS

We need to talk.

In through my nose, out through my mouth. In through my nose, out through my mouth. I keep the calm, steady breaths going as Jes disappears inside the hospital.

Right about now, I wish Graham and I had a different relationship. And I don't mean I wish I'd been telling him about every blow job I ever got, either. More like, I wish I could call him and say, *don't ask, just get down here,* and not expect the inquisition. But if I go to jail, I'll call him. And that's going to be... fuck.

To be fair, if he called me and said *come bail me out of jail,* I'd never let him get away without telling me what happened. Never.

Fuck. This was such a bad idea.

I hurt her.

I fucking hurt Jes.

The consequences of my actions swarm me in the most unpleasant ways, not unlike bees. Hell, I wish I were caught in a swarm of bees. That pain would be fleeting. The ache of humiliation lingers far longer than a bee sting.

And fuck what people think of me. All I care about is Jes. How will her friends treat her? How will people look at her at the grocery store or at the school when she drops the boys off when the whole town finds out I was arrested the same night she *coincidentally* got her shoulder dislocated?

We'll have to move.

I'll have to sell AgDev. There's no way any of the good old boys in Oakcreek are going to give business (and more importantly, *money*) to a *wife-beating rapist.*

"Fuck!" I slam my fists into the grating in front of me, hating myself. I knew this was a bad idea. I knew it. When she caught me and I came clean, that was right. There was no escaping her knowing my truth. But *acting on it*? Letting her convince me that I somehow deserved to act on these dark desires? I don't deserve it. Look what I fucking did to her. "Fuck!" I shout again but before I can rail the back of the car with my anger, the door abruptly swings open, sending a rush of cool evening air into my face.

I suck it in, taking the edge off my anxiety as I look up at Officer Drake, one gloved hand gripping the top of the door.

"Don't fuck up my car," he deadpans. Tossing his head over his shoulder, motioning behind him, he says, "Come on, let's have a talk." He gives me room to step out, and as I rise, I'm met with a palm straight to the center of my chest. "Don't make me use cuffs, okay, man?"

I shake my head vigorously, my mind spinning even faster. I can't believe *I'm* the man that this Officer thinks could be violent.

Then again, *I was* violent. I *did* hurt my wife.

I get dizzy but refuse to be the jackass that faints as a result of his own stupid fucking actions. I'm grateful the bench is near as I sit down with a sigh. Officer Drake sits next to me, silencing his radio when it comes to life just as he begins to speak.

"Fucking thing. It never quits," he bemoans, then turns his torso to face me. I match his position and take him in. Really look at him for the first time, considering back at the hotel I was on the brink of heart attack. He's young. Early thirties, maybe. Jes's age.

Hell, he could be Jes's husband. I look at his hand resting on his thigh, and a gold ring glimmers on his ring finger. He's married.

So he must *really* think I'm a fucking creep. Think I stalked my wife then raped her. And hurt her, no less. Jesus Christ. I lick my lips, my tongue peeling from the roof of my mouth, everything so goddamn dry. I force myself to speak.

"Officer, I see you're married." I press my hand to my chest. "I love my wife. This is the weirdest fucking case of *'it's not what you think'* but I swear to Christ, *it's not what you think.*"

He narrows his eyes behind his frames, and I feel guilty even though I'm technically not. Not of anything criminal, anyway.

"It was consensual… roleplay, I guess." I scratch the back of my head and analyze the concrete beneath my boots. Concrete is not interesting but it also doesn't judge.

"Like, um, rape roleplay type of stuff? Consensual nonconsent?" he offers, tone almost... nonchalant?

"Yes," I say immediately, a little ashamed that my response is almost breathless. But yes, that's exactly it. "That's, fuck, that's exactly it. And... the ropes...' I shake my head because I have no idea how to explain it. But since I'm sitting with a cop in front of a hospital, I have to try.

"I like tying her up. I work with ropes, I'm good with ropes and seeing her in them, I just... I guess I've always wanted to see her tied up." Finally, I meet his gaze. I'm confused by his expression. He nearly looks... *understanding.*

"Sometimes, you want something even though it's wrong." He holds a hand up between us, eyes stern. "Not saying illegal," he clarifies. Then he tips up his baseball cap and scratches at his head. "But something... you feel you *shouldn't* want."

I nod. "Yeah. I shouldn't want to tie up my wife but I do." I snort at the truth. "She actually really likes it."

He tugs his hat down. "Listen, your wife is inside with a friend of mine. I think she'll be able to help you guys."

I raise my eyebrows. "Is she a lawyer?" It's partially a joke.

"She's a nurse," he says, annoyed. "Come on."

We take a few steps before he stops, and I nearly run into his backside. Which I think may hurt, considering this man looks like working out is his favorite thing to do. Show off.

He lifts his fist, a single finger outstretched. "I'm still talking to your wife with the nurse before you can come in." Gaze pinched, he studies me for a second then turns around, saying something into his radio. Inside, he makes me stand in a hall while he goes to interrogate my wife.

I can't believe he's in there saying things like, *You can tell me, don't worry*, and asking shit like, *Has this happened before?* because even if he really does understand and believe that it was just roleplay, still, he has to ask.

Hell, I want him to ask. I want him to give her the chance to disprove those things.

But it still feels like shit.

Minutes feel like hours, but then he whistles, and I go. She's not behind a literal curtain, but in an actual exam room. Officer Drake holds the door open, and it pricks on my skin that he was in a room with my wife where she could've been only partially clothed without me there.

When I meet her eyes, one step into the room, I see she is in a hospital gown, but her pants are still on. I don't like that he was here first. But I go to her, catch her face in my hands, and share the most desperate kiss of our lives. I swear, we must look insane.

But we had an insanely erotic day. We'd been emotionally edging for hours. All to end in an accident turned nightmare, we haven't gotten to process it yet.

There was no aftercare, and now more than ever I'm realizing just why aftercare is such a big thing. You're emotionally balanced with it, but completely off without it.

I'm off, more than ever.

She peels her lips from mine with a soft laugh. "I'm fine. She put my shoulder back in right away. Less than a minute."

I jerk back and stare down at her, in complete awe. "Are you on pain meds?" I question, because she looks so... good.

She shakes her head. "They don't give pain meds for this. Just Advil, or whatever."

"The off-brand," the nurse says. Then she turns to me, and peels off a glove before outstretching her hand. "Hi, Laws right? Nice to meet you. Anxious to meet you, actually because we need to talk."

I swallow, my mouth dry.

I shake her hand. "What's your name?"

She smiles. "Sammy."

Twenty

JES

Lesson learned.

Laws kisses me like our lives depend on it, and for a second it feels like they do. I didn't realize how much I needed the connection until our lips parted.

After Sammy introduced herself, he came back to kiss me, and now, when he stands back up, I see the grouchy cop is back in the room.

"Hi," I lift my hand to him, as if he didn't just interrogate me about the man I love most, eyeing me suspiciously. I swear once he even looked down at me over his glasses as he wrote in his little notepad. I wanted to slap that stupid thing out of his oversized hands.

He nods. He doesn't even verbally respond. Ugh. My focus goes to Sammy, whose hands are braced on her hips.

When Officer Drake brought me in just ten minutes ago, he was adamant I see Sammy. When she came into the room, she greeted him by Van, eyeing him knowingly, then turned her focus on me.

I wondered why I had to see her specifically but then she held me by the shoulders, looked into my eyes and said, "Honey, I'm gonna need you to tell me if you're in trouble."

I thought then maybe she was a trauma nurse and this protein bar with a baseball hat thought I was lying to him about us roleplaying.

I explained to her, calmly as ever, that we were roleplaying a fantasy involving force and rope play, and things went awry. She blinked at me. I blinked back because I thought it was a test. To assess my honesty or something.

Then she took me by the shoulders again and said, "We need to talk."

I think the first five minutes of our talk was just her questioning me on what happened, what we'd done in the past, and how I was feeling. I realized she was proving to herself that I wasn't actually a victim, but early on I could see my truth in her eyes. She nodded along, sometimes even shaking her head knowingly, and in her presence, I somehow knew it would be okay.

I calmed down, and then she told me a whole lot of things while fitting me for a sling. Things that... quite frankly, made me teary eyed. To know this accident won't ruin our lives, to know that there are things to be learned and that this happens to people often—that we didn't ruin our ability to indulge, but we do have work to do. It was all so enlightening.

She asked if she could speak to Laws about all of it, and I

nearly leapt at the idea. She warned me, though, that the officer would be giving me a full interview about the evening.

And he did.

But now, Laws is here, and he's about to hear a lot of things he needs to hear. The first thing being, it's not *his* fault.

"You're both kinda stupid," the plucky nurse says, arms folded across her chest. "Laws, it's not your fault and Jes it's not your fault. You're both at fault for taking on a big scene outside your comfort zone with very little experience living the kink."

I chance a glance at my husband, whose eyes are wide. "I'm sorry, what?"

Now her hands are on her hips, and as she steps closer, I feel the stupidity of what we did, more than ever. "The scene. The rape," she whispers the 'R' word, protecting us from whoever roams the hall near the door. "You guys haven't been doing it for more than four months and you decided you'd try two ties at a hotel room after teasing each other all night?" She slices her hand through the air. "I don't want to hear how you had safe words and tap-outs. You shouldn't be doing anything elaborate anywhere but your home base for a while."

She said this before, when it was just us, and I didn't get a chance to ask exactly why, so I do now. And I think Laws could better understand this. His face is so twisted up. He's aged a year, still looks even better, stress and all.

"Why not?"

Her eyes come to mine, and the seriousness she imparts with just one look is impressive. I see a ring on her finger.

She's probably got her partner wrapped around that ring finger.

"So if you have an accident," she says, drawing the words out slowly, and they sting as it is. Because *this* is why, *clearly*. "You're home and don't risk legal repercussions. Among other things."

"Makes sense," Laws says in a very light laugh, one that makes my stomach clench. He likely thought he hurt me and he'd be going to jail. I can't imagine how he must be feeling, but I want nothing more than to know.

I can't wait to be alone with him again and talk out this entire mess.

I know now where it went wrong. We were doing too many big things at once. Sammy is completely right.

"I live the lifestyle," she announces, making Laws startle. I notice that the cop doesn't bat an eye, and I wonder... are they married? Oh, wouldn't that be too good. I can't help myself. I waggle a finger between the two of them, despite the big space.

"Are you two...?" I leave the question hanging.

The officer snorts. "Gross. No."

"Gross?" Sammy says, folding her arms over her chest. "You didn't think I was gross when we were thirteen and you wanted to take me to the movies."

"I wanted to put my soda in your big purse. Get over yourself."

Sammy rolls her eyes, and turns back toward us. "He's my husband's best friend. And normally his beat partner. And we've been friends since we were like, twelve." She shrugs. "Small towns."

"Anyway, I live the consensual nonconsent lifestyle with

my husband. We call it a lifestyle because of how seriously we take our rules. We've had accidents before and we learned very quickly to respect the kink, whatever it is. Learn it, live it, breathe it. Explore its ins and outs, what works and what doesn't, and do the good things over and over."

She shakes her head. "It takes at least a year before you should be trying anything wild. And a public scene?" She shakes her head, dark eyes wide with shock. "Bad idea." She faces only Laws now, and my pulse quickens. "You could have been arrested."

His head falls. "I know."

She sighs, and says, "Look, I can help you guys. But this is a warning. What if there's a next time and I'm not here? Van's not on call? Not everyone is cool about this stuff. Most people don't even know what we like," —she motions two fingers amidst us— "is a thing at all. So you can never, ever be too careful."

"Lesson learned," I say, reaching for my shirt on the bed.

She pulls out a notepad and clicks her pen, tip hovering over the surface as she blinks at me across the room. "I'm going to give you some resources. I want you to use them. One of them is a paid membership to a community full of people who live their fetishes, it's worth the money." She scribbles and my heart races.

I came here depressed, thinking we would never be able to live this kink again, to give Laws all the things I know he so desperately needs and we're going to leave here better off. A bumpy road and a sore shoulder, yes, but... better off.

I look at Laws and realize I may have to convince him of that. At first at least. He's frowning, and pale, and my heart literally throbs that he feels so at fault and ashamed. It's practically radiating off of him. Sammy eyes me, then Laws, and clears her throat.

She rests her hand on his forearm, getting his eye contact. "It's okay. You had the easiest of accidents. No broken bones, didn't get arrested, and Van says nothing in the hotel room was broken." She cracks a smile. "Not too bad overall."

"I would like to have had none of it happen," Laws admits.

"But it did. So learn, take these resources," she rips the paper off, and hands it to him. "My husband and I are active members in the CNC community here. So you'll likely see me if you join." Her eyes come to mine now, head tipping to the side. "Join. Kink can be confusing, even to the most skilled there are still times when emotionally it can be hard to... reconcile. Communities help. Honestly."

I nod, wondering what's on the paper, but excited to see.

"You know," she says, tucking her hands into the pockets on the front of her scrub top. "Once you're more experienced and have things a bit more figured out, you can do public things. You just need someone to stand guard, in case. There always has to be a safety in case, no matter what."

"You... you mean like, someone standing watch who knows what we're doing?" I cringe at that idea.

She nods. "Yeah. And as cringe as you are thinking that is, isn't one trusted person knowing much better than the situation you're in now?"

I blink at her, horrified at the idea of having... who? Ruthie stand by? God, she'd never let me hear the end of it.

"Does someone stand guard for you and your husband?" I ask, curious.

From the corner of the room, with his back against the wall, boots crossed at the ankle, head tipped down, Officer Drake lifts his hand silently.

"Small town," Sammy says.

I snort.

"Anyway, real life isn't like a porno or a romance book. You can't just be a shibari master because you tie up trees, man. I get it, but it's just not the same. And likewise, you guys can't be having public scenes where the cops get called. Ever. It's not cool. When your kink is public in that capacity, you force other people to partake just by witnessing. And that's not consensual for them."

From the corner, the cop adds, "What she said."

"So public stuff is outside, but not near people. Think, parked car on a relatively empty street, with your lookout parked a few cars behind." She tucks a piece of dark hair behind her ear, then pops a piece of gum from her pocket, no big deal. "Stuff like that. Just don't subject people to be a witness to your show. It's not fair."

"That's... we never considered... God," Laws rubs his forehead, "I'm... I don't know, I'm sorry?" He faces me, expression pained. "I'm sorry? I don't even know what I was thinking."

"Me either, though," I add, because in truth, this was my idea. I remind him of it. "Laws, I planned this. All you did was go along with it. I thought we were ready—"

"We both did or else we wouldn't be here," he says, and it's true. If I really didn't want this, I wouldn't have planned it, and if he was truly in fear that we'd have a situation on our hands, he would never have gone along with it. That's not how our relationship works.

Van's radio chirps, and it breaks the dense silence that settled momentarily. "I gotta go make a call. Sam—you discharging them?"

She nods. "Yeah, they'll be ready in five."

I look at Laws. "When he drops us at the truck, do we need to go back inside the hotel for anything or can we just get straight in and head home?"

He kisses my forehead, and cups the back of my head. "We'll go straight home, baby. Straight home."

And for the first time in a few hours, I feel totally at ease.

LAWS

How do you feel about five?

The drive back to our place, which should only take half an hour, takes nearly one full hour. My mind is everywhere, and I'm so distracted that I force myself to be gentle with the gas pedal and stay focused on the road.

We talked. I started. Because I had to look at the road, knowing I didn't have to soak up every morsel of understanding I knew I'd find in her gaze made it much easier to be honest.

First thing I did, clutching her hand across the cab, was apologize. For hurting her. For trying two ties at once, which I realize now I had no business doing. Trees aren't humans, and understanding how to rig Jes is different. I should've known that.

Arbor rigging took me years to learn, too. This is something that requires more finesse and skill, and I went for a big move after just a handful of months.

I apologized for not checking in; at no point did I ask for a color. For losing the shears, for cutting her clothes, shit... I think at one point I apologized for knocking over the lamp. Once I started, I couldn't stop.

I apologized a lot, and she only tried to stifle me the first time. I raised my voice, and I told her that I needed her to hear it and accept it. I think we both knew that was more for me than her, my personal aftercare, but again, Jes is a giver.

Then I explained how I felt, because as we have learned in our research thus far, communication is key. And it's kind of funny because we're good in the communication department when it comes down to it. We've established safe words, talked about the things we don't want and the reasons why we don't want them, and have been good about talking about the scene during aftercare, to make sure everything is always addressed.

We just got complacent, we both felt overly confident—I know I did—and in turn, we overlooked some major things. *Like practice, time and patience.*

I told Jes I was disappointed in myself for always telling the boys that practice is what makes a man good at something, not luck. And here I was, thinking of myself as the lucky man whose wife lets him enact his ultimate fantasies with her. Really, though, I hadn't practiced enough and my ego led us to disaster.

She raised her voice a little with me when I said that, telling me that she wouldn't agree to that. "*Our* egos, our excitement, *us,* Laws, that's what I've been trying to make you understand from the start. Jesus. What you want is an *us* thing, not a you thing. Tonight was us. Both of us, okay?"

There have only been a handful of times in our marriage that I've ever heard Jes raise her voice out of anger. I'm the one that loses my cool and gets frustrated with the boys over stupid things like not picking up their schoolwork off the table all weekend or leaving clothes strewn about their floors for days. Jes is one of those quiet parents, soothes with her soft voice and calms with her caring demeanor. Once she yelled at Lex but only because he terrified her by sticking his wet finger right into an electrical outlet.

He got shocked, but he was okay. But that's the last time I can remember her really yelling, and that was out of fear.

On the drive home, it started as a raised voice but quickly turned into what I could see was a frustrated shout.

Frustrated with me, and it had not a goddamn thing to do with how the evening went. It was how hard I'd made things, how much guilt I had. It was on the drive that I realized that I'd been making her feel guilty and salacious, too.

I apologized, again, to her, and promised from then on out, I'd handle it all as an us, rather than bearing the burden of my fears myself. I admitted to her that I didn't like breaking the contract with the photo.

"Why didn't you tell me how you felt that night?" she asked, tipping her head to the side, expression full of empathy. The woman who just had her shoulder popped back into the socket and was wearing a sling because of it, was feeling bad for *me*.

I laughed, because the truth was kind of funny, and with the night we'd had, funny was a must. "I mean don't get me wrong, I *wanted* the picture of my hot as fuck wife." She laughed, and then we both just fucking cried laughing for the last few minutes of the drive. She wiped tears from the corner of her eyes, and I don't know if we laughed over the fact that the big head relinquished control to my little head, or what.

But the laughing was cathartic, and now, I lock up the garage and mudroom doors as Jes kicks off her shoes and flicks on the kitchen lights, a more somber me has taken over again.

I'm glad we talked. I am.

But I'm feeling the drop. It's a lot like that first time we experimented—again, foolishly—without any rules or parameters set. And afterward, we both went to bed feeling empty and terrible because we didn't balance the emotional scale for how much we'd tipped the physical. What I'd done to her body—physically, it was a lot.

We didn't handle it, and we experienced severe emotional drops. Valleys so low that I'd wondered if I'd ruined the best thing to happen to me—my marriage to my best friend.

That's how I feel now, watching Jes plug her phone into the charger in the kitchen. The rest of the house is dark, and the boys are still with my parents. After all, we should be having the most intense sexual experience of our lives right now. In a hotel room.

"Quit thinking about what happened and let's have a nice night," Jes says softly. I abandon my train of thoughts, because I promised her I'd treat this as an us thing, and secretly thinking about how fucking shitty I feel for what I did isn't going to help.

"I'm feeling..." I struggle to articulate myself, though I

know what I feel. Low. Down. Inexplicably depressed. "Shitty."

A moment later she's in front of me, her petite hand sliding up the side of my arm, her touch so fucking reassuring and gentle that my head falls forward, and she caresses my cheek as I lean into her touch.

"We're home," she whispers, but then... she flicks the top of my ear. I pull my head from her and find a cheeky grin on her lips. The curve of her smile makes my cock ache. The despair and depression I felt less than a minute ago is draining from me. "So let's have a good night." Her fingers find my neck and sifts through my hair. Her nails teasing my scalp have my groin pulsing, and I draw her close to me with both arms, holding her tight.

"What do you want, Jes?" Our lips move against one another because our faces are so close. The warmth of her breath on my lips has me fucking throbbing.

"Pain," she says simply, our eyes connect and as we breathe together, I seem to understand exactly what she wants, and why.

We need a release. She releases all her body's tension and her brain's discomfort when she's dealt pain. She looks like a fucking goddess doing it, I might add. And I have this part of me, a masochist I suppose, that needs to inflict that pain. Equally, that pleasure. It's a heady, powerful thing and I... I'm at the point where I'm comfortable admitting: I need it.

I need it to feel balanced.

She slides her hand into mine, and my instinct is to close my fingers around hers. To grip her tight. She tips her head against my tricep, and it makes my chest tighten. We walk slowly through our home, up the stairs, in no hurry, and go to our bedroom.

After everything we've been through, we're doing this tonight. It feels symbolic of something bigger. Like our commitment to honor our deepest needs, no matter how hard they are to talk about.

Not just sexual, of course.

But sexual too, because holy shit—my wife bought a dildo and I didn't know about it. That's... I don't want that. I want to watch her use it, for fuck's sake. I want pictures of her using it when I'm away. But I don't want to be living in a home where there's a rubber cock in a shoe box that I'm unaware of. No. Not happening.

She takes her clothes off, places the sling on her bedside table, and I close and lock the door, out of habit, but maybe also out of ritual. A step we take that starts the scene. She doesn't stop me, and it's a good habit to keep, even if it's not needed tonight.

Seeing her completely naked, strawberried skin along her wrists and neck, and a little pink around her ankles, my dick gets hard. Or maybe it was already, but I feel it pulsing against my thigh as I take her in.

"You're fucking gorgeous, you know? The most beautiful woman ever."

She rolls her eyes, flipping her hair over her shoulder. "I am not, shut up."

I shake my head at her, because I've never been more sure of anything in my life. "I'll shut you up with my cock in your mouth because you're saying some crazy shit right now, baby."

She giggles, and I shuck off my jeans and hoodie, but not

working too fast. We're not engaging in a full scene, but I am giving her a healthy dose of dirty talk, that's for sure.

But I know she likes it. When I slip my fingers into her panties after I talk to her this way, she's always drenched. Fuck, I want to come at just the thought of how swollen and wet she gets.

"Do you want my hand, or the whip?" I ask, my voice husky but soft, letting her know I'm ready to start. Ready to make her feel good. Ready to hear her cry out for me.

I think that's what I've come to learn about loving the dominant role. I like inflicting some pain or discomfort because I thrive when I get to care for her. We both feel more connected than ever.

It's... wild. What I thought was my worst nightmare has been maybe the greatest blessing. In disguise, of course. With a stop at the hospital along the way, but still. A blessing.

"Your hand," she whispers, and then she's out of my grasp and leaning over, her creamy ass making my mouth water. I love taking her from behind this way, driving my tongue into her pussy while I hold onto her ass. But right now, she needs something else.

"How do you feel about five?"

She nods, swinging her hair so it's off her back. The curve of her spine sends a jolt of lust down my body, landing like an explosion between my legs. My balls ache, my cock bobs, opaque beads pulsing at the slit.

I stroke myself once and choke on my moan. Her pussy lips are flush, swollen, the center shiny from her arousal. Arousal that would feel so fucking slick against my fingers, taste so sweet on my tongue. Arousal that, right now, I can't indulge in.

I hit her across the ass, hard. She yelps as she starts to topple forward, and I reach around her rib cage to stop her fall, protecting her shoulder. She hums in appreciation and leans back towards me, wiggling her ass, a whimper in her breath as her ass heats and turns an angry red. I know it hurt.

It's meant to hurt so it can feel that much better. It just can't hurt too bad.

"Remember your safe words," I remind her. Before our talk on the drive home, I probably wouldn't have said anything. I didn't want to kill the mood, or ruin the scene. But I realized that I need to hear her consent or remind her she can opt out. Maybe a few times throughout each experience, but I need it. For my peace of mind as her husband and her dominant.

She agreed.

She nods and whispers over her shoulder, "I know, baby."

"Color?" I rasp, and I get the breathy response, "Green."

I release her torso to stroke myself, then hit her again, just as hard. She doesn't move quite as much on this one, but she still has to adjust to prepare for the next bracing with her uninjured arm.

Her pussy glistens, arousal coating her thighs now. Everytime she readjusts, it spreads, and she's getting wetter by the second. Striking her for the third and forth times, I pause.

Sweat glistens on her skin, and her shoulders bob a little with her jagged breath. Enduring pain is work, but watching her do it is a fucking pleasure.

I'm stroking myself as I stare at her red-stained ass, plump and perfect. "Five, and I'm fucking you."

She nods, her chin coming to her shoulder. "Make me your wet fuck hole already."

I don't know what it is about that phrase that turns me into a barbaric deviant but fuck, it just does. My hand comes down across her ass, and she screams in response. I grab her hips and spear into her, earning me another scream, this time huskier. Because now, it feels good.

Gripping the tops of her ass cheeks, I massage her where I've spanked her, and drive my hips into her in timed strokes.

I know after impact play, she needs slower sex, slow but deep, too. So I fuck her that way, the way that makes her toes curl and her eyes roll closed. I can't see her face but I know she's getting just what she needs, as her head falls forward and her ass presses against me.

"Laws," she sighs, her voice shaky, trembling with need. "I'm gonna come," she moans, and there's not a chance in hell I can hear her say that and not immediately feel the same way. It's impossible.

"*Fuuck*," I grind out, still kneading the darkening handprints on her ass, making sure the skin no longer stings. But she's not concerned with that now, and she moans loudly as her orgasm begins.

"Laws, Laws, *oh God*," she mumbles, her cunt tightening around my cock like a fist. Fuck, the way she spasms around me while doing these tiny little movements—it's so intense. I never last more than thirty seconds.

She feels that good.

"Come, baby. Back that ass up and come on my cock like the filthy little whore you are. My dirty slut. All. Fucking. *Mine*." I rasp, my voice husky, barely hanging on. She clenches around me again, milking me, like her cunt is ravenous for my cum.

I remember when we were trying to have a baby.

All the times I'd whisper to her, "I'm fucking my cum into your hungry little pussy." I feel that way now, without the urge for offspring. Only the desire to own her orgasm in some primal, *see what I can make you feel* type of alpha way.

Her ass wiggles as she rides out the last of her orgasm, and that's as long as I can hold off for.

I come in rhythmic pulses, so hard that my vision goes blurry momentarily as I grip her hips and fold over her.

I'm buried deep as I fill her, and she pants my name as I do.

And even though it's after midnight, somehow, the evening seems redeemed.

Twenty-Two

JES

I'm going to tease you with the photo of your own spanked ass.

I wanted to feel him, warm and sticky between my legs, damp in my panties. So I told him no bath, which is sometimes part of what we do after. Instead, he rubbed me down with lotion. Now, we're cuddling and I am admitting something I'd realized while being spanked.

"I don't even think it's being spanked, for me, as much as it is, *you showing me what you need.*" I pause, attempting to make sense. "The biggest good guy on the planet." I sigh as he strokes his fingers through my hair, my head on his chest. 'It's just so... *hot*, knowing you have this side and need these things." I say, feeling so silly but I don't know how else to describe it. But I don't want him to misunderstand me, so I attempt to make sense of it beyond *that's hot*.

"You've always been really good in bed. Always. But the other side of you. That side of you is desperate for power and he's somewhat ruthless. I guess what I'm saying is, somewhere inside me, I was dying to be a damsel in distress. And now I can be."

"And I'll rescue you," he says into my forehead, still stroking my hair.

"Yeah, you will… you do," I reply, letting my eyes close. "I like when you use your hand because I get to feel the two versions of you that way. I get to feel the strike of the Laws that needs control and pain, and then when you hold me and touch me softly afterward, I get the Laws who loves every part of me."

"But the actual impact," he starts, fingertips trailing down my arm. "You actually like it, don't you?"

I stroke my fingers along his bare chest, twining my fingers in the coarse hair he keeps nearly trimmed. He leaves some, though, because years ago, one of the first times we got naked together, I told him I like the hair on his chest, that it reminded me that I'm dating an older man.

I think that reminded him that he was dating a twenty-two year old, but he has groomed himself the same way all these years. And I still love it.

"I do. I really, really do." I can't believe it really, because the wildest things we'd ever explored before were anal sex and face sitting. But I do like it, and I love being the person to bear his secrets and experience his pleasure.

"How about our luck tonight, huh?" he says, cricketing his feet with mine beneath the blankets. "Getting a cop who is the lookout for a couple who likes rape roleplay, too." He shakes his head.

I shrug. "Small town."

"Yeah," he chuckles, stroking his fingers up through the top of my hair as we settle more comfortably into the pillows. "Small town."

A thought crosses my mind as I adjust against Laws, the comforter grazing my bare ass, still tender. "Hey," I say, sitting up, disrupting our comfort and descent into sleepiness. "Before we go to sleep, I want you to take a photo." I lick my lips. "Of me."

I want a photo for both of us. I know Laws will look at it, and the idea of him looking at a photo of my marred flesh—pinkened from his hand—and getting hard? Maybe even filling his hand with his thick, long dick and making himself come all over the shower wall at the thought? It makes me wild.

But it's symbolic, and we both know it.

He felt we'd called a bad omen into our lives by breaking the contract. We discussed at length that yes, the contract is very important but so is pleasure. We want this, and adjusting the contract to better reflect our needs is something that has to be done when living a kink. Kink is customisable, and tastes evolve over time. We have to communicate and *keep* communicating. We can't be complacent again. We have to grow *together*.

And there's no such thing as a bad omen or ill luck. We make choices and those choices have consequences. That's it. A photo doesn't change our fate.

"It's okay, you know?" I reassure him, but when he reaches to the nightstand for his phone, keeping his eyes on me, I realize we're on the same page. He smiles.

"Turn around."

I turn, arching my back to make my ass pop. With my elbow out, fingers tangled in my hair, I look back over my shoulder and our eyes lock as a seductive smile sweeps us both.

He groans and when I hear the phone slide against the nightstand, I turn back around and flop down into his arms.

"How'd it look?" I ask.

He pinches my nipple. "Hot. It looked... fucking hot, Jes. And I'm not going to show you right now. I'm going to wait until you're begging for a scene, desperate to play, and then I'm going to show you, and I'm going to tease you with the photo of your own spanked ass."

I sit up, staring down at my husband who so easily rumbled that delicious warning without so much as batting an eye.

"Wow." I shake my head, loving the smirk on his tired lips. "That was a mix of Laws and *Laws*," I say, emphasizing that the second is a different man, the man that likes rope and surprise. "I like it."

He pats his chest, and I lay back down against him. "You know what? I like him too." He yawns, and those are contagious, so I yawn too. "And I have you to thank for it all."

My eyes close, the hum of his voice rocking me toward sleep. "Thank yourself for not locking the office door."

He laughs, and it's the last noise either of us make before falling into a warm, deep sleep.

Twenty-Three

LAWS

I like you in that shirt.

Aside from the gnawing chirp of your alarm, the second worst way to wake up is your phone ringing with the work ringtone.

I scrub a fist over my eyes, taking a second to calibrate. My ringing phone isn't just waking me, it's grabbing me by the throat and tearing me out of bed. I was in a deep sleep. The deepest fucking sleep I've had in years.

I grab my phone off the side table, anxious to answer and not wake Jes. But when I press the phone to my ear and say a groggy "Hello?", I sit up in bed to find Jes's side neatly made. On her night table, her clock reads eleven fifteen. Holy shit! It's nearing noon?! I haven't slept in on a Saturday morning like this since I was in high school.

My legs are hanging off the side of the bed in a panic as Greg's voice comes across the other line. Immediately, as he begins to speak, I wonder - did everyone find out? Is it everywhere? Laws and Jes Briggs at the ER last night, a cop with them. I can fucking hear it now.

"Hey, you there, man?" Greg asks after I ignore the first question. I tune in, pinching the bridge of my nose.

"Yeah," I say, forcing a rough exhale to steady my anxiety. "I'm here. What's up?"

"You okay?" he asks, voice thick with concern. "Did I... did I wake you, Briggs?"

I shake my head. "I'm up. What's up?" Until I know what this call is about, I'm not going to be able to stop my racing heart. Or thoughts. I may not have been arrested, but now that light is shining into my eyes through the windows and there's not an intimate moment to be whispered with Jes, reality is here and now.

My actions, though not arrested, may be enough to ruin me. And I have to be ready for that.

"I got kind of a weird question," he starts, and my pulse skitters, my stomach lurches, and I stare at my bare toes curling into the shag rug on the hardwood.

"Yeah?" My voice is hoarse as shit.

"Would it be super inappropriate for me to ask Jes's friend Penny out for a cup of coffee?"

"It's not—" Wait, what? "What?" I ask, his words not quite making sense. Did he ask about... "Penny?" I question, sounding like I've never heard of her due to my extreme whiplash.

"Jes's friend, Penny. I've met her a handful of times at the boys' birthday parties and stuff."

"Yeah," I nod, "I know. I'm just..." self-absorbed. "Surprised, is all." I scratch the back of my head as I stare down at my feet. "Penny has a partner," I say, though I've never loved Garth, still, they're together.

"I just ran into her at the grocery store this morning. Addie called and needed some things for breakfast and invited me over."

"That's good, that's a step in the right direction," I hear myself saying just as I realize what he's asked. He wants to know if it's weird to get coffee with Penny. "But... you want to work it out with Addie still, don't you?"

There's a pause and it hits me then that maybe Greg knows about Addie having... well, already moved on.

"That's not in the cards. She's... moved on. Anyway, I'm not asking about Penny for any reason other than a friend."

A friend? Penny has friends. And I don't think Garth would like that. "Penny's–"

He doesn't let me finish, and I'm relieved. I'm still trying to wrap my mind around the fact that if Greg isn't calling to question me about last night, there's a great likelihood that we are, as nurse Sammy said, *Fucking lucky*.

"She was crying, in the middle of the grocery store, staring at this package of soft cheese. Boursin, I think. And I mean, I recognized her and even though she didn't see me, what was I going to do? Walk away from a woman crying?"

I shake my head. "Fuck, that's brutal. What did you say? What was wrong?"

He clears his throat. "She split from Garth and it had just happened a day before. She was feeling really... raw," he says, almost as if he's explaining it from her perspective, understanding and gentle. "She kept saying how embarrassed she was but I reassured her that I knew just how she felt. And she said, I highly doubt that, and I said, actually, I'm going through a divorce and I just found out my wife has a boyfriend who is..." he clears his throat, "moving in with her and my son at the end of the month."

"Oh fuck, Greg. I didn't know. Jes heard something yesterday but didn't know that. I'm sorry, man, that's fucking rough." I can't imagine another man sleeping under the same roof as my boys, and my blood boils for my friend.

"Well, anyway, I just wanted to see if it would be weird to ask Penny out for coffee?" He sighs, and I hear him dragging a hand down his face. "I haven't sat with another woman and talked in... years. But I think we could both benefit from spending some time with someone who gets it."

I nod. "I think that's a good idea." I cast a sideways glance at the bedroom door, wondering if Jes would think this is a good idea. Wondering... where Jes is at all? "Want me to run it by Jes and call you back?" I ask.

He chuckles. "Nah, that's okay. If you think it's not a bad idea, then I'll roll with it."

"Alright, well, shit man. I'm sorry about Addie." I don't know what else to say, because I am sorry he's not getting what he wanted. "You never know though, Greg," I tell him, rising up from the bed to stretch my spine. "Life may not look just how you pictured, but I see you being happy."

He chuckles again. "Optimistic asshole. Alright, well, I gotta go. I'll see you on Monday. And I'll let you know what she says."

We end the call, and I leave my phone on the night table before heading toward the door to find my wife. Once I pull it open a crack, noise and life rush up the stairs, flooding my ears.

Jes is laughing, and so are the boys. They're home. I glance back at the clock to verify I wasn't sleeping when I read the time earlier. It is indeed nearing noon. I'm sure my parents dropped them off at ten in the morning so they could make their bridge game.

I hear the plastic clattering of Legos, and Lex's triumphant cheer at finding the right piece and more soft laughter from Jes and Des.

At the bottom of the stairs, I stop to take in the sight. The dining table covered in Legos, my sons' hair sticking up everywhere from a night of fun, music playing softly from the Alexa in the kitchen, traces of a late breakfast littered across the counter.

Jes's face is free of make up, her hair twisted into a bun atop her head, a few pieces stray around her face. She's got on an oversized AgDev t-shirt that falls nearly to her knees, I'm assuming because it was easier to get on over the sling but having her branded in my company logo stirs my possessive nature. Paired with tight black leggings and bare feet she looks goddamn gorgeous, and I have to run my knuckles along my sternum to dislodge the emotion that hits me at the sight of them.

"Morning," I call, grabbing their attention. The boys leap from their chairs, racing to me with open arms.

"Daddy!"

"Dad!"

I crouch and embrace them, knowing very well that Lex is close to being too cool for this. I savor every moment as I pull them in tight, inhaling the smell of pancakes and bedsheets. "Hey guys. How was Grandpa and Grandma's place?"

Lex peels back first, returning to his Lego creation, but Des stays in my arms, his fingers sticky against my bare chest. I threw on sweats but nothing else, and as I eye my wife, I see she appreciates my choice.

"Good," Lex says, settling back into his chair, feet tucked beneath his butt. "We got to eat pizza and Grandpa let us watch *Die Hard*."

I blink at him. "*Die Hard*... with Bruce Willis?"

He nods, like it's fine. "Yeah but we got bored and did a puzzle with Grandma instead."

Jes hides a snicker as she says, "It's a Christmas movie anyway."

"We went swimming and I got water in my ear but Grandpa taught me a trick to get water out. Do you wanna see?" He asks excitedly, escaping my arms to run to the center of the room. Dramatically, he whips his head from one side to the other, as hard as possible. "Grandpa says it always works but it makes you dizzy."

I watch him jerk his head from side to side. "I bet. Well, you got it out now, right?"

He nods triumphantly. "Yeah. You wanna see the castle I'm building?"

I get back to my feet and make my way to the table, a mess of brightly colored bricks scattered everywhere. From the rubble, Des grabs a small castle, and holds it up to me.

With admiration and pride, I tell him all of the things about his creation that I like, and I do the same for Lex's build—which, he says, is going to be a dungeon.

Then I finally get a moment with Jes, as the boys' attention goes back to their toys. Looping my arms around her waist, I press her into the fridge, and crush my mouth to hers. "Thank you for letting me sleep in."

Her breath brushes my lips. She smells like coffee and toothpaste, and somehow that makes me hard. I reach between us, adjusting myself, earning a toothy grin from her.

"I like you in that shirt," I whisper to her, explaining my situation. She pats my chest.

"Thanks. And I think you needed the rest. Why don't you head out to the patio and soak up some sun? I'll bring you a fresh cup of coffee." She rocks to her toes to press her lips to mine again. "Let's just enjoy the day."

Once outside, I settle into an Adirondack chair. One I built with Jes at my side, bare feet outstretched in the lawn, belly round with Lex. My fingers trace the grooved edge of the armrest and I take in the lush green lawn and the gentle swaying of the mature oak in our yard.

Whatever I'd envisioned life to be like as a married man and father, the truth doesn't even compare. Because I know I'm one lucky bastard to be this happy.

Tipping my head back, I let out a long sigh. It's from this angle I see a white envelope resting on the table between the two chairs. On the front, in the most beautiful cursive, is my name.

I reach for it, sliding a finger beneath the flap, letting the tri-folded letter slip free.

Spreading it open, I keep it pinched in my hands as my eyes find the start.

Lawson,

I debated on whether or not I should write this, after all, communication is key, right? And something about a letter feels like a cop out. Like I'm resorting to writing words that I'm too shy to say in person.

That's not true, though.

I wanted to write this letter for you. For you to be able to hold, to touch, to look back on when and if you will inevitably question things. For you to have something tangible to put your worries to bed.

I love you, Lawson Briggs. I love you for everything you give daily. Your friendship, your passion, your laughter and ease, your endless support. I love you and I love the life we've built together and the children we've made.

I never thought I could love you more than I did a few months ago. And when I found you in your office that night, I wondered if we'd break. If we'd found a fissure so deep it couldn't be repaired. Instead of break, we built. We stacked more bricks up together, building more and more around us, making it hard to take us down, to break us apart. Now consider this letter a way of strengthening the foundations of what we've built.

I gave you time, and you needed it, but you told me how you felt. You gave me a gift the first time we talked because knowing you completely is all I've ever wanted. To be your best friend and your wife, to know you better than anyone else.

Then you kept giving. You let me talk and ask and approach. You were open, putting aside all of the discomfort I knew you felt. You were vulnerable with me, Laws, and that hasn't gone unnoticed.

I love you for sharing. I love you for allowing me to love you that way, that personally, that intimately.

And now we have this new thing. Driven by need, desire

and passion, we both now want to roleplay. Want to indulge in those fantasies. I feel like I've been awakened. The pleasure I feel from the force, the shock, the dirty talk, the rigging, the surprise... all of it, I want it, Laws, and I'd never have known I wanted it if it weren't for your openness and honesty.

We've got a lot of learning to do, and I know there will be ups and downs. But this letter is for the lows. For when you need a reminder of why we push ourselves to explore our needs.

Because it brings us closer than ever and that's all I've ever wanted. To be as close to you as possible.

I love you. And I'm so honored to be your wife.

Love always

Jes

Folding the letter back up, I slip it into the envelope and keep it between my fingers. I don't want to set it down. In fact, I want to put it in my nightstand right now, to know it's safe, to know exactly where it's at so I can take it out and read it later.

Because I will.

It doesn't escape me that Jes could have easily pretended to try what I wanted and kindly backed out. Hell, the night where we sat opposite the bathroom door, she could have begged me to keep it to myself. There are about a hundred outcomes that could easily have come to be, but I'm living in the best outcome. The ideal reaction, the optimal result.

And I fought with her to get here, too.

I owe her a lot. And as she tiptoes onto the patio with a cup of coffee in her hand, I'm overwhelmed with how I feel. I pat my lap, and take the coffee from her, setting it aside. She settles onto me, but not before peering up at the boys through the window, making sure they're busy enough for us to have a few minutes alone.

My lips connect with her temple as I figure out what exactly I want to say. Her weight and warmth, paired with words far more eloquent than I could ever be, have me *feeling*. I wrap my arms around her, losing my lips in her hairline, along her forehead, down her temple, to her cheek. Then her lips sync with mine, and we kiss long and slow, our tongues dancing together to their own secret music. Every part of this exchange is intentional, meant to seal all that we've discovered and discussed in the last few months.

"Thank you," I finally say, once I'm fully hard beneath her and we're both breathing too hard for the patio mid morning. "I read your letter and thank you for everything you wrote and all you've done, Jes."

She just smiles.

"I know that it felt like I was hiding parts of me from you and... I don't know just how that made you feel, though I can guess. When I found that... toy..." I say, careful with my words because daylight and children are ten feet inside, "I just stared at it. Like, whoa, this is Jes's but more than that, I envisioned you thinking about it, searching for it, selecting one then anticipating it's delivery." I kiss the tip of her nose, then take her mouth again. "I didn't like that some part of you felt compelled to keep that secret. So I put that feeling on a really big scale, and I'm sorry for making you feel that way."

"It's okay. I mean, I understand. I'm just glad we're here." She gets off of my lap and peers back into the house again, her face softening as she presumably sees the boys. "Anyway, I meant what I said. You can stay out here and just... relax. I know last night was a lot and you deserve the morning to just decompress." She winks as she hands me my coffee. "How'd you sleep?"

I take a sip of the fresh brew. "Slept better than I have in years. In fact, I'm glad Greg called. I almost died when I saw how late it is."

Her expression shifts at the mention of his name. "How is Greg?"

I take another sip and lower the mug to the table, careful not to place it on the envelope. That letter is special to me.

"Greg wants to ask Penny to get coffee," I announce, because Greg didn't say don't tell anyone and also, I'm forty-four so I don't abide by grade school gossip rules. "Did you know Penny and Garth split?"

She winces a little, her nipples hard through the thin fabric of my old work shirt. "She texted me last night but since we were... busy," she grins, and I love that we can already start to laugh about our experience last night. Because we were so excited and foolish. It feels good, in some way, to still be able to be foolish and giddy at our age. That we still bring out the joy in each other. "But I called her this morning when I got up and yeah, I heard."

Despite the fact we're home and not near anyone, she whispers when she adds, "I always wanted her to leave Garth. I just didn't want her to do it like this."

I lift my eyebrows. "Like how?"

"Because he made her doubt herself so bad she had to leave!" she sighs. "There were things she wanted in the bedroom—"

I hold up my hand. "Listen, I'll talk about railing your pussy until I'm blue in the face. But I don't want to hear what Penny wants in the bedroom because chances are, she and Greg are going to get together. And Greg is my friend and my foreman. I don't want to know that Greg is doing whatever it is that Garth isn't. That's just not how it is with my friends. Okay?"

I could never look him in the eye if I found out he liked dressing up like a fox while railing Penny, or whatever is she wants. Hell, if he found out what I like? I'd likely never look him in the eyes again.

Jes leans down to give me a kiss before heading toward the sliding door.

"Hey, you wanna barbecue steaks tonight? We throw some corn on the grill and eat out back. Let the boys toss the football and have some wine?" she offers, one foot in the house, one out. I smile at her.

"As long as you don't lift a finger. Woman, you dislocated your shoulder less than 14 hours ago. You should have woken me up to help with boys this morning, and if I catch you so much as loading a mug in the dishwasher I'll spank you so hard you wont sit for a week." I say with a playful smile on my face. "But for dinner? Your plan sounds perfect. But I'll be cooking."

"Fair enough, husband," she smirks, turning back towards the door. "Oh and... Laws," she shouts back to me, "Penny wanted Garth to collar her. If I have to know, you have to know." And she darts back into the house.

"For fucks sake, Jes!" I mutter as I hear her laughing from inside. She may be a bit of a brat, but she's *my* brat. My wife. My everything.

Once she's gone, I drink my coffee and survey my yard, feeling more content than ever before. Turns out, if you're honest about what you want, there's a strong likelihood that your life can be exactly what you want it to be.

So simple and yet so fucking powerful.

I'm glad Jes helped me learn that lesson. And I'm even happier to have her to live my darkness with. In fact, my needs no longer seem dark and deplorable. They now seem exciting and hot, and again, like most other things in my life, I owe it all to my beautiful wife.

Twenty-Four

JES

ONE YEAR LATER
Seeing him that way makes me crazy.

"Ah, ah, ah," he growls, "you come off that cock when I say so, not a second earlier." With that, he shoves me forward and the dildo spears my throat, making my stomach clench.

A year ago, this would have likely made me vomit. But it's been a year of playing (and roleplaying) and I've learned a lot.

Right now, I'm glad one of the things I've learned is how to breathe through my nose with my mouth full. Under the spray of water, no less.

"Now," he grates, dragging me back off it. "Deeper." This time, he gags me on *his* cock, salty from being inside me.

He reaches out and a moment later, the water raining down on me turns icy.

I hiss in reaction, my core clenching and my nipples hardening as I go from comfortably numb to painfully aware. His grip in my hair tightens, making my face ache. "Take it all until I tell you," he warns, his tone dripping with unspoken promises. Reprimands in store for me if I disobey him. I gag, but lean into him until my nose is pressing into his groin. He smells like sex and him, and both things make me moan.

With his free hand, he swats beneath me, slapping my breast. He means it as a punishment, to fill my flesh with a sting so sharp that I mewl, audibly ache. And I do, because he'll fuck me harder that way, when it's time. The truth is, though, I've grown to really enjoy impact play with him.

I've learned that my skin doesn't react well with cheap leather, which is what most toys are made of. I've also learned that 'you get what you pay for' definitely extends to sex toys... and rope.

There's been a lot of trial and error, complete with a Google search history that would make anyone shy. But we've been honest, and open. And we've explored beyond his original needs, while always maintaining an element of the consensual nonconsent roleplay.

Sometimes he just ties me up and watches me flounder while he teases me. And on those nights, he comes right there in the bedroom, walking around my suspended body. Without touch or anything.

The sight of me bound is his Achilles' heel, his guaranteed trigger, and the way he melts for me always makes me feel so good.

Of everything we've tried and done, we've put our safe words to use a few times. And after the first time, I think we were both a bit jarred. But as we continued on, trying new things, we realized, it's part of the journey. Knowing what you don't like is as important as knowing what you do like, and understanding why we need what we need.

We've never understood each other more, because you never need to trust someone as much as you do when they're stringing you up bare, holding, in theory, your very life in their hands. They can do anything to you while you're tied up. Take anything from you. And when they don't? That's a bone deep trust.

"Turn around," he growls, spinning me to face the wall where the dildo bobs. "Choke on this while I take your ass." His hand comes down along my bare ass, and my entire body vibrates from the smack. My pussy throbs as he slides the blunt tip of his cock up the split of my ass.

"No," I whimper, but he shoves me forward, and I gag on the salty rubber dick. "No," I manage, as he jerks me off to let me breathe. He releases my hair and then his hands are gripping my hips with a possessiveness that makes me feral. A grunt followed by the most shameless noise of him spitting on his cock and then he's pushing inside me, one thick inch at a time. My ass burns, and somewhere low in my belly aches.

"Deepthroat that cock," he commands, still sinking deeper inside me. When he's all the way in and I'm aching all around him, tears stinging my eyes, he moves. Slowly, he strokes out and in, the head always staying inside. I can't believe it, but it does start to feel good. My pussy throbs from the pressure, and as the dildo tickles the back of my throat, I start to come.

Laws moves the tip of his finger between my pussy lips, and groans, holding his cock motionless inside my ass. "Look at that little cunt go," he says, drifting his finger through my lips again.

I come so hard I'm gasping around the cock, and I can't help it but my ass begins to bear down. There's so much pressure from my orgasm, I push back against him, but he lets go of my hip to slap my ass.

"No, no, you don't get to come and then kick me out." He bends down, his body heat melting off of him over me. "Open that ass and let me fill it, or you'll fucking regret it."

Panting, I relax myself for him, and he sinks inside quickly. I gasp around the cock in my throat, beginning to bob on it. Imagining it's him as he pumps into me from behind, nothing more than groans and curses.

The cold water feels welcome now, because I'm so fucking hot. From the inside out, I'm burning up, my body spasming around his, around the fake dick, twitching and pulsing.

But then he hits my ass hard, making me gasp and pull off the dildo, taking in a deep lungful of air with my head down when he slams into me full force. A heat spreads through me, and then he grunts, ragged and raw.

Jerking back, he slips out of me, his cum streaming down my thigh. I've come to realize that when I'm on my period, sex in the shower isn't half bad. I get the icky feeling of being sticky and messy immediately washed away, and I'm not forced to see a bloody mess—which was the big deterrent for me—it took me out of the mood.

Laws, on the other hand, is surprisingly into it.

He isn't exactly sure what it is about it he likes, but something about me streaking him, leaving him a little red and how sensitive and swollen I am during - it drives him mad. And seeing him that way makes me crazy.

And on his 46th birthday last month, I gave him something he'd been wanting for a while. A redo of our night gone wrong. The kids went to his parents house but this time, we stayed home, opting for an in-home scene.

He was the intruder.

And we had so much fun and being in the house alone meant we really let loose. There are some pieces of furniture I will never be able to look at in the same way again. I was defiled on so many different surfaces. He cuffed me, he fucked me, he held his cock above me as he streaked my body in his release. We laughed when he admitted he googled what he should say as an intruder in roleplay.

Trial and error, exploration with some paths leading us backward, but all in all, it's been one of the best years of our marriage.

And things were perfect before.

We even took the advice of that nurse and joined an online community of couples who like to engage in consent based roleplay. We started there, but are now active in other communities, too. Now when either one of us has an idea of something we're thinking of exploring, we log on to our shared Fetlife account and talk to people—see what to avoid, things to expect, safety precautions to take.

We've been active online for over eight months now, and even have plans to meet up with another couple at the end of the year.

"Pass me the soap," he says over my shoulder, the aftercare that I've come to adore already beginning. As soon as he's come, my raw version of Laws disappears, and an attentive, beautiful Laws returns. It's the best of both worlds.

I hand him the soap and we take a hot shower together, though the water is still turned to cold.

LAWS

ANOTHER YEAR
Where are your panties?

"She's just," I shrug, shaking my head as noncommittal as possible. "Under the weather. I'm gonna take her this," I say, lifting the can of 7Up. Addie nods, but I don't miss the way her eyes narrow on me just a second, as if she doesn't quite buy my bullshit.

I don't really care. I'm not selling it. She can take it or fucking leave it.

I push inside the bathroom, wait for the door to slowly seal closed, then twist the deadbolt. There she stands, fingers curled along the hem of her black skirt, green eyes pinned to me. "Anyone catch you?" Jes asks, chest heaving. I can see the dark outline of her areolas through her blouse, and I want to spank her because of it.

But we don't have time.

"Addie was going to check on you, I told her I was bringing you this," I hold up the 7Up before setting it down along the small stainless ledge above the sink. From my pocket, I produce the item I *really* came in here to give her.

She eyes it between my fingers and thumb, licking her lips. I close the distance between us, and plunge the plug between her lips, making her coat it in saliva. She moans around the plug, holding eyes, her green piercing gaze making my cock thrum.

Her eyes, always grounding me. Bringing our life together into focus, making me cherish everything we've been through together. How we've grown, how we've learned. How we play.

"Now turn around," I tell her, plucking the plug from her mouth with a pop.

Her fingers, still curled around the hem of her skirt, lift, exposing her pussy to me.

"Where are your panties?" I ask, and then she holds out her hand, shaking them.

"I took them off to get ready for you."

I pull her silk hair tie off her wrist and feed it into her bratty little mouth.

"Bend over."

She turns and bends at the waist, the split of her ass opening slightly, giving me a peek at her tight holes. And fuck is she tight. Sometimes I last a shameful amount of time. But right now, I'm not getting any. All I'm doing is putting her plug in.

In the bathroom.

At the church.

After a baptism.

Yeah, it's not optimal. But she teased me all morning at home. Sucked the head of my cock into her mouth, and fucking suckled me slowly for an hour. At one point, she just kept her mouth around me, not moving, just letting my dick rest on her tongue.

She was driving me wild.

Then she got up and said, "We have to go to the baptism. But bring my plug, and once we get there, punish me for edging you with it." Then she got in the fucking shower like that wasn't the most insane, but hottest thing ever.

Her plug glistens with spit as I find her hole and press it in. She does this breathy little gasp that makes my cock hard, but I have to ignore it. We won't be home with the boys squared away for literally fucking hours.

So we're edging each other until then.

I don't have a plug in. Watching *her* have a plug in is enough.

She spits out her scrunchie. "How's it feel?" she asks, dropping her skirt as she steps into her panties.

"Shouldn't I be asking you that?" I ask, tossing my tie over my shoulder to wash my hands in the small sink. She hands me a paper towel.

Her grin makes me throb. "You know how I feel. It's you I'm worried about, having to think about how good I feel. It must be agony."

I groan, drying my hands in the brown paper. "I'm going to take it out with my mouth when we get home. That's a promise. You better hope it prepares you for how savagely I'm going to own your ass later."

She pulls open the door. "Don't forget your 7Up," she says, stepping out.

I grab it off the counter and follow behind. Annoyingly, Addie is leaning against the wall. I guess I should be grateful she wants to know if Jes is okay, but ever since she and her boyfriend broke up and Greg and Penny started dating, she's been around more.

I think she believes we can talk Greg into going back to her, but the truth is, I wouldn't want him to go back to Addie. She cheated on him, but that's not even all. They could've worked through it, I think, but she was so unwilling to talk to him about anything.

I remember his face that day of the choir concert last year. I don't want to see my friend like that again. And he doesn't look like that now, not with Penny.

They became friends. That first coffee date led to many, and I think that's why they're so happy now. They built a solid foundation first, and love came second. They've only been dating a handful of months, but he's in love with her. I know this because he helped her move into a new apartment instead of watching the Super Bowl.

"I'm fine, really," Jes insists as I walk up and loop my arm through hers.

"Let's go find the boys, baby," I say, giving Addie a small nod to let her know we're taking off. I don't hate Addie for how she treated my friend because everyone makes mistakes, and everyone is entitled for a shot at redemption. I know that. But I can also not want her in my friend's life as more than a co-parent, too.

We wander through the groups of families, and spot Mae with their daughter tucked tight to her chest. Graham's arm is draped around her, a mile wide grin on his face.

Des and Alex are nearby, standing with a few other boys who have a frog—lord only knows where they've got it. But they're entertained and relatively quiet, and since the baptism is over, we let them play.

Small talk around the church leads to a long lunch out where we pass Graham and Mae's daughter around, reminisce about when the boys were little, eat too many french fries, and in general, spend a long afternoon with family and friends. It's great—and the entire time, I'm fighting a hard-on knowing that each time Jes wriggles in her seat, she's doing it to adjust the plug in her ass.

When we get home, Jes heads upstairs to change into sweats and set up a board game with the boys at the dining room table. After she's changed, they start the game, her agreeing to take my turn until I'm out of my dress clothes and in sweats, too.

Pushing open our bedroom door, my eyes fall to the pillow.

All the arousal I've been fighting all day comes to a head when I see the dark side of the satin case exposed. A grin curls my lips. Beneath the pillow, the tail end of blue-dyed jute sticks free. Our new conditioned rope for full-body ties.

After that board game and bedtime for the boys, it's on.

Officer Dononvan "Van" Drake has a book of his own! The first book in the Men of Paradise series, **Where Violets Bloom** is a stalker romance (an interconnected standalone).

Sammy, the helpful nurse from the second half of this book, has her own book, too. The third book in the Men of Paradise series (also an interconnected standalone) features Sammy and her brother's best friend Mally, who is also a cop. **With Force** is a CNC roleplay book of a different nature.

Both books are available to **read with your Kindle Unlimited membership!**

Resources

I'm no expert! Learn from Laws and Jes - engaging in and/or exploring any sexual art form or kink requires an investment of time - there's lots of learning before the fun!

Here are some of the places I visited while researching for this story.

https://www.shibariacademy.com/pages/ties

https://www.theduchy.com/tutorials/

https://shibarisanctum.com/category/education/tutorials/beginner/

https://jaderope.com/us/rope-bundles-sets/introductory-bondage-kits.html

https://www.etsy.com/shop/KinbakuStudio

Bonus Content

Want to know how things work out with Penny and Greg?

Sign up for my Patreon and check out their short story now!
   Patreon.com/DaisyJane

Want to know how Graham and Mae fall into parenthood?

Keep reading for an exclusive bonus short story!

Graham

Walk and sway. Walk and sway. Maybe that's how sashay was invented? Someone was walking and swaying and said, *hey, you know what? Let's call this sashay!*

Yawning, I *sashay* my way into the nursery, fully aware I'm having an internal one-sided conversation with myself about how the word sashay was formed. Sleep deprivation manifests itself in weird ways.

Slowly, like a sniper sucking in a breath for the big shot, I lower my daughter into her crib, sliding my hands from beneath her sleeping body as slowly as possible. *No sudden movements.* Hell, I've learned to not even take actual steps when I sneak out because my ankle might pop and undo an hour of *hardcore sashaying.*

Can't risk that. Moonwalking, because it's not just awesome but also silent, I exhale quietly with relief once I'm back in the hall. As slowly and quietly as ever, I make my way toward our bedroom, closing the door with impressively little noise.

Turning, I press my back to the door and let out the sigh I've been holding in for the last two hours. Because before the hour of swaying and rocking and singing, there was one whole hour of consoling. Shushing and back pats, leg bikes to get out gas, pointing out the window at all the colors of leaves —I played every card in my deck. And when I got through the deck and she was *still* crying, I reshuffled and started again.

Some babies just cry, and Mae and I are quickly learning our baby cries *a lot*. And to make matters a touch more stressful, Dahlia is also a light sleeper.

But finally, she's down.

"How are you?" I ask when I open my exhausted eyes to find my wife in the center of the bed, hair wet from her shower. She's wearing a nursing bra and pajama pants, and even though it doesn't seem like it would be sexy, it is.

She is sexy at all times, with or without trying. Simply put.

Watching your wife bring a child into the world is a fucking trip. At one point during labor, Dahlia was almost all the way out and Mae reached down and literally pulled her the rest of the way out of the birth canal, draping the baby on her chest.

Women are so much stronger than men, I don't care what anyone says.

But it wasn't just her strength during labor that has me falling in love all over again. It's every single moment since we came home with Dahlia six months ago. She's patient and loving, tender and sweet, but still makes time and space in her very overwhelming day-to-day for me and her friends and family.

My brother Laws warned me there'd be a dry spell after the baby was born, and rightfully so, there has been.

But around month three postpartum we started to get frisky again, and *holy shit*. Sex post-baby is fucking incredible. Raw and carnal, we make the most of every fucking second knowing a baby could stop the entire thing. She's wild and unfiltered, grabbing, sucking, licking, riding. She takes, moans, cums and it's hot as hell.

Tonight, though, neither of us have the energy for any of it. I swear.

Dahlia's been cutting teeth, and she's been taking it out on us.

Mae smiles, but it's riddled with stress and worry. "I'm okay, how are you? Thanks for taking over bedtime. I really wanted to work out this clogged duct in the shower."

I pad my way to the bed and flick on the baby monitor on the nightstand. Dahlia's crib is visible on the screen, and I glance at it quickly to make sure she's still alive and asleep.

I flop onto the bed and peer over at Mae, who has one hand cupped to her face in a yawn, the other clutching her right breast.

"Did you get it?" I ask, reaching down to cover her bare feet with the comforter.

"Thanks," she says, wiggling her toes beneath it. "And no, I didn't. And I'm trying to not freak out but I really don't want to get mastitis again." She sighs and lets her eyes fall closed as she summons a deep breath. Though when she exhales, I can see all her worries still etched into her forehead.

"Here," I say, reaching for my phone next to the baby monitor. "Have you Googled? Let's Google what else you can do." I drape my hand on her lap, and stroke her inner thigh as I thumb in a quick search and wait for answers to populate.

"Did you try the pump on the highest setting for twenty minutes?" I ask, reading off the first recommendation from the top webpage result.

I look over at Mae, who looks goddamn gorgeous even in her fatigue. She rolls her eyes. "Yes, Graham, I tried to get Dahlia to feed off that side all day, and I've tried the pump a thousand times. I've tried hand expression, I've tried heating packs, I've tried it all."

"Okay," I say calmly, knowing how much misery she was in with mastitis two months back. I don't want that again, either. "Let me see what Reddit says."

I don't see her but I know she rolls her eyes again. "And before you say don't, I'm telling you Mae, I've read some helpful stuff on there."

"About cars, maybe," she debates, but her voice holds no fight. We're both so tired, I don't even think we could argue right now if we wanted to. "But not about clogged milk ducts."

A moment later, I hold my phone out to her, screen glowing with my victory. An entire 247-comment thread about solutions to clogged ducts for those who do not or cannot take antibiotics for mastitis. "Boom," I say, and she surprisingly collects the phone from my hands.

I let her read, wishing I could do more to help her than Google shit. A moment later, she locks the phone screen and hands it to me, turning to get comfortable on her side.

"Nothing good?" I ask, reaching back to set the phone down. I check the monitor again and everything is okay, so I face Mae. "You could not have read *all* those responses that quickly."

She wrinkles her nose. "I read the top five. They had the most upvotes, so those are the responses most people agree with."

"Oh yeah?" I tuck my pillow beneath me and match her position, her elbow crooked, palm propping her head up. Lying on our sides facing one another, she smiles.

"Yeah. And guess what everyone says is the fastest, easiest way to unclog a duct?"

My head wobbles in my palm a little. "Not sure. What?"

She reaches up, releasing the clasp on her bra. The fabric covering her breast folds back, and I get hard at the sight of her naked tit. She's got great fucking tits and now that we have a baby, her areolas have gotten a little darker, nipples a bit bigger. And all of it is incredibly fucking hot.

"You need to unclog it, Graham." She taps her nipple and grins at me. "Get to sucking."

"What?" My head slips from my palm and I topple forward, crashing into her chest. She hisses, yanking back, thrashing in the pillows to sit up.

"Oww!" she complains, and despite how bad it likely hurts for me to headbang her breast with the clogged ducts, Mae still manages to scold me quietly, not to wake the baby.

"I'm sorry, I'm sorry," I say, scrambling to sit up in bed too. "I just, that surprised me."

She shrugs, pushing her hair behind her. She unlatches the other side of her bra, exposing both breasts to me. "You don't have to swallow it if you don't want to, but I need you to suck, and *suck hard.*"

"I..." I blink at my wife who, in the years we've been

together, has *never* been the bold sexual aggressor between the two of us. In fact, in the past, we've actually discussed that we both thrive from me being the deliverer of all the dirty words, from me taking control.

"It's not about sex," she amends, as if seeing the confusion on my face. "It's about my personal misery." She licks her lips, her eyes pleading. "I'm so uncomfortable, Graham. *Please.*"

I consider her request, and not because I won't do it because uh, fuck yes I will. In truth, sometimes when I walk into the room and she's feeding the baby and I wasn't expecting it, I linger a little. Watch for a few extra seconds. I've never admitted to Mae that something about watching her feed our child does things to me below the belt because it feels weird and wrong.

I shouldn't be tugging one out in the shower to the vision of milk leaking from Mae's breasts as she collects them with her palms, looking at me with seduction and desire. Yet, I have been doing that.

A lot.

I want to help her, but I see an opportunity here, and I'm not going to miss taking it.

"Okay, first, I want you to know, I will absolutely do it. I just reacted the crazy way I did because I was completely taken off guard."

She nods, excitement bringing color to her cheeks. She's excited to feel better, but I want to do more for her than that. I want to *actually* make her feel good. And I think it's possible.

Fuck, I'm already hard.

"But... I see an opportunity here, baby, and I'm gonna go ahead and shoot my shot."

She arches a brow, but remains quiet.

I look at her bare breasts, and my erection intensifies. Looking up to her eyes again, I grin. "I've kinda been fantasizing about playing with your tits while you're breastfeeding."

Her head tips sideways. "Really?" I love that her singular question bears no judgment or shame, just genuine interest.

I nod. "Really. I may or may not have been thinking of your tits a lot in the shower lately."

She flushes. "Graham..."

I scoot closer, and our knees touch. "If you don't want me to make it a sex thing, I won't. But if you're open to it, I'll unclog your duct and make you cum."

Her eyes go hazy and heady with just the mention of an orgasm. We've been having sex but not nearly as much as we'd like, and I know she needs more. I need more too. Now's a new opportunity.

"You... what do you wanna do?" she asks, her hand sliding up the ends of my pajama pants, over my bare calf. Goosebumps break out along my neck at her touch.

"I don't have a plan, but I just want to know if you'd be okay with me touching you while I *relieve* you?"

She nods, and removes her hand from the leg of my pants so she can pull her hair up. With it in a loose bun and out of my way, she slides off the bed and strips naked.

The pink and purple marks painted along her belly make me groan, gripping my hard cock through my pants. I loved her body before, but now? I'm possibly obsessed.

"Get naked," she commands. Obeying, I rise and hook my thumbs in my pants and yank them off before sliding back into bed.

On her back, completely naked, I sidle up next to her, balancing my body weight on an elbow, surveying her beauty.

"God, baby, you are so fucking sexy, do you know that?" I tell her, my voice growing hoarser by the moment. My hard cock rests on top of her thigh, and I suck in my breath when she reaches down, taking my crown in her fingertips.

She plays with my head as I hold her eyes, slowly bringing my mouth to her breast. Our gazes hold as I press kisses around her areola, loving the way her breath grows wanton and lazy.

"I'm going to drain you, Mae, and I *am* going to fucking swallow."

Her lips part, but all she manages is a tiny nod of her head.

"And while I do, I'm going to grind my cock against you and let you feel just how fucking hot you and your perfect fucking body make me."

She nods again, liking my filthy talk the way she always does. Only this time, she's in control. Her fingers feed through the back of my hair as my lips traverse her soft skin, finding the nubbed peak of her breast.

Slowly, I curl my tongue around her nipple, flicking and swirling as it hardens in my mouth. She sighs, and my cock leaks against her thigh in response. She's breathy like just the flick of my tongue has her close. I reach out and find her naked cunt, sliding two fingers between her lips.

"Yes," she says softly, her legs widening, making more room for me. "That feels good. All of it, Graham, *oh God.*"

I love when she says my name when we're being intimate.

I find her clit, swollen with need, and begin rubbing, using her arousal to make smooth circles. She moans and then, while I know she's feeling good, I latch.

I'd be lying if I said I hadn't wondered way too many fucking times what this would be like. How would her nipple feel in my mouth now? How fast does her milk come out? What does it taste like? How would swallowing a mouthful of her make me feel?

My hips take up a motion of their own, grinding against her as I begin to suck. I blink up at her, and between her lazy, sated grin, her wet pussy on my fingers and her hand teasing the back of my head, I've never felt so fucking close to Mae before.

She smiles at me over the swell of her engorged breast, and just as her eyes flutter closed to enjoy the moment, the first spurt hits my tongue.

I open my mouth in a moment of shock before sealing my lips around her nipple again, resuming what clearly was a great latch considering I'm already getting milk.

Her eyes pop open and for whatever reason, I open my mouth just a little to show her my reward. She peeks inside, eyes going hooded, her breathing intensifying.

"Swallow," she whispers, pulling at the ends of my hair as she watches.

I swallow and my hips thrust forward, the taste of her making me insane. "Fuck, baby, you taste so goddamn good."

She giggles, but presses my face back to her breast. "Drink me, Graham. Drink me and make me feel good."

Holy fuck.

The three hottest words I'd ever heard from Mae until

now were "fuck me Graham." But "drink me, Graham" definitely takes the fucking cake.

With my latch tight, I begin taking long, hard, deep pulls from her breast, loving the sweet, rich warmth that floods my tongue. Her milk is sugary and creamy, and my cock against her thigh has never felt so fucking good.

I'm going to make a mess on her, I already know. My spine tingles with an impending orgasm and with each suck and swallow from Mae's breast, it gets closer and closer.

If I'd humped Mae's leg and cum on her belly in five minutes before we had a baby, I'd probably beg her to never mention it. Now, though, it feels like a compliment. Because I'm so turned on by everything about my wife right now, that not cumming is impossible.

She kneads her breast, and our eyes catch as she does. The more she kneads, the more hot spray fills my mouth as I suckle her. Her eyes shine and I groan against her flesh as I swallow her down, committing her sated and loving gaze to memory.

Still stroking her pussy, I'm surprised when she whimpers "I'm close" because she's never cum this fast, either.

Milk dribbles past my lips, curling around her breast, dripping into the bed sheets. Just the sight while tasting it makes me rabid. I thrust my hard cock against her, and she moans while wrapping her hand around me. Smearing her thumb over my head, she strokes me harder, using my precum as lubricant.

Then I get an idea, and I don't know how she'll feel but we're both so fucking close to coming, I'm trapped in the coital bliss of the moment and go for it.

I spit milk into my palm and stroke myself once,

replacing her hand over my milk-sticky cock. She whimpers in delight as she strokes me, and while it doesn't feel too different than before, just knowing her milk is on my dick seems to make us both a little wild.

Resuming my latch, I continue to suck and drink from her breast, swallowing each mouthful as I do. She moans, she whimpers, and a second later she's cumming. Her thighs smack together, her spine rolls, and I stroke her swollen clit as she thrums all around me, vibrating with pleasure in our bed.

When I look up to find her watching me nurse, my resolve breaks. "A little more, and then you're done," she whispers, and it's so fucking unexpected and erotic that I grind against her one final time, the first rope of my orgasm rocketing from me.

I streak her belly and the underside of the very tit I'm still sucking as I come violently, urgently, painting my wife in the biggest release I've had post-baby.

When I'm done, I slowly release my latch, letting her breast-- now visibly much smaller-- free.

"It worked," she says quietly, collecting her spent breast in her palm, kneading it. "The clogged duct is totally gone."

Then she bites into her bottom lip, glancing over her body, the canvas streaked with my cum. "You liked my milk."

I bend down and take a quick nibble of her pebbled tip. "Fuck, babe. I really did. Does that make me weird?"

She cups my cheek, stroking her thumb across my bottom lip. "I don't know. But if you're weird, so am I, because that was the best orgasm I've had in a while."

I nod, knowing I need to clean her up but loving the sight

of her naked and covered in cum, milk dribbling down her breast. She's a goddamn sight. "Same."

She strokes a finger through the mess I made on her. "As long as I'm nursing, I want more of that."

Easily, I agree. Because if there's anything I want more of? It's that.

Acknowledgments

Laura, thank you so much for all of your hard work. Your developmental editing, feedback and our open dialogue about the story and characters have been such a gift to my storytelling and craft. You are so sharp and insightful and I'm so honored to be working together. You are truly amazing and I value and appreciate you so much!

To Randi, my content creator and social media guru, thank you so much for all your work. Equally, for your friendship and positivity. You are an incredible woman!

To Jes, thank you for your support and friendship. Whether it's a text message, Discord message or social media image, you are always there and come with sweetness and care every single time.

To Kris, your aesthetics are such a vibe, and it amazes and honors me that you create those pieces of art to honor my books.

To Marissa, when our similarities begin with smut but know no end! I'm so glad to call you a friend. Glad and lucky!

Lauren. Your friendship and support means more than you will ever really know. I'm so glad we took that cabin trip!

Daisy's Basement! My Discord server has quite literally become my favorite social hangout. Buddy reading, sex talk, relationship chat, lingerie shares, coffee favs—whatever it is, I genuinely feel at home with you all. Thank you so much for your friendship and creating such a beautiful, safe, fun community.

To everyone reading my books - thank you so much.

Finally.

To my husband, for everything.

Reviews

I hoped you enjoyed Laws and Jes's story. A while ago, I asked members of my Patreon what they'd like to see in a book of mine. As it turns out, a few of those ideas ended up in this very book! So thank you to my Patrons!

Thank you for taking a chance on me and thank you for reading my book.

Your feedback and opinion matter to me! If you have a minute, you Amazon review is greatly appreciated!

Thank you again for spending your down time on my book. It means so much to me!

XO

Daisy

Also by Daisy Jane

Series:

Wrench Kings (3 Books)

The Wild One / a reverse age gap romance / MF / Book 1

The Brazen One / a grumpy/sunshine romance / MF / Book 2

The Only One / a femdom romance / MF / Book 3

Men of Paradise (3 Books)

Where Violets Bloom / a stalker romance / MF / Book 1

Stray / a femdom romance / MF / Book 2

With Force / a CNC romance / MF / Book 3

Oakcreek (2 Books So Far)

I'll Do Anything / a bully femdom romance / MF / Book 1

After the Storm / an alpha MM romance / MM / Book 2

The Millionaire and His Maid (3 Books)

His Young Maid / an age gap boss/employee romance / MF / Book 1

Maid for Marriage / an age gap romance / MF / Book 2

Maid a Mama / a surprise pregnancy romance / MF / Book 3

The Taboo Duet

Unexpected/ an age gap Daddy figure romance / Book 1

Consumed / a Daddy kink romance / Book 2

Standalones:

The Other Brother / dual POV / MF

The Corner House / single POV / MFMM, MFM, MFM with an HEA

My Best Friend's Dad / age gap instalove novel / MF

Waiting for Coach / age gap novel / student teacher / MF

Hot Girl Summer / a taboo step sibling romance / MF

Pleasing the Pastor / an age gap virgin romance / MF

Release / a taboo MMF, MM, MF romance

Raleigh Two / a taboo MFM romance / MFM

The Man I Know / a married couple romance / MF

Novellas:

Cherry Pie / very taboo why choose / MFMM

Printed in France by Amazon
Brétigny-sur-Orge, FR

28897082R00192